THE SOLACE *of* LEAVING EARLY

ALSO BY HAVEN KIMMEL

A Girl Named Zippy

$\mathcal{D}oubleday$ NEW YORK LONDON TORONTO SYDNEY AUCKLAND

THE

SOLACE

of

LEAVING

EARLY

Haven Kimmel

PUBLISHED BY DOUBLEDAY
a division of Random House, Inc.
1540 Broadway, New York, New York 10036

DOUBLEDAY and the portrayal of an anchor with a dolphin are
trademarks of Doubleday, a division of Random House, Inc.

Book design by Pei Loi Koay

Library of Congress Cataloging-in-Publication Data
Kimmel, Haven, 1965–
The solace of leaving early / Haven Kimmel.—1st ed.
p. cm.
1. Women graduate students—Fiction.
2. Mary, Blessed Virgin, Saint—Apparitions and miracles—Fiction.
3. Murder victims' families—Fiction. 4. Indiana—Fiction.
5. Orphans—Fiction. 6. Clergy—Fiction. I. Title.

PS3611.I46 S65 2002
813'.6—dc21
2001054810

ISBN 0-385-49983-3

July 2002
First Edition

1 3 5 7 9 10 8 6 4 2

For my children, Katie and Obadiah:

EVERYTHING

THE SOLACE *of* LEAVING EARLY

Pulchritudo eorum confessio eorum: Their beauty is their testimony.

SAINT AUGUSTINE

It wasn't given to Langston Braverman to know the moment she became a different person; she only knew later, looking back on the afternoon a simple storm arrived and stayed for days, the afternoon she first saw the children. The woman Langston had been was immune to visions and visitations; she was a head-dweller, an Attic Girl who could quote theologians on the abandonment of reason, but who, nonetheless, trusted reason the way one trusts one's own skin. Not that the scene wasn't rational: the accoutrements, the props, the slip of light that first brought the children into focus, were grounded in actuality. There were shadows on Chimney Street, to be sure. A canopy of maples stippled the pavement in front of her house. And further down the block, in front of the mobile home where the children had come to live with their grandmother, the sky was tinged with green, the light anyone from the Midwest recognizes as foreshadowing; it was into this sort of day they walked, at first not visible to Langston, and then undeniable.

And their gowns! the older girl in lavender and the younger in pink (and the caps, of course, the pointed hats worn by women in a medieval court, with long, ribbonlike scarves trailing from the top, in colors that matched the gowns); even the gowns could be explained. They had been sewn by the girls' mother, and lovingly so. Langston didn't know then why the gowns had been made, perhaps for a parade, or more likely for school, but there was a strange prescience stitched into them. The necklines and the sleeves were elastic and able to stretch for a long time (longer than most mothers would have had the sense to predict), so the girls were free to grow. The hems were wide and could be let down a few times.

Even their names, the names they asked to be called, were simply words they had heard all their lives, and in their desperation attached to themselves. There was no real miracle there, apart from the miracle that simply is: the world coming into concreteness again and again, our witnessing of it. The weather was hot that day, and Langston was sitting in the open window in the attic, and she was a fool thinking fool's thoughts, when the girls came around the corner of Chimney and Plum Streets (Plum Street, where a few blocks down Amos Townsend lived alone). She could barely make them out at first—they looked like two little clouds, darkened before the coming storm—and she stopped thinking whatever had been plaguing her. She felt her breath quicken (*what on earth am I seeing?*) just slightly. She squinted (*are those children on the corner?*) and then they stepped out of the lower branches, and she knew even then. She knew the light wasn't there for her, she knew it wasn't really her vision. She knew the planet tilts on its axis to nearly the same degree that a woman's womb is tilted outward, that we are all walking into and out of the light, every day, and a thousand million times, more than we can ever count or claim to recognize, all the elements converge toward what can only be called a miracle, so often it happens that it must be the very nature of the world. It is the nature of the world that we miss the moment our fate changes, but can recall it later with perfect clarity.

At any rate, there they came. Immaculata, the elder girl, eight years old, and her younger sister, Epiphany, who was six, walking down Chimney Street toward her house in silky gowns that allowed for a breeze. Little girls is all they were.

PART ONE

Chapter 1

AMOS AWAKE

Because he believed in leading a disciplined life, Amos Townsend tried to go to bed at the same time every night, eleven o'clock, or close to it. Some nights he fell asleep right away, and even as his grip on consciousness slipped he felt a flood of gratitude for the loss. Most nights he lay awake an hour or more, enduring the contours of his pillow and the fact of his bones pressing into the mattress. Sleeplessness bred in him the most desperate irritation; he realized he hated flannel sheets (although he loved them earlier in the day, or at least the thought of them), and that the length of his legs made him furious (length and knobbiness inherited from his father), legs that consistently tangled in the ridiculous sheets and kept him from sleeping. What disturbed him most was simply the hour of midnight, and the dark bedroom, and the waves of fatigue and pity that stole over and seemed to steal something from him. Amos believed that both discipline and grace were muscles he had to keep exercised, oxygenated, in order that they might be called upon in an emergency, and nights for him were often an emergency, and sometimes he muttered low and exasperated, "Dear Lord, please just let me fall *asleep* already," and then waited for grace to descend on him with a shadowy nod.

A single thing gnawed at him at night, an idea he had no name for, although if anyone asked him he could have written a book, as they say, on the subject. Perhaps he was even called to write it, but he was vexed by the how and the why. Amos knew as well as anyone what went into writing a book, having written a master's thesis, and he considered the process to be akin to having one's nerves stripped with a curry comb. A ghastly experience, not to be endured. He imagined the tower of reference books clotting his study, and the notecards he would use to try to keep his thoughts straight, and the inevitable architectural work that would need to be employed, and the hours spent in the overstuffed chair facing Plum Street, lost in thought and picking at the threads in the upholstery; and most of all, the way writing a book makes a person feel that he'd rather be anywhere than inside his own skin. He'd rather be on Plum Street, that's for sure, kicking along in a tangle of leaves or stopping to pet one of the litter of mountain cur pups born next door (beautiful little dogs that would be feral in the blink of an eye—he knew he should pet them quickly, before he lost his chance). But if he were on Plum Street his mind would be drawn to his own study window, and he would think with longing of the work he could be doing and how work is the only thing that saves the soul, the only thing that makes a man a man, as he remembered Emerson saying, or something like it. Writing a book brings a single, irreducible truth right out to the edges of a person: there is no place to *be*, there is no place in this world, it is impossible to be happy.

And why? why another book in the morass of Self-Improvement and the self-published, all those elegant novels remaindered and shelves of poetry unread? Why Amos Townsend's ideas, when there are such game and handsome exegetes for the world's mysteries as Richard

Feynman and Brian Greene and that bald man with the big glasses who can connect everything in the world into a single theory? Psychics and expatriates and musicologists and postmodernists, not to mention Harold Bloom, or Updike with his fifty novels (good ones, too), all typing away while the world sleeps, or is sleepless: no. A book by Amos would be unnecessary.

At 11:47, thinking of Updike, Amos smacked his own thigh in frustration and performed the fourth quarter of what he thought of as his Human Drillbit routine, in which he turned from his right side to his stomach, and from his stomach to his left side, and from his left side to his back, and from his back to his right side, on and on, drilling himself closer, he hoped, to sleep. Amos liked to consider himself a man with a cynic's smile, more apt to turn it against himself than against the world, and did so, on his back once again, staring at the shadows on the ceiling. He smiled at himself and his own suffering. His suffering. Every evening of his growing-up years he sat at the dining room table with his parents and his younger brother, Samuel, in front of the cold fireplace, and watched his father say a simple prayer and then look at his family with his habitual expression: a closed-mouth grin, the barely discernible lift of his eyebrows that said, *Well, here we are again.* And his mother had her own version of it, didn't she? patting her napkin in her lap or straightening her skirt, the way she pursed her lips and let her gaze fall to the floor.

A life within limits, that's what his father had taught him to live. The elder Townsend might as well have taken young Amos by the hand and walked him to the seashore—except they lived in southwestern Ohio—and pointed to the shoreline and said, "Do you see? It's insurmountable." Best to smile, and offer your neighbor an extended hand, and be thankful for your roast beef and linen napkins. Amos remembered how, in the end, his father spent almost every day with his face in his hands, sobbing dryly. No one could unearth the reasons for his sorrow, and Amos didn't try. ("Isn't it enough," Amos finally whispered to his mother, after watching her claw at his father's pajama top for the hundredth time and beg him, *beg* him to tell her why he wept so, "isn't it enough that he's crying?" His mother had looked at him like he was a stranger, and surely he had felt like one.)

7

Somewhere in those years at home with his parents, living the odd life of a preacher's child (in which he was part of his father's pastorate and part of his father, too, which granted him privilege in the congregation), Amos learned to smile patiently at everyone in town—the members of Lost Creek Church of the Brethren, kind, pious, hardworking people who were committed to community life—but also at the conservatives of the town, and the gun owners, the cruel, florid men who attended the town's other churches devoutly, men who, even holding open the door for a neighbor at the diner or speaking to Pastor Townsend on the street, were inches away from something guttural, some crassness or abomination. "All God's creatures," his father used to say, walking home in the bright Sunday afternoons of Amos's memory. Pastor Townsend loved, it seemed to Amos now, the worst aspects of human nature, because the display of such validated in him his long-held and hopeless belief in something Calvinistic. (Although the elder Townsend would never have admitted such a thing—heavens, no. The Church of the Brethren—the faith of Amos's father and of his father before him—broke away from the Calvinists during the Protestant Reformation, but Amos couldn't shake it, this feeling that a trace of the old world, of the Old Man, remained.) Doom or damnation or predestination, all revealed providentially through our unkindnesses and injustices and unchecked appetites—this is what Amos learned to look for from his good father.

I cannot write a book and I will not write a book, Amos thought, drumming his fingers against the mattress, *but if I were to write it, where would I begin?* He would begin not back there in rural Ohio in his father's church, although that would have been an interesting place to start, but in his very own heart, in his second year in seminary, when he first read Paul Tillich's *Dynamics of Faith.* It was a small book (compared to the rest of Tillich) and the argument being made seemed deceptively simple: we all have an object which represents our Ultimate Concern. For some the object may be celebrity or personal power or money, or even something like romantic love and family. Institutions, including Christianity, have historically elevated the moral good to the status of the Ultimate. But there is really only one ultimate, unconditional concern, and that is for the Unconditional itself, what Tillich called our "passion for the infinite." We grasp the notion of the infinite immediately and personally, and yet it is seldom the object to which we dedicate our lives, and this is where Amos began to feel nervous. We elevate the finite, which has as its only power that of flux and decay, and when our ultimate concern fails to achieve ultimacy, we live lives that are hopelessly broken, and we know it.

On the day they were to begin discussing the book, Amos walked into the classroom feeling both thrilled and sick, because how was he, how were any of them, to go on, now that they realized who they were and how they had been living? He watched his fellow seminarians enter the classroom one by one, until all nine were there, fine people, all of them, but none seemed to realize what they held in their hand, the localized nuclear event. They chattered, they rearranged their book bags, they set out portable tape recorders. One man systematically offered everyone a stick of gum. When the professor walked in, a middle-aged and serious man Amos trusted without hesitation, and put his book down on the desk and said, "So. Are we ready to discuss Tillich?" Amos felt his stomach lurch sideways and then turn over. It was the same feeling he had watching newsreels of bodies being bulldozed into an open grave: the approach of the bottom line, life irreducible.

They began to discuss the book, and Amos could see that his professor took it as seriously as Amos himself did, the revolutionary idea that even Beauty and Justice are only concerns of the highest order, and do not achieve Ultimacy. God alone. *Sola Deus.* And who manages that, in this hardscrabble and knocked-together life? Well, almost no one, Amos realized, sitting there in class. His father hadn't, his mother hadn't, no one from his congregation—those carpenters and farmers and quilters, sincere, gentle people—had managed it. His professor had not, although he clearly wished it possible. And it was then and there that the idea began to form in Amos that there is a universal element in the human condition, something alchemical, and it's nearly visible, it radiates off people in waves, and you can see it everywhere, all the time.

His thinking was interrupted by Mike, a man in his forties who always wore short-sleeved dress shirts washed thin. "Listen, I worked in middle management at IBM for sixteen years, and I can tell you, business people don't know they're broken. They don't care about ultimacy or the lack of it in their lives."

And then Anita, who had grown up in a series of foster homes, said, "It seems to me that the farther away a person moves from thinking about what does or doesn't achieve ultimacy, the happier he is. The happiest people I know in the world are the cruelest. They *rest* in it, somehow." And on around the table it went, one student after another disagreeing with Tillich's proposition.

The professor asked, "What about when the middle managers at IBM look in the mirror first thing in the morning, or last thing at night? What do they see there?"

"They see profit and loss," Mike answered, "and I don't mean metaphorically. They see the company they work for."

Amos said nothing; his tongue seemed to have failed him. But he thought one thing over and over, the way he used to think a single thought in church on Sunday until he nearly choked on it: You are all wrong. You are all completely wrong about this. We live lives that are hopelessly broken, *and we know it.*

*

At 12:22 Amos decided his imaginary book needed anecdote: everyone loves a story. But more than that, he would be remiss if, in making a claim about the nature of humanity both broad and oblique, he failed to include humanity itself. So he would begin with Steve and Lydia, because that was where he first truly understood the idea, the nameless idea that rendered him sleepless.

Could it have been ten years ago, or closer to twelve? Amos was not yet thirty, and just out of seminary, when he was called by his district to a small congregation in a town called Mechanicsville. Mechanicsville was little more than two streets crossing, surrounded by farmland; the only business was a general store that offered dusty loaves of bread and canned vegetables. Most of the people who lived there worked in Dayton, fifteen miles east, all the family farms having long since been sold to corporate agribusinesses. The first time Amos drove through town his heart felt leaden, and he could hear his father offering his perennial advice: *Unhappy? Can't get started? Lower your standards.*

He sank into the little white cottage behind the church, put his books on plywood bookcases, bought a tea kettle, took up his post. But Amos was frightened every Sunday as he stood before his congregation (eighteen people if the sun was shining), and felt he had no authority, God-given or otherwise, nothing like what his father had provided on his darkest day. Who was Amos to comfort the sick or the bereaved; who was he to give advice or explicate the Scriptures?

And who were these *people*, anyway? All through the late fall and early winter, in order to pick up his mail at the local post office, Amos had to walk past the home of a man named Skeeter, and there was very often a large dead deer hanging from its back feet (or worse, on a hook through the gut) by a series of winches and pulleys on a tree inches from the sidewalk. Amos's hometown had the only opera house in the whole of Ohio; there were no dead animals in the trees of his youth.

The deer were hung to bleed, Amos knew, and he was able to take that in stride, but he began to be bothered by the sight rather deeply. He began to see the deer in his sleep (and certainly when he couldn't sleep), and not so much the carnage as the details: a whorl of lightened fur just above the thick muscle of a hind leg, or the delicate curve of a nostril. They had beautiful eyelashes and their lips looked like velvet, and the way they hung made them appear to still be running, or reaching with their front legs for the safety of the ground. And he couldn't walk on the other side of the street because on that side was a family whose name he was never able to learn; they had a standing army of delinquent teenagers and a vicious pit bull on a chain that could reach the sidewalk and then some, a dog that was frantic to kill a grown person.

Neither Skeeter nor the Pit Bulls attended Amos's church, and just as well. But they were there, the feeling of them, and they represented one of the basic facts of the town. The people who did attend were not so different (they had all grown up together), but they had the depth and decency to wonder about the unseen world, and to ponder an ethical system, outdated and unreliable as it increasingly seemed to Amos.

Steve and Lydia were typical, really, of the town and of a certain way of life. Steve was short and round, with dark hair that never seemed clean, and large, brown, watery eyes. He was jovial and appeared to have a good heart. For years, since he'd graduated from high school, Steve had sold campers and RVs at a lot a few miles outside Dayton, and he seemed to make a comfortable living. He loved Lydia, who was shorter and rounder and talked too loudly. She sold, Amos wasn't sure what to call them, knickknacks? ornaments? things with which to decorate a home? and they were uniformly ugly and caused a bubble of despair to rise in Amos's esophagus each time Lydia brought him a catalogue. They had two children, Brian, who was twelve, and Karen, who was sixteen. Both kids were dark like their dad, silent, and overweight. They were involved in nothing, no sports, no activities or clubs. The few times Amos tried to talk to Karen she had blushed furiously and answered him in a mortified whisper. Every week when Amos saw them he couldn't help but wonder if there was ever a conversation about *anything* in Steve and Lydia's household, apart from grocery lists and car maintenance. They all seemed so resigned and complacent; so blank. They were curious about nothing, they exhibited no restlessness, they seemed to want nothing more than they had. The slightest reference, on Amos's part, to an inner life, seemed to bounce off their collective surface like a foreign language, and finally, Amos was forced to consider that perhaps there was simply no there there. They were human, yes, and they bore immortal souls. All God's creatures. But Amos didn't understand them any more than he understood bison or oak trees.

One Sunday, as they passed through the receiving line, Steve shook Amos's hand and said, in a sly and conspiratorial way, "Were you at the game last night?" And for a number of empty moments Amos couldn't imagine which game he was meant to remember. A card game? a game of chance? Rook, Scrabble? and then realized Steve was talking about the county basketball team, of which the members of his congregation seemed inordinately fond.

"Oh, no. No, I'm afraid I missed it."

Steve leaned in even closer, so that his mouth nearly touched Amos's collarbone. "We're hotter than a popcorn fart, this year." And then he backed away, pleased with his analogy and his daring, to have said such a thing in the vestibule of a church. Steve's eyes shifted left and right to see if anyone had heard him, all the while leading Lydia out the door by the elbow and nodding his head in agreement with his own pronouncement.

The phrase rang in Amos's head for a day—he had absolutely no idea what it meant—and considering it was a form of torture. The fact of the phrase caused the sky to bleaken and his skin to itch, and by Monday night, when he was unable to sleep, Amos despised his own sensibilities and also despised the world. He smiled in the dark and drummed his fingers against his chest. He even laughed, some, before he fell asleep, and then Tuesday morning the organist at church, May, called him much too early, earlier than he ever liked to be awakened, and told him that Steve and Lydia's daughter Karen had died in the night of peritonitis, after her appendix burst at home. They hadn't known she was sick, and hadn't heard her calling weakly and in terrific pain from her bedroom, because they all slept with televisions on in their rooms. May mentioned this detail in passing, as though it were the most obvious thing in the world, but Amos was struck dumb. They were all in their separate bedrooms on a Monday night, asleep with televisions on? Their daughter, a sixteen-year-old girl, was *dying* and they couldn't hear her? This great and mysterious thing, this outrageous event, happened to those people?

"I thought you ought to know," May said, sniffling, into the silence.

"Yes."

"Because you're their pastor and maybe you want to head over to the funeral home."

"Oh God. Of course. Thank you, May," Amos said, hanging up. He reached for his clothes and tried with all his heart to imagine what he might say to Steve and Lydia, but there was nothing. And so he tried emptying out his mind and heart and allowing the Holy Spirit to fill him, but the nothing was then full of nothing. He was out of his league, he was no match for this one, and more than anything, it had happened to *them*? What comfort could there be beyond the most wretchedly platitudinal? And if, finally, he was called upon to offer those platitudes, could he do it?

It was worse, of course, than he could have imagined: when Amos arrived in the funeral director's office Steve was doubled over in a chair and gasping. Lydia had been tranquilized and simply sat, staring out the window. Brian had been sent to his grandparents. As Amos turned the corner into the arrangements room, the funeral director met him with such a look of gratitude that Amos was filled with foreboding, and then Steve realized Amos was standing there and rose from his chair with a force that caused it to topple over backward. Lydia never flinched.

Steve threw himself on Amos, wailing, "Oh my God oh my God oh my God," in such a piteous way that *Amos* began to weep, all the while thinking, *This won't do at all,* and finally it was the funeral director who calmed them all down, who spoke the phrases Amos couldn't have allowed himself to say, and thus Steve and Lydia settled the business of burying their daughter.

At the funeral Amos delivered the kindest eulogy he could have written, about the light in Karen and how that light had rejoined the eternal light of God, which he believed. He said things he didn't believe, about how we will all be transformed in the blink of an eye, about how we will all be reunited in heaven, where there is neither suffering nor death, anymore. The church had been filled with hysterical teenagers, more teenagers than Amos had ever seen in a single place. Even the Pit Bull children were there. Amos had no idea where they had all come from or who they were or what they wanted; certainly Mechanicsville couldn't lay claim to this much youth. He knew from May that Karen had had few friends, and yet there they all were, wailing and comforting one another and distracting Steve and Lydia, which was maybe good in the end but seemed cruel at the time.

Amos stayed in Mechanicsville for a year after Karen died, and the church closed in around Steve and Lydia, in the way that small towns and certain denominations take care of their own. Amos, too, did what he could. He offered to counsel them, and when they failed to keep their counseling appointments, he offered them anything else they wanted: to cook their meals or keep their dog while they went camping for the weekend. He tried to cut their grass, but Steve waved him away, despondently. They continued to come to church every Sunday, wrapped in a silence and vacancy Amos doubted they would survive. They survived.

*

He would use those images in the early part of the book (if there were a book, and there never would be): the deer on the hook. The dog flying out to the end of its chain. A father knocking his chair backward. *This is evidence*, Amos would say to Mike, his fellow seminarian from long ago.

Evidence of what? Mike would ask, genuinely curious.

Amos pressed the heels of his hands against his eyes and prayed for sleep, trying not to consider the events of the last week, the final chapter added to his bleak metaphysics.

I don't know, Amos would answer. I simply don't know.

Chapter 2

LANGSTON COMES HOME
AND SAYS NO

She had been home only a few days, hidden away almost exclusively in her attic room, when the church bells began to ring for Alice Baker-Maloney's funeral. They would ring on the hour, every hour until noon, when the services were set to begin. Alice's mother, Beulah Baker, was burying her in the Sycamore Grove Cemetery, just a quarter mile east of town.

It was the middle of May and already hot in Haddington. Langston lay on top of her quilt and watched a combination of dust motes and pollen swirl in the shaft of light saturating the air over her bed. An old, black, metal fan her daddy found who knows where was directed at her from atop her desk; the blades appeared to be lethally sharp, and the cloth-covered cord had been gnawed upon by generations of vermin. A hum that was also a whine, a serious and direct complaint, issued from the motor. She was nervous for a variety of reasons, and the possibility of an electrical fire was only one.

Langston had always been opposed to perspiration, for one thing, and her situation had become painfully clear to her in the past few, humid hours. She no longer lived in her beautiful old apartment off-campus in Bloomington, which had been remodeled just enough to provide its tenants with climate control. She was, in fact, in her childhood home, in her childhood room. The house was entirely free of comfort throughout the long, hot summer months. Her family baked, they mildewed, they shone, they stuck to furniture. Langston's mother, AnnaLee, outlawed any articulation of discomfort. (The house was cold all winter, for that matter, but the cold seemed less oppressive, somehow.) Langston was embarking on a new career in perspiration, one that could potentially last for months.

In addition: she was broke, had no prospects, was unemployable, and found all forms of employment untenable, anyway. She had walked away from a Ph.D. in, not midstream, exactly, but some location more horrifying than that. She had stepped out of her program the way one might step out of an airplane 30,000 feet above a bean field in the dead of night. In truth, she walked out of her oral examination, just stood up and walked out. She collected the few things from her office she thought she might need, then went into the main English department office and resigned her fellowship, withdrew from the program, and said some things. The few things she said were like kitchen matches applied to a gasoline-soaked bridge.

Then she drove her Renault (an old car, faded burgundy, with a stick shift; so old, in fact, that there were icons on the dashboard which no longer meant anything. Cultural symbols divested of meaning, by time) to her lovely apartment building, the Greene Arms. When Langston saw the name the first time she felt she had found a way to participate in some very subtle ceremony for a dying and rising god. *I live in the Greene Arms*, she thought. *I am safe within the Greene Arms.* On her last day as a Ph.D. candidate she stayed there only long enough to load her car with a few belongings, and to collect her dog, Germane.

(Named not after Germaine Greer, but as in: Germane to this conversation.) He lay on the floor with his head resting on his front paws, a look of profound worry on his face. Langston didn't speak to him, not knowing what to say. She gathered up clothes and books and toiletries; Germane's bed and squeaky hamburger, his food and water dishes.

After loading everything in the car, she stopped at the apartment of the landlady, an old woman named Mrs. Shekovsky. Langston had already paid May's rent and had not yet extended her lease into the next school year, so it didn't matter if she left early. Her father would return to collect the rest of her things, Langston told Mrs. Shekovsky, who nodded. Her rheumy gaze filled Langston with unhappiness.

"I'll miss that dog of yours," she said. Mrs. Shekovsky was absent a number of teeth, and in their place was a darkness to which Langston could not become reconciled.

"Yes, he'll miss you, too."

"I always felt safe with him around."

"Dogs are good for that."

They were silent a moment.

"Take care, then."

"You, too."

It was so easy to walk away from the life she'd spent years building that for a moment Langston thought she might levitate. Everything is so temporary, she thought, so unrooted, and any one of us can just stand up and leave. She tried to imagine the world, even just one square mile of it, from the point of view of God—the appearances and vanishings, the abandoned objects, doors left open in haste—how it must look over centuries, but she felt her breath catch in her throat.

Germane and Langston took the stairs down to the first-floor hallway, which was tiled in black and white marble diamonds. A radiator painted gold shone from the corner. The inset mailboxes were military green. She memorized it all. Then they walked out into the courtyard. The fountain in the center burbled a bit listlessly; the baby frog who spit water out of his little froglips seemed to be clogged. She ran her fingers over the black iron benches surrounding the fountain, studied for a moment the flower garden, where the spring tulips were blooming red and yellow. A small, coral-colored stone got stuck in the bottom of her shoe,

.

and she reached down to pull it out. She thought that if evidence were ever necessary, there was, no doubt, a laboratory somewhere that could test the dirt from the bottom of her shoe and locate with utter precision the last place she had been. She could hold out this rock to anyone passing by and say, "Look here! Here's the proof: I *did* leave home."

*

It was hot in her childhood bedroom; she had walked away from her life and her vocation; her parents would surely try to force her to get a job, and the church bells were ringing for Alice Baker-Maloney, another unreconciled bit of Langston's history, a girl she'd grown up with who was now undeniably dead.

They'd gone to school together, and attended the same Sunday School week after week, year in and year out, and so had cobbled together a friendship during a time when friendship was determined by proximity. For a few years Alice had been Langston's only playmate (with the exception of Taos), but Langston couldn't remember loving Alice or feeling jealous of her affections or desiring her company. She couldn't remember *knowing* her. Alice had been a quiet girl with a plain, flat face and an overbite. Her hair was blond and listless. The only magic she seemed to possess were dimples; her appearance was changed entirely when she smiled.

Langston listened to the bells. There was something anachronistic in the way they rang out against the bright afternoon air. She tried to think about anachronism—what it means in literature, what it indicates about our confusion regarding the nature of space, our own persistent perishing—but found she was unable to hold on to the thought. She couldn't think about much of anything at all. Alice had traveled only as far as an old farmhouse on the Crooked Tree Pike, two miles west of town. She'd married a man from Hopwood, converted to Catholicism, married, had two daughters. Neither Langston nor Alice had traveled far, but here they both were, home again.

*

When Langston was in college, and later, in graduate school, she often found herself staring at strangers, wondering what they knew that she didn't. In the library once, for instance, she saw a young man whose slight build and scuttling carriage (along with his chaotic hairstyle and eyeglasses) suggested to her that he might genuinely understand the connection between the most esoteric reaches of the Eastern religions and quantum mechanics, a subject in vogue at the time. She would have loved to understand such a connection herself, but found that she was too busy to learn what she considered the crushingly tiresome foundations of physics. Alice, of all people (and Langston could suddenly recall that she had an unfortunate cowlick right at her hairline, which caused her limp hair to grow, for an inch or so, backward) now knew something Langston did not. Alice knew how it felt to have children, and how it felt to die, and she had seen, most likely, the entrance to heaven.

Langston most devoutly wished, while not daring to expect, that many things might be restored to her in heaven; some things she simply lost, and some things she never had. In heaven she would see again the wooden swing set in the backyard where her brother Taos and she used to linger as children, he so fair-haired and she so dark. She'd see his legs shooting out with enough force to propel him higher and higher, nearly out of sight, the dying summer light held captive by their simple joy. The old barn that used to sit in the north corner of the yard would be resurrected, and the terrible events Langston came to associate with it would be wiped away. She suspected there would be, in addition, a room built especially for her, a room lined with shelves like the showroom of a sacred toymaker, and on those shelves would stand all the immortalized and misplaced objects of her life—some things she would be stunned to see again and some she would barely remember having owned.

And in Langston's heaven she would attend dinner parties with Alfred North Whitehead and his lovely wife, and she'd take as her guest John Donne. And since this was heaven and not just any heaven, but Langston's, she'd ask Emily Dickinson to join them and Emily would say yes without hesitation and never behave strangely. They would stand at Dr. Whitehead's picture window and watch the snow descend on heaven, which would look remarkably like Cambridge. The wine and conversation would be so sublime that their very bones, if bones they had, would shine; at the end of the night Langston would walk home alone and hear behind her on the cobblestone street the muffled sound of all the world's good dogs running toward her, going home with her, and the silence and the snow against their fur would amount to a sort of transport.

In heaven many things would be restored to Langston, and also she would be able to begin the story of her earthly life differently; she would construct a fiction that was nonetheless legitimate—it would be the story she told and therefore true—and it would not begin with her in exile in her thirtieth year, in this attic room, at home with her parents in Haddington, Indiana. It would not be a tale in which her life grew smaller and smaller, as if she'd been moving through ever-tightening concentric circles toward a vacant and inexplicable center.

*

Langston heard the low coursing of her mama's voice on the telephone, so she snuck down the attic stairs to the wide hallway on the second floor, and then into the bathroom, next to her parents' bedroom. By placing her ear against the cool radiator, she could hear, just barely, what was being said. Not that she cared. Her mama was forever talking to someone, going on about something. When Langston casually mentioned, just two days ago, that she thought her mother might find less frivolous ways to spend her time, she had been met with a blood-curdling look. But today Langston thought her mother might be talking about Alice, and the puzzling circumstances of her death. Not that Langston cared.

". . . the two children. It's hard to even *take in*." AnnaLee's voice was like a river. She paused, and Langston could tell she was crying. "No, I know. Yes, she's here. I have no idea—no one does. And who would she tell, who does she have? Let me call you back a little later."

Langston slipped out of the bathroom while AnnaLee was blowing her nose (quite loudly, for Langston's taste) and up the attic stairs. By the time AnnaLee knocked on the door, Langston was sitting in the window, casually watching the comings and goings (such as they were) on Chimney Street, as if she'd been sitting there for hours.

"Come on up," Langston called. Germane's tail began to thump on the floor, but he didn't rise. He knew the sound of all their footsteps.

"It's hot up here," AnnaLee said, turning the corner of the staircase.

"And it's only May."

"Hmmmm." AnnaLee sat down on the bed, pushing her hair off her forehead. She looked—as always—Langston felt, disheveled. Her hair, which had been red in her youth, was now a sort of strawberry-blond mixed with silver, and she still wore it long, even though she was over fifty. She most often gathered her hair up in some sort of bun and stuck a chopstick through it (or a twig, if a chopstick wasn't handy), and if there was the least amount of humidity in the air, tendrils and curls sprang out from everywhere. And she insisted on wearing strangely antiquated housedresses, the sorts of dresses that had little glass buttons, or embroidery on the pocket.

"I want you to go to Alice's funeral with me today, Langston."

"Excuse me? No." It was just like her mother to spring such a thing.

"I ask you for nothing, and I'm asking you to do this with me. It isn't much. Your father is at work, I don't want to go alone, and I think it would be a good way for you to, I don't know, come back to town."

"Mother. No."

They both sat in silence a few moments. Not a single thing moved on Chimney Street. The hum of the fan rose and fell, as if it might burst into flames or shoot up like a rocket.

When she spoke again, AnnaLee's voice was strained, but Langston was relieved to see she wasn't crying. "Look. Let's just say on this one day, May 14, 1998, just today and perhaps never again, say yes to me. Make this easy. I want you to go with me. You grew up with Alice Baker; her mother lives right across the street, for heaven's sake, and, *and* it's the polite thing to do."

Langston clenched her jaws against her own conflictedness until she thought her teeth might crack. Of course some part of her wanted to say yes; of course she wanted to be easy for her mother, but there was another part, a whole other side that stayed hard and resistant. She was afraid to give in, ever, for fear that all personal standards would be abrogated at once. Each time she tried to compromise or broker some emotional bargain with her mother, she saw again in her mind a nightmare figure she'd invented for the occasion, a dark figure riding into town like one of the Horsemen of the Apocalypse. She called him Squander, and his sole purpose on this earth was to make Langston behave.

"I can't, I can't," she said, and immediately felt desperate, chattery and crystalline. "I can't bear it, the horror of that church and those tragic, large people and the look on their faces, that stunned look, and I never really knew Alice, did I, we played together *briefly*, when we were very *small*, and the hymns, and the weeping, the handkerchiefs, the eulogy, please. Don't get me started. I don't want to hear how Alice is sending us a postcard from heaven saying 'Wish you were here!' or how she fulfilled the greatest ambition of a woman's life, mothering, or how Jesus is waiting to gather us all in like little sheep. No. Absolutely not." She finally had to sit on her hands to keep from waving them in the air like someone drowning.

Her mother sighed, but didn't move. "I," she began, then stopped, taking a deep breath. "I've tried to tell you, I've begun to tell you half a dozen times about our new minister, Amos. I don't understand why you won't *listen* to me, Langston. He's wonderful, he would never—"

"He would never have come to Haddington if he was wonderful, that's *a*; and *b*, he's the minister for a failed nondenominational Christian church that's become, what? The Brotherhood? Is it some kind of cult? And he—tell me again—he floats around to churches that need him, like a spore? No, thank you. I've been to that church a thousand times and I've heard the sermons of six different ministers, and they are *soul-sucking*, Mama, they pull my soul right out of my body and devour it with their banality and their, their inability to perform a close reading of a text."

"Langston, he went to seminary at—"

"I don't care."

"He wrote his thesis on—"

"I'm not listening."

Her mother stood up quickly, more quickly than she usually moved.

"It's ten o'clock now. Two hours, Langston. The funeral is at noon. You have two hours to grow up." She turned around and stomped down the stairs, slamming the attic door behind her.

"Yes, well," Langston said to her mother, quite a few minutes after she was gone. "I'd take you a lot more seriously if you ever wore shoes."

*

The bells rang a dozen times. Langston lay on her back, staring at the unfinished attic ceiling, the old wiring snaking along the lengths of board. Germane studied her some, then slept, then studied her more. At 12:15 she decided she could do with some lemonade, so she wandered down to the kitchen and drank some. The house was strangely still— the *town* seemed still.

At 12:20 she thought she'd feel the weather, so she walked out onto the porch and down to the sidewalk. It was hot, as she'd suspected it would be. Germane followed the progress of a squirrel up a tree, but stayed close to her side. She could see the cars gathered tightly around the church, down on the corner of Chimney and Plum, and the hearse waiting with a grim patience at the bottom of the outside stairs. *A gay, ghastly holiday,* Emily once wrote. Langston headed in that direction, thinking she might wait on the corner and walk her mother home, and at the corner she thought she'd just step on into the vestibule and wait for her there.

She could hear the last strains of the last song, but didn't recognize it. Someone, a woman, was weeping with abandon. The vestibule felt pressurized—what was that pressure?—such that she held her fingers against her temples and closed her eyes, waiting for it to pass. She decided to open one of the swinging doors between the vestibule and the sanctuary, just a crack, just enough to see her mama. Instead she slipped inside, finding herself in the midst of a standing-room-only affair. The man standing next to her, middle-aged with a black pompadour and a blue polyester suit, smiled at her kindly even though his face was streaked with tears. Langston had never seen him before.

Robbie Ballenger, the owner of the local funeral home, and one of his assistants were just beginning to escort the family out of the church and into the waiting coach. Langston saw Beulah, Alice's mother, stand, sway, nearly fall. Robbie caught her under the elbow, solidly, and led her down the aisle. Beulah seemed to have aged fifteen years since Langston was home last Christmas. Her hair had gone completely white, and the dark circles under her eyes made her look like her own mother, Alice's grandmother, who died the year before. Just as Beulah reached her, Langston stepped back and out of the way, but Beulah saw her anyway.

"Thank you for coming, sweetheart," Beulah said, but her gaze was so unsteady Langston was unsure if Beulah was talking to her. She glanced behind her at the blue-suited man, but he just nodded as if he were thanking her, too.

"Me?" she mouthed to him. *But I didn't come,* she wanted to say. *I'm not really here.*

Then other people were streaming past, the stunned, the shuddering, the sober, and for just a moment Langston caught sight of the man who was surely the new preacher, but he was out the door quickly. He was tall and thin, with dark, unruly hair and a gauntness, a bone structure that reminded her of Ichabod Crane, and the look on his face was so unbridled, his pain was so evident that she had to look away.

AnnaLee saw her from across the church. She had changed into a dark dress and all of her hair was in place, for once. Her eyes were bright with tears, and when she saw Langston in the doorway she pressed three fingers against her lips and kissed them, and Langston did the same.

Chapter 3

GENIUSES

"God is of two minds about the world," Amos wrote, trying to prepare the sermon for the coming Sunday. He scratched it out, filing it in the category of pure projection, and started again. "God has two minds." "God *is* two minds." He dropped his pen and rested his forehead in his hands. Every week was the same; he began writing his sermon in faith he would be able to say what he meant—or more importantly, say what he believed, and what he felt should be said—and every week the whole enterprise fell apart, and early on. The desk chair, an old wooden captain's chair that both rocked and swiveled, groaned as he leaned back. Amos worked at his father's desk, which had been *his* father's desk, as befitted a succession of preachers. When he was a young man Amos had been moved by such things as heirlooms, and by continuity, the march of certain objects or inclinations across time, but now he wished, as he always wished while sitting at this desk trying to write, that if continuity were something truly to be desired, his father had been a miner or a stonemason or a grocer. *Anything* but a minister. It was a *dreadful* profession.

He recalled an evening at dinner when he was twelve or thirteen; his father had seen a nature program on herding dogs the night before. "There are two varieties, apparently," his father said, while Amos's mother sat tucked in and enthralled, and Samuel, already half-gone from their lives, moved his peas around on his plate. "One herds by running at the sheep and nipping at their heels—he commands, he stands apart, he declares his authority with his teeth, if you will—while the other simply pretends to be one of the sheep." His father sat back in his chair, a scarecrow of a man, all angles and laugh lines, his head tilted slightly to the left, as it did when he was either genuinely taken with a notion or wished to appear so. "It put me in mind of my own profession," he then announced with his rueful smile, which brought instant relief to Amos and his mother. The punch line had been delivered, the analogy successfully revealed. The meal was concluded with good feeling all around, because the Elder Townsend was no heel-nipper; absolutely not. He was the sort who patrolled the edge of the herd, pretending to be one of the sheep.

*

"When we consider the universe, we believe we're encountering a dualism: the material and the ephemeral, or the seen and the unseen, but in fact, all we see and all we know are One in the mind of God." Amos wrote at night, in his study where two tall windows faced Plum Street. His desk sat in front of one of the windows, and the streetlight cast shadows of the old maple tree on the wall beside him. "The wall, and the shadow on the wall. Plato's cave. Memory. Immortality. Image. Which is causal; which the initial aim?" Gibberish. He marked it out.

As a child he had loved *The Dick Van Dyke Show;* years later, in seminary, he had watched the reruns and found, to his delight, that he loved it just the same. He chose his favorite episode unwittingly, the way children do: Rob Petrie, trying to write a novel, found himself with writer's block and decided to go to a mountain cabin alone, to get some work done. He needed space, freedom from disturbance. The only scene Amos could remember was toward the end: the wooden crate on the cabin floor overflowing with discarded sheets of paper; Rob wearing a cowboy hat, smacking a ball on a string against a paddle over and over. Rob didn't put on the cowboy hat or pick up the paddle-ball at the beginning—oh, no. He tried hour after hour to get something written. The cowboy hat came on by degrees. Amos laughed aloud in his study, thinking of the scene. The *slipping down* of it was so delicious, so cathartic. Because for that half hour the slide was happening not to Amos, who thought himself a humble man edging toward some everyday lunacy, but to Dick Van Dyke, who could take it. A man of rubber. That wide, sweet smile.

"Perhaps I have suffered some right-brain injury," he wrote, "because I look at my hands and they don't appear to belong to me." It was true, Amos's fingers were so long they seemed comically unfamiliar. Each knuckle had a will of its own. What he wanted to explicate (in his unwritten sermon) was Amos's favorite, most fundamental understanding of God—it was Whitehead's idea, but he was trying to avoid Whitehead's language because it simply didn't, well, it didn't *preach*—namely: the Primordial and Consequent Natures. What might be, what is, what has been. In God's Primordial Nature there exist all the pure possibilities for every moment (every actual occasion, Whitehead would say) of concrescence; in the Consequent Nature is the world as we chose to make it: every actual occasion and every actual entity, *every single moment*, rendered objectively immortal. Amos still felt a chill when he considered the reach of this idea, and how he felt when he first heard it discussed in seminary.

"Whitehead's not for me," Mike had said, shaking his head with great skepticism. "I'm an Aquinas and Luther sort of guy. Anybody who takes God's thumbprint off the world? Huh-uh, no way." Amos had smiled at him, unable to respond. God's thumbprint on the world? It was an inelegant description, but if Mike couldn't see it in Whitehead, he was dreaming.

The fine people of the Haddington Church of the Brethren, newly designated, would kill for some immortality just about now, Amos thought, and he would love to give it to them. Perhaps he would say, "Eternally, immortally, Alice Baker-Maloney is held in the Consequent Nature of God; God recalls her rising up and her lying down. She is safer there than she ever was among us." But that wouldn't do, would it? because the congregation would be reminded not just of her rising up—not just the little girl with flat blond hair who looked like she'd never be memorable—but of her lying down, those final minutes. Amos closed his eyes and pressed against them with his thumbs until he saw stars. What might comfort him theologically would provide no comfort to his flock, and it was there, again and again, that he failed. He failed to give comfort. He failed to say the words that normal, heartsick people needed to hear: Death is not a cosmic accident, not a nightmare, not evidence of a punishing, all-powerful God. Instead he said almost nothing, and ground his teeth against his desire to tell them the truth: God is helpless. We are at the mercy of our own radical freedom, and all God can do is take into God's self the grief, the violence, the sublime acts of kindness, the good sex. God comes to us from the future, and has only one godlike gift: the *lure*. We are lured toward truth, beauty, and goodness . . . the lure is pulling at our hearts like some lucid joy inside every actual occasion and all we have to do is . . .

Say yes. He stared out the open window at Plum Street, where nothing had been happening but a little wind and few shadows, and saw, suddenly, a girl walk into the arc of the streetlight. No one in Haddington walked after dark, although it seemed to Amos to be one of the safest places left in the world. He pushed his glasses farther up on his nose and leaned forward, greatly interested. She had a dog with her, a big shepherd mix, from the look of him. The girl stopped and looked up at Amos's window. She was not such a girl, he realized, but full grown, and all long lines: long, dark hair in a braid down her long, straight back. A white T-shirt that held the light. Blue jeans. Heavy black shoes. A narrow face, so different from most of the faces in Haddington. Walt Braverman, that was who she looked like—this must be— She turned abruptly and walked on, into the darkness on Plum Street. Without a word from her, the dog turned and walked beside the girl, like something from a myth of companionship. Long after she was gone, Amos raised his hand in a greeting.

*

After Mechanicsville and before Haddington, Amos was sent farther south, to an even smaller Ohio town called Mt. Moriah. The parsonage was a mobile home that smelled like cats; the Mount in the town's name was ironic, and the church had approximately eleven members, with a collective age of nearly a thousand years. But the church itself was beautiful and spare, a clapboard church in the wildwoods, as the song went, outside what was left of a failed farming town. The Mt. Moriah cemetery lay behind the church, and part of Amos's duties included the caretaking of the cemetery grounds. It was the most peaceful job in the world. There were no Wednesday night or Sunday night services, because the Survivors, as Amos liked to call them, had such a hard time getting to church on Sunday morning. The woman who had played the piano, Esther, was so overcome with arthritis that she could no longer lift the piano lid, and the one remaining deacon, Brother Roy, had glaucoma and so had abdicated the passing of the collection plate. On Sunday morning Amos just chose what he felt like singing and stood in the pulpit and belted it out. The game congregation sang the songs they knew and nodded when they forgot the words and didn't seem to mind that Amos didn't use the hymnal.

"Friends, let's sing 'Home of the Soul' again," Amos said almost every week. It had become his favorite song, and the old people were beginning to pick up on the words. In the beginning he'd had a hard time with it, given that it was written in overlapping parts and he had to sing all of them, but finally he'd worked out how to get Esther to hold the soprano part (tremulous and tuneless) and James to mumble the tenor while Amos threw his body into the bass line. *Home of the soul / Blessed kingdom of light.*

Amos would be the last minister Mt. Moriah saw; at the annual conference the year before, the vote had been, memorably, "to allow that body to lie down." There were 1,100 Brethren congregations in the

U.S., and they were kind enough to see that one through to the end. The assignment suited Amos fine.

It suited him fine at the beginning, that is, when he first got to Mt. Moriah and took the full measure of his new constraints. Working in the cemetery in the summer mornings, trimming around the crumbling tombstones and white crosses erased of their bright messages by wind and weather, Amos used to periodically tip his head back and laugh aloud. *Dear Father,* he would write in his head, although his father was by that time three years gone, *you would be so proud if you could see my new assignment. I have lowered my standards almost to the grave.* He'd even felt waves of bleak amusement pass over him during Sunday services, faced with the steadfast eleven, their blindnesses and hearing aids and tremors, their walkers and catheter bags. He'd wished for some clever, sardonic sibling to share this story with, a clear-eyed sister, or a brother born too late to really be a part of the family. (But all he had was Samuel, an ear, nose, and throat doctor in California. Samuel had responded to his Anabaptist, social-gospel-based upbringing by becoming conservative, marrying an anorexic, and severing all ties to the Midwest, to his past. The last time the brothers had seen each other was at their mother's funeral, two years ago, and then they'd had nothing to say.)

But it hadn't lasted long anyway, had it, that amusement? It ceased to be funny almost immediately, as soon as he realized that every member of his church, to a person, had a plot in the Mt. Moriah cemetery reserved in his or her name. The grounds were just waiting to swallow them. And then he began to notice strange things about his flock, like the way Esther had just the trace of an English accent. He learned that she was British, and had an M.A. from Oxford in economics. She'd moved to the Midwest with her husband, a native, after the Second World War. She was widowed and had outlived all three of her children.

Amos had called on James once at home, when James was ill and couldn't come to church, and had found James's farmhouse, which sat down a short lane lined with dogwoods, to be one of the most beautiful houses he'd ever seen; the starkest, sanest aesthetic. Singular care. The light in the entryway ceiling, for instance, was surrounded by yellow roses that swirled out in a tangle. James had painted them himself, years before, when he could still hold a brush and climb a ladder. Amos had brought dinner, and James's kitchen was like something in a painting by Chardin; every object was resonant with its own usefulness and nothing was out of place. In the center of the oak table, handmade and shining like glass, there sat a single lime with a leaf still attached, and a pewter salt cellar that probably dated from the Revolutionary War.

The more he knew the less he could look at them, Esther and James, and Brother Roy, who in his day could tame a wild horse, deliver a baby, and play bluegrass mandolin. Lila, who had a secret and wept through every service. Israel, the last of eight brothers, who wore braided leather suspenders and who, as a boy, had memorized most of Tennyson. Ralph, who prayed every week that his right arm, which he'd lost to a thresher fifty years before, would stop itching. All of them, all of them, the hobbled and the grieving, Amos loved them all, and watching them arrive on Sunday was an assault against his very nature. They sat in the first two pews as patient as saints; they weren't waiting for him to tell them anything they didn't know; they sang whatever he asked.

He wrote to his mentor and begged to be transferred, and received a gentle but firm no, and then they began to go, one at a time, James first, in his sleep. Amos would do anything to forget those years, the way Lila groaned in her dreams and reached out to him in panic from her hospital bed. And it wasn't so different with the others, was it? their confusion, their tears, their humiliation. He stayed until the very end, putting a final coat of paint on the church before locking it up the last time, until the three in the nursing home four miles down the county highway were dead, and the Mt. Moriah cemetery was lush and green and busier than it had been for years. He began every funeral the same way: *This poor, sweet world has lost another of Her geniuses. Let us pray.*

＊

Amos began writing his sermons on Monday night, and, invariably, finished them late on Saturday night. He worked on them every evening.

The days were busy in Haddington, the largest town he'd been as-
signed to (population 3,062); his little church alone had forty members
who attended full-time. There were shut-ins to visit, and people in the
hospital. Babies got born. Amos engaged in more pastoral care than
ever in his professional life: marriage and premarital counseling, career
advice, and sometimes, real and interesting conversations about religion. Along the way something admirable must have happened in this
town, because the people were generally kind and intelligent and good-
humored. Their intentions were honorable. (There was the usual small-
town Indiana mix, of course, no different from small-town Ohio:
hunters and alcoholics, men nearly a decade past adolescence still driving hot rods, vicious gossips, lonely families addicted to drama; on the
whole, though, Amos was happy there.) He gardened when he could,
and wished for more hours to read.

*

The Primordial and Consequent Natures of God were necessary steps
toward the place he really wanted to go with this sermon, which was the
concept of pure possibility. "Think of it," he wrote in his old-fashioned, rural-Ohio script, "at the outset of every moment of concrescence, there is, in the Primordial mind of God, all the pure possibilities
for the outcome of that occasion, moment by moment, day by day, for
every actual thing: you, me, the dogs, the government, geraniums. And
all God desires is beauty and goodness, the harmonious resolution of
contrasts. We are happiest, I believe, and God is certainly happiest,
when we allow ourselves to fall into beauty. God is luring us there, even
now, breath by breath." That wasn't what he really wanted to say. What
he was aiming for was nostalgia, heartache, homesickness. Or stranger
yet, the heart's desire to return to someplace it had never been. He
thought of his own bizarre tendency to long for other lives; just a few
days ago, on the four-lane highway between Hopwood and
Haddington, he'd been passed by a decrepit, fumy old Cavalier, packed
with people. It was an Hispanic family, the father driving and smoking,
the mother looking out the window with a wistful expression on her
face. There must have been four children in the backseat, and two more

between their parents, and for just a moment, Amos couldn't swallow, so dearly did he wish to be one of them. This is madness, he had thought, shaking his head. Who would choose such a life, a life free, as it were, of choices? Who would want to be one of six impoverished children living in a foreign and hostile place, squashed into a car with no room to move? And who on earth would want to be those parents? Amos did, and it wasn't the first time. Certain houses caused the same wave of longing—the look of a particular curtain in an upstairs window, or a bike left on the lawn—and some movies did it, too. Why? he wanted to ask his congregants. "Why does this happen to us? Because we have abandoned an infinite number and variety of pure possibilities, and perhaps they live alongside the choices we did make, immortalized in the cosmic memory. Perhaps there are unknown lives walking alongside ours, those paths we didn't take, and we reach for them, we ache for them, and don't know why. We have, none of us, lived our lives as we ought to have, and maybe that's a good, working definition of sin. God doesn't care, the angels don't care, no one is mad at us for our failures. But what agony, to know our better selves, the life we might have lived is there, just out of reach!"

Amos put down his pen, took off his glasses, pressed his eyes. No, no, it was all wrong. Possibility, infinity, beauty—none of those words were right. He was begging for recognition, he was asking his congregation to tell him they were with him, that they understood this particular knot because it is the problem of the world, but he knew he couldn't ask this way. Using Whitehead was too academic, too circuitous. What he really wanted to say was: have you felt this? this phantom life streaking like a phosphorescent hound at the edges of your ruin?

*

But he didn't ask. In bed that night, unable to sleep, Amos went over his schedule for the next day: breakfast at the hospital with the Waltzes. Premarital counseling with Joannie Johnson and Jim Cross, seventeen and eighteen years old, respectively, and pregnant, collectively. A quiet lunch at home. An emergency meeting with Beulah Baker on the care and raising of two little girls. The thought of Beulah made him clench one of his fists with apprehension. Alice and her husband, Jack, had attended his church, and Amos had counseled them together and separately, and he imagined, wide awake, his eyes shining against the shadows, the pure possibilities for what he might have said or done, where he went wrong. A chasm, this one. He remembered everything about Alice—the clarity was suffocating. She had blond hair on her arms, and she was able to sit perfectly still for long periods of time, so still that she appeared to be absent. But she wasn't absent. She was unfathomed, deep and bright. A smile like the northern lights, and gone.

He would rely, finally, on Scripture to begin his sermon, as he usually did. Most people (even in Haddington) believed in the authority of a sacred text, regardless of how corrupt or inappropriate it turned out to be. *Come, let us reason together,* he would say. It was as good a place as any to begin.

Chapter 4

HOW DID SHE DIE?

"I started early, and took my dog," Langston quoted to Germane as they headed out for their Sunday morning ramble. Germane's intense civility, as a dog, came about in part, Langston believed, because of his early and repetitious exposure to Emily Dickinson. Other poets had done him no harm, but Emily seemed to understand the metaphorical relationship between women and dogs in a way that elevated Germane's status beyond the literal, and thus, Langston concluded, he behaved more like the Platonic ideal. He exhibited more Dogness.

Like many towns in the rural Midwest, Haddington seemed most comfortable with two directions, as opposed to the standard four; everything in the town that was not residential lay either east or west on

Main Street. Langston and Germane turned right off Chimney Street and onto Main, toward the "downtown." Haddington had no library, no place to hear live music (with the exception of the Full Gospel Tabernacle Church, half a mile to the west of town, which was subtitled The Israeli Church and Her Army—no one who attended the tabernacle would reveal the meaning of the name), no bookstore, no restaurant of substance, not even a bar. There was, however, at the west end of town, a little free-standing liquor store that sold cheap beer and grain alcohol mixed with lemonade; a retail outlet called Kountry Kids and Kousins, where one could acquire a wide variety of stuffed rabbits in gingham dresses and wooden little black children for one's front yard; a convenience store/gas station combination, which also sold a species of Pizza King pizza out of what had formerly been a hydraulic bay; a beauty shop; the Farmers and Mechanics Bank; a rickety building, once the hardware store, where Haddington's weekly newspaper, *The Crier,* was produced; Lu's Diner; and a small grocery store wherein all the floors tilted to the west. (Woe to the child who dropped a gumball there.) This comprised the downtown. There were a few more establishments at the east end of Main (a veterinarian, a post office, a junk shop), but they were no different in quality, and if anything, were even less interesting to Langston than Kountry Kids and Kousins, which she had picketed one summer during her undergraduate years for its exceedingly poor taste. Farther east, all the way out of town, was the pesticide plant where her father, Walt Braverman, worked. The plant was called Jo-Gro, after the owner's wife. The owner took over a series of airplane hangars built on a whim by a survivor of the Second World War, Jed Kelso, who believed he would be able to buy vintage aircraft from the government and open his own tourist attraction. When he died he owned exactly one plane, the crop duster he used on his fields, which Jo-Gro left sitting in front of the plant as an advertisement for its services.

They crossed Main Street and headed north, toward the park. Germane didn't walk on a leash, so he and Langston were acutely aware of traffic noise, of which there was little. Just after they had safely covered the distance from one side of the street to the other, Langston heard the rumble of a large truck in the distance, and reached down and looped her hand through Germane's collar. He didn't chase cars—he didn't, as far as Langston could tell, misbehave in any way—but she wouldn't take chances. The truck lumbered up the street, switching laboriously from one gear to another, and she could smell who it was before she even turned and looked. It was Lars Yoder, with a load of pigs headed for auction. As he passed he waved at Langston. She waved back. They had gone to school together, Lars and Langston, and never exchanged a single word. Langston was so confident of this fact that when she met her maker in heaven and was asked: Did you ever exchange a single word with Lars Yoder? she would say, even if her salvation depended upon it, "No, I did not." And yet he waved every time he saw her. She could only assume that he waved at everyone. The pigs were pushing their noses through the slats in the truck bed, which made Langston so unaccountably sad she thought she would have to sit down on the sidewalk. How is it possible, she thought, that a person can drive a thinking, feeling animal to slaughter and not become less than an animal himself? And what were the pigs searching for, after all, but air and freedom? She considered purchasing a copy of *Charlotte's Web* for Lars and sending it anonymously through the mail, and at the same time she knew such a gesture would be fruitless. All around her people participated in occupations they neither advocated nor condemned. They simply acted. Her father, for instance, had never expressed any excitement over pesticides, and her mother's own garden was organic, and yet he drove to work every day and loaded his Jo-Gro truck with toxic chemicals and sprayed them on the fields at various farms, and her mother lived off his paycheck and no one said a word about it. (And this particular irony—her father, her mother, chemicals, money, given the nightmare they had lived through and continued to endure—this one caused Langston's heart to stutter in its traces, when she was able to think about it at all.) Every time Langston came home she felt this way, both appalled by and curious about the methods her family and fellow townspeople employed to navigate their various discrepancies. The longer she had been away the more obvious their pathologies or blatant fictions seemed, but she found herself unable to speak. She didn't know what to say.

They wandered through alleys and back streets on their way to the park. Germane ran ahead of her sometimes, but always turned and looked back to make sure Langston could keep up. When they got to the playground she found a stick of the appropriate size and began to throw it; in moments of inner candor Langston was able to admit that there was something in the discourse of "fetch" that Germane did not understand. She picked up the stick. She looked Germane in the eye. She said, with authority, "Fetch!" and threw the stick and Germane tore after it and even skidded on his stomach to catch it, and then threw it in the air and would not return it to her. This happened repeatedly. She ended up having to gather a number of fetchables, and after two years, Langston continued to uphold her end of the conversation and Germane did not.

She primed the pump at the edge of the park and gave Germane a drink. The well water was undoubtedly the retirement community of a thousand different types of parasites, and yet Germane drank it every day and never became ill. Langston hoped he was building up immunities that would see him through a very long life.

After his drink they wandered back toward the downtown, where they made their daily stop at the grocery store. Because of the severe and possibly illegal angle of the floor, the store's ancient front door didn't open or close without a fight. She pushed against it for a few seconds without success, and then finally put her hip against the glass and gave it a hard bump.

"Yer gonna go through that glass someday, missy!" Mr. Clarence Burton, the proprietor of the eponymous Grocery Store, said as she walked in. He was standing behind the counter, scratching the top of his bald head with a pencil. Mr. Burton was a stout man who always wore a butcher's apron that tied at his "waist" and hung down past his knees, although no butchering occurred in his establishment. The closest thing to fresh meat carried there were Dinner Bell sausages. Mr. Burton's hair, when once he had it, had been something of a phenomenon—it was the color of a ripe cantaloupe and so curly it couldn't be combed. All that remained of it was a U shape that went from temple to temple, curving around the back of his skull like a long, skinny, orange S.O.S. pad.

Langston pushed the door closed with great effort, and then turned and nodded at him. "Mr. Burton."

"Miss Braverman. How's the folks?"

"They're well. And Mrs. Burton?"

"Ahhhh," he said, waving his hand dismissively. "She's a tough old heifer."

"Is she recovering from her hip replacement?"

"I'm a' tell ya! I wish't we'd never did it!"

As usual when speaking to Mr. Burton, Langston flinched. "And why would that be?"

"Because used ta I could always know where she'd be! Used ta I could put her in a place and say, 'Stay right-cheer,' and she'd not move! And now she's up as she pleases and movin' around and what all. I'm a' have to put a cowbell around her neck so's I don't lose her!"

Langston tried to nod pleasantly, but ended up just sighing. She knew as well as anyone that Haddington was no place for feminist militancy (as far as she could tell, the women's movement was still three decades and four hundred miles away), but for the love of God! A cowbell!

Mr. Burton went back to scratching his head and Langston wandered down the middle aisle toward her favorite section. Germane clicked along behind her. She didn't know what kept him from sliding westward, but somehow he was able to stay on his feet. They pretended to look interested in the potted meat, bleach, and dry cat food that was the Grocery Store's stock-in-trade. Langston was trying to work up the nerve to ask Mr. Burton a terrible question, a loathsome inquiry, but found herself unable to form the words. Finally, she picked up the one grand and anomalous product Clarence stocked that she could find nowhere else: Giant Fizzies. Fizzies were two big tablets that looked like Alka-Seltzer and which foamed mightily when dropped in a glass of water. They had an ersatz fruit flavor, but mostly just color. In addition to being delightful, Langston believed they aided one's digestion, because she always felt better after drinking one.

Mr. Burton rang up her purchase. "That'll be sixty-seven cents, missy," he said, as usual. As far as she could tell, Clarence had never told anyone about Langston's lifelong attachment to the Giant Fizzy.

"Clarence," she began, "do you ever find yourself in need of . . . what I mean to say is, are you ever tempted to take on a . . ."

"Whatcha fixin' ta ask me there, Langston, because I've got to be gettin' on home to the missus."

"I'm asking," she cleared her throat, "if you need any assistance with—"

"Well God love ya! Thanks for askin', but no, we get along fine. Mrs. Burton is happy to stay on the couch watchin' her programs while I'm here at the store. But I'm a' tell her that you asked."

Langston nodded, humiliated, and walked out of the store into the bright morning. *That's it!* she thought, stomping down the street. *That's the end of that particularly hideous road. I'll tell Mama when she brings it up, because she's about to bring it up, I can just feel it, that I cannot possibly get a job, I'm not ready to get a job, there is absolutely no suitable employment for a person of my education and my temperament in this town. I will even be able to say that I humbled myself once, dear Lord, I all but maligned myself, by asking for a job in Clarence Burton's Leaning Grocery Store!*

These thoughts were followed by the encroaching shadows, the dark visages of her former professors and colleagues witnessing her plight in Haddington, hawking crafts in Kountry Kids or serving pie at the diner, and there was no end to the pain of such an encounter, even in imagination. It was the stuff of literature, Langston very well knew, it was *overrepresented* in literature, this failing in increments. She was no Lily Bart, nor even Bartleby. Haddington was a destination no respectable writer would choose as the fate of a character; it lacked the power of the tenement, the beauty of the gothic ruin, the geometry of the heartless city. She wondered if she were about to become one of them: the hog farmers who waved at everyone while driving live animals to slaughter, or broken-hipped Mrs. Burton, absorbed in daytime television, or Alice Baker-Maloney, laid waste. Or even worse, Langston's own mother.

*

As she approached her house, which was built at the turn of the century and used to be just a white, wood-sided farmhouse like any other in town, but which her father chose to cover with avocado-colored aluminum siding, highlighted with brown shutters, thus causing it to look, from a distance, like a salad going bad, she noticed her father sitting in the wicker glider on the front porch, drinking a cup of coffee and enjoying the fine Sunday weather. He raised his hand in greeting, then patted the seat next to him, inviting her to sit down.

"Morning, Langston."

"Hi, Daddy."

He was no Atticus Finch, her father. Painfully shy and hard of hearing, Walt had recently started wearing two little flesh-toned hearing aids that sent Langston into spasms of heartache. She didn't know why. He was handsome in a hardworking, laconic, salt-and-pepper sort of way. Something about him was even a bit elegant (he would probably disagree); his finely shaped hands and black eyebrows, the straightness of his nose, his wide mouth, added up to make him look different from the other men in town. All Langston's life he wore essentially the same clothes, first at the grain elevator (gone now), and then at Jo-Gro: a red shirt with blue trim (the sleeve length varied by season), his name sewn over the left pocket, and blue pants. Even after a shower he seemed to retain some of the dust of the shelled corn, and a certain chemical sheen.

"Is Mom still at church?" Langston asked, sitting down.

"She'll be home directly."

The glider eek-eeked back and forth on its track. Walt pushed them with his dusty work boots.

"It's a shame about Alice Baker," Langston said.

"Sure is."

They glided.

"You hear how she died?" Walt asked, looking a little to his left, away from Langston, shyly.

"No. I assume some wasting cancer. It seems to be how everyone dies these days."

"That's not—"

"I know she's dead; I don't feel compelled to know the details. Why explore the nature of her wound? As Mercutio said, 'It will suffice.' I paraphrase."

"Hmmmm."

"I've remembered a lot more about her in the past two days," Langston said. "Like how she was one of the first girls in our class not to have a dad. I'm sure it's quite common, now."

"He died."

"I remember. We were in the second grade and our teacher said he'd been in an accident. Alice wasn't at school for a week, and then she came back and I don't . . . I don't know what happened after that."

They glided.

"Was he, wait a second. Was he electrocuted?"

Walt nodded. "Trimmin' trees."

Germane stood up, circled, lay back down.

"And also how Alice was the best in our class at making those string designs, those little string things you made with string. Do you know what I'm talking about? how you hold a string over here and over here and then do something with your fingers and it makes a little, what, a little design?"

"Cat's cradle, Jacob's ladder."

"Right. And she could also braid things, braid hair or strips of leather, very elaborate things." Langston thought a moment. "There's a connection, isn't there? Moving her fingers, seeing a pattern where there is none."

"She went into textiles."

"Excuse me?" It had never occurred to Langston that Alice might have had a profession.

"She was an artist. Made baskets, some as big as a room you could walk into. Shown all over the country."

"Are you *sure*?"

"Taught it, too. Went around to schools. Children loved her."

This stunned Langston into silence. That little flat-faced girl with the overbite and the cowlick? She was an Artist in the Schools and children loved her?

Germane's tail started to thump and Walt said, "That would be your mama," and then AnnaLee came into view. Oh, she was a mess, her mother, Langston thought, but at that moment she looked so pretty.

Langston didn't look anything like her—she favored the Braverman side of the family (it was Taos who was so clearly AnnaLee's child)— and this distance, this lack of a resemblance, allowed Langston to see her mother, sometimes, the way strangers surely did. Everything about AnnaLee was strong: her chin, her jaw, her shoulders, her upper arms. Her calves knotted into muscle with every step, even though the only exercise she took was walking and gardening. She had broad, flat hands; widely spaced, narrow green eyes, thin lips. She never wore makeup or jewelry, apart from her wedding ring. When she smiled she had thin wrinkles everywhere—they radiated out and then connected in the middle of her cheeks, and even those looked lovely on this Sunday, to her daughter.

"Hey, you two," she said, walking up to the edge of the porch.

"How was church?" Walt asked, as he did every week, although as far as Langston knew he never went to church and probably didn't actually care how it went.

"It was good. Amos . . . he's a good preacher. He gets to me, somehow."

Walt nodded.

"You should come with me sometime, Langston. I think you'd find him interesting."

"Mmmm-hmmm," she tried to sound pleasant, but noncommittal.

AnnaLee held out the index finger of her right hand, positioning it so that when Walt and Langston glided forward her finger touched her husband's knee. Langston pretended to concentrate on Chimney Street. Her mother could be so *unconscious;* it was exasperating.

"The little girls are coming to live with Beulah next week, Walt," AnnaLee said, and her eyes instantly filled with tears.

Walt shook his head in sympathy but didn't say anything.

"It's just . . . it's so . . . Beulah can't take care of those children. She was past forty when she had Alice, which would make her almost *seventy*. And she spent the past ten years caring for her own mother, it seemed like she would never die, and I think Alice was planning to do something special for Beulah this summer—send her to Ireland or something as a way of saying, 'Okay, that's over, now you can enjoy the rest of your life.' "

Walt shook his head and clucked his tongue. He was moved.

"The whole situation makes me feel like," AnnaLee looked down the street at Beulah's mobile home, where nothing moved, "like we're never actually out of the woods. Beulah must have thought she'd seen the worst of it. She must have thought she was going to have some peace, and now this."

"Wait a second," Langston said, realizing for the first time that no one ever mentioned Alice's husband, Jack Maloney. "Why doesn't Jack just keep the girls? They're his children, too."

Her mother didn't say anything right away, but looked at Langston as if she'd suggested the children be sent to the moon.

"What? We're creeping up on the twenty-first century here, Mama. Men are not actually helpless. Jack can probably be taught to turn on a washing machine and make a bed. The rest of the world is examining postfeminist constructs, and Haddington is still handing out cowbells. I don't know which is worse."

AnnaLee shook her head as if to dislodge water from her inner ear. "Langston, don't you know how Alice died? Where have you *been*? What goes on with you that you are so completely free of anyone else's story? My *God*."

Langston was surprised to see that her mother was both really angry and really crying. "For heaven's sake, Mama."

Walt stopped gliding and took AnnaLee's hand.

"I didn't really feel, I've already said this to Daddy, that it was my business to pry into the nature of her illness, or the details of her death, that's all."

Her mother looked at her a moment, then wiped her face with the back of her hand. "That's not all, Langston. If you gave yourself even one hard look, you'd see that's not it." She squeezed Walt's hand. "I'm going in and make some lunch. Come with me?"

Walt stood up and Langston noticed for the first time how he favored his lower back, how he walked with a slight limp. *Dear Lord*, she thought, *he's in his fifties*. He had been just a boy when Taos was born, only nineteen, and just twenty-two when they had Langston, and she'd always thought of them as being so young, younger than other parents, but here they were, middle-aged.

"How did she die, then?" Langston called out to her mother as AnnaLee walked into the house.

Just before the door slammed, Langston heard, "It doesn't matter."

Langston glided a few times. "Exactly. That was exactly my point."

Chapter 5

THE SACRED HEART

Madeline and Eloise, eight and six. Amos had never met them, although he'd seen pictures. Alice had begun coming alone to his church a year before she died, and after a few weeks Jack came with her, but the girls had continued to go to Sacred Heart of Mary, in Hopwood, accompanied by Jack's devout aunt, Gail. Alice didn't want to confuse them or disrupt their lives, she'd said, and they loved Sacred Heart. They'd both gone to preschool there; they had friends; they were attached to their teachers.

Amos remembered, sitting at his desk after talking to Beulah about the fate of the children, the first time he looked up and saw Alice in the congregation, beside her mother. The sermon that day had been on sacrifice. He'd begun literally, with the animal sacrifice of the First Testament. "It is difficult to truly consider, with our late sensibilities," he'd said, "the blood steaming on the altar; doves, goats, lambs, calves." Then there was a whole section he'd had to remove, if he remembered correctly, that began: "Trust me: this is a *book* we're reading." He would have held up the Bible, a dramatic gesture of the sort he ordinarily despised. "It has a message for you, but there has to be foreshadowing, tension, resolution. We have to be exhausted, sickened by all those corpses, the slaughter of innocent animals, in order to truly recognize the new witness of Jesus in Nazareth. There must be continuity." The typological lamb. The Hebrew people made animal sacrifices; Jesus put an end to animal sacrifice with his own innocent death. Amos quoted from the Letter to the Hebrews 9:11, and 10:1–18. He was leading up to his favorite Christological position, which is that everything recognizable is inverted in the Christ-event: the strong are made weak, the prostitute is invited to the table, the Law is replaced with the Spirit, the sacrificial animals are set free. Christ's task is *immediacy,* he doesn't have time for anything but *metaphor,* he doesn't have time for actual *cows,* to literally sacrifice is demonic (or as Tillich would say, to literalize any event in the myth of Jesus is idolatry). That's what Amos wanted to say, and then he wanted to go on saying it for a few days or a few hundred pages, at least until he or someone in the audience had some idea what he was talking about. He ended the sermon with yet another banal plea for responsible stewardship of the earth, the same sort of plea that could be heard in any vaguely liberal church on any given Sunday. As he joined the congregation in silent prayer, a small voice repeated in his head, *Are you going to write bumper stickers next? "Love The Little Animals: Jesus Did"?* And when he opened his eyes, he saw Alice staring directly at him as if he were profoundly interesting, or of another species. The stare was almost rude, and Amos had looked away long before she did.

But he had seen her long enough to form an impression he would remember, undoubtedly, for the rest of his life: her straight, blond hair hanging to her shoulders. Brown eyes, widely spaced; her face, broad and square, with high, pronounced cheekbones. A slight overbite, the sort that seems so sexy and heartbreaking in an actress in a black-and-white film. And dimples—visible even when she wasn't smiling. Alice wasn't beautiful, not really, but she was conscious. She took in the whole world at a glance, and in doing so, drew the world to her. How could he have known what he knew in that moment: that Alice was kind and competent, and possessed of an enviable stillness, that she was lovely all the way down to the source of her nature? He did know: he knew her right away, and he felt known by her, and that was where the trouble really began. She could have been a lingerie model sitting half-naked in that pew and he wouldn't have noticed. She could have been exotic or worldly or a Valkyrie and it would have meant nothing to him. But that Alice saw him—that was a feeling Amos had never experienced before, and it felt like a revelation and also like a virus.

She didn't speak to him that Sunday, or the next, or the Sunday after that. She just stood up when the service was over, kissed her mother on the cheek, and left. Amos didn't ask anyone about her and mostly didn't think about her during the week (but his nights were worse, and this was something he admitted to himself when he was able to admit anything at all). He wasn't in love with her—no, no, *not* in love with her—because although he was capable of any sin or transgression or pettiness, he thought, he would never have allowed himself that one. He was not that sort of man. He had never, ever been the sort of man who fell in love, and that was what plagued him when he saw Alice, that was what kept him awake at night, during those first few weeks. No woman had ever moved him to such thoughts. Alice was another of those wrenching shadows, the shade of a pure possibility unchosen and un-lived, and at night he was almost able to feel her lying next to him in his bed, nearly in his skin: the heat and the pull and the breath and the sanity of a woman. Life. Life itself.

*

On the fourth Sunday, Alice brought her husband, Jack, to church with her. While they sang and even during his sermon, Amos surreptitiously studied this man who was married to a woman like Alice. Jack was tall and broad, very handsome in a rugged way, nearing forty. All through church he kept a hand on Alice, sometimes rubbing one of her shoulders, sometimes clutching her fingers. He wasn't just proprietary; he was worried about something. Alice permitted all of Jack's various physical manipulations with a pliant unresistance. She sat up when he wanted to put his arm around her waist. She leaned in when he pulled her, offered her hand when he reached for it, but didn't initiate any contact. *What does this mean?* Amos wondered, trying to imagine how it would feel to have another person controlling his body.

Alice and Jack stood around in the pews talking to Beulah until all the other church members had gone through the receiving line, until just the four of them were left in the church.

"Pastor Townsend, I don't believe you've officially met my daughter, Alice Baker-Maloney," Beulah said, as he approached them.

"How do you do," Amos said, offering her his hand. Her handshake was firm; her palm hot and dry.

"And this is my husband, Jack," Alice said, directing Amos's attention away from her. Jack wore dusty cowboy boots, blue jeans with a hand-tooled leather belt, and a soft, white cotton work shirt. Either he was a man who always looked a part, or he was the thing itself. As they shook hands, Jack nodded his head once at Amos.

There is something so grim in his— Amos was interrupted before he could finish the thought.

"I'll be going, Alice," Beulah said. "Come by the house when you're done here."

Beulah turned and walked down the aisle toward the swinging doors that led to the vestibule. Alice and Jack were there for him, apparently.

"Could we have a moment of your time, Mr. Townsend?" Alice asked.

"Of course, yes. Of course. Do you want to go to my office?"

"No, thanks. This will be fine." She smiled at him, and then looked at Jack. "We're seeking your guidance, actually."

Amos was struck again by how completely at ease she seemed. There she stood, a virtual stranger, asking Amos for a favor, and she didn't seem the least nervous or sheepish. But she also didn't appear to feel entitled, and that was a line Amos had seen few people walk successfully.

"I don't know how much guidance I'll be good for, but please. I'll help if I can." *Genuine*, he thought. *She's just genuine.*

"Jack and I are having problems—we've been having problems for a few years now. We've done pastoral counseling with the priest at our own church—at the Sacred Heart of Mary, in Hopwood—that's Father Leo, a dear man. We've seen him once a week for a year, and also we've seen a, what do you call him, a secular therapist, I guess you'd say. Robert Collins? Do you know him? We've gone together and Jack has gone alone. And Jack also has a, well, mentor in this organization he belongs to—"

"My goodness."

"Yes. I think we've explored the range of possibilities. My mother said you had been very helpful to a number of people in this congregation, and I just thought. You know, the people in this church didn't really have anyone to talk to for years."

"I've gathered that."

"Pastor Schaeffer didn't, it wasn't that he didn't care about people, it's just that he didn't see how anything was going to be solved with talking. He believed you just found the piece of Scripture that applied to the situation, applied it, and went on living a righteous life."

"I'm starting to feel the same way myself," Jack said, surprising both Amos and Alice.

Amos tilted his head at Jack as if Jack had said a puzzling thing, something that required examination, hoping Jack might say more, but he didn't. He looked down at his boots, squeezing the back of his own neck as if he were developing a migraine.

"Do I understand that you're asking me to provide you with marriage counseling? Or additional marriage counseling, something like that?"

"Well, yes, I guess so. I, for one, would just like to hear what you have to say about a life, about our life. Marital problems are often religious problems, aren't they?"

"How so?" This was actually a thought Amos himself had entertained on occasion, without knowing how to articulate it.

Alice shrugged. "A life well lived, a life badly lived. General confusion. Despair, regret, failures of sympathy or empathy. Kindness, good humor. Those are all religious issues. And in a marriage, too."

Amos nodded, pushed up his glasses, tapped his finger against his nose. He was just about to lean against the pew, to settle in comfortably and discuss it more, when Jack cleared his throat and put his arm around Alice. "We need to go. The girls are waiting for us," he said, without room for discussion.

Alice didn't seem offended. "Thanks for your time, Pastor Townsend," she said, extending her hand.

"Amos. Call me Amos, please." He shook her hand a second time. "Could you come in on Wednesdays, early evening? After work, Jack?"

Alice looked up at Jack, who gave his assent. "Thanks," she said. "That would be fine. And thank you for agreeing to talk to us. I know it's probably strange to be approached by people unfamiliar to you, but who do you know, finally, in this life, right?" Alice asked it in a light-hearted way, her face tipped up toward Amos's, not expecting an answer.

I know you, Amos could have said, but didn't.

*

The parsonage Amos occupied in Haddington seemed modest from the outside; a two-story rectangle, built in the 1930s on a long, narrow lot. The exterior was covered with gray asbestos shingles, the roof was gray, and the small front porch was painted a blue that might as well have been gray, as if the church had decided, long ago, to make the house invisible to everyone but its occupants. Inside, the house was tasteful and spacious. The living room ran the width of the front of the house, with hardwood floors and aging wallpaper patterned in reckless peonies. In the dining room a chandelier hung in elegant torpor over the oak dining table (which sat eight); the wallpaper in that room was cream with a pattern of maroon velvet pheasants. The railing on the walnut staircase had been rubbed smooth by sixty years of hands. Upstairs there were three large bedrooms, each fully furnished and comfortable (preachers almost always have families), and the study facing Plum Street. The kitchen was Amos's favorite room, although when he first moved into the house he thought he'd enter it only to keep from starving to death, so intimidating was the design: white tile floor, white tile halfway up the white walls, glass-fronted cabinets. Someone in the past twenty years had replaced the sink and countertops with stainless steel. The room was a single, continuous, hard-bright surface, except for the old, butcher-block table at which Amos took his meals with a book. (The most intractable aspect of his bachelorhood was that Amos was uncomfortable eating without reading; he felt as if he were wasting both time and food.)

In the two years he'd lived there, Amos had added a screened porch onto the back of the house, facing the narrow backyard and the gardens he planted, and the white, tumble-down garage he used as a storage shed. Living there in Haddington, in this beautiful house, Amos was happier than he felt he had any right to be, or he had been happy, any-way, and for quite a long time. In the late afternoon and early evening, when he didn't have obligations at the church, he loved sitting on the screened porch with a glass of wine and a book, although he had to be discreet about drinking wine. He was a Pietist by profession, and the peace churches felt strongly about sobriety. (The authors of the Bible seemed not to have felt so: wine is mentioned 520 times in the First and Second Testaments.) And there was virtually no social or casual drink-ing in the small towns of eastern and central Indiana; either one was a drinker, and belonged to a drinking class, or one was a teetotaler.

An alley ran next to Amos's house, and there was another at the south end of his property, where the gardens ended. On the opposite side of that alley was an abandoned warehouse, large and constructed of wood so dark it appeared to have been dipped in creosote. Amos faced this building when he sat on his screened porch, and he spent a long time studying it. In certain lights he could see the faint traces of an old Pepsi advertisement shining up like chiaroscuro: the bottle (at an odd angle, as if it might be flying through space) surrounded by bub-bles that were probably dazzling when first painted, and the logo, un-changed for decades and instantly recognizable. The logos of soda. It was a funny idea to a man like Amos, the changing location and exten-sion of the sacred. The Pepsi sign suddenly revealing itself in the dying light, intruding on his evening, had the potential to haul up a freight car of cynical resignation in him, but for some reason it never had.

Indiana was a world-class firefly state, and time and again Amos watched them come out in the evening. There were always a few moments, warm from the first drink of wine, when he felt he was living in the fantastic air between seasons: there were the morning glory vines in the collapsing fence; the beans climbing the poles; the slate flagstones that led to the porch, silvered; the white shed; the lightning bugs' green bellies; and suddenly, out of nowhere, the airborne Pepsi bottle, a knock from the past. For Amos the painting was both more and less than the merely commercial: it was nostalgic, and thus served to remind him that he was lost and far from home. More importantly, it was a message. *The signs are fading, just like you always knew they would.*

*

Just before the streetlights blinked on, Amos saw AnnaLee Braverman walking down the alley toward his porch. She was carrying a basket over her right forearm, as if she'd brought Toto with her. AnnaLee was one of the few people from whom Amos didn't need to hide his wine glass, which made him especially fond of her. There were, in fact, countless things he appreciated about AnnaLee. He liked her wildness, the way she carried herself like a great ship through the world; her grief, and her great mind; the way she listened in church, her strange vulnerability to her mother. She had a resilient, perfectly normal marriage, she was afraid to drive, and she dreamed primarily in smells. She interested him.

Rising, Amos opened the screen door. "Don't think I can't see you haunting my alley, AnnaLee Braverman."

She raised a hand in surrender. "You caught me."

"Come on in," Amos said, gesturing to the wicker furniture on the porch. "Is that a present for me in that basket?"

"As a matter of fact." AnnaLee sat down in the rocker and opened the basket. "Dill bread. Fresh butter from the dairy. You're too thin."

"Hmmmm. I only *look* too thin so people like you will bake for me." He went into the kitchen and brought out two plates, napkins, and a knife. "In fact, I only became a minister because of the alleged Sunday dinners I would be invited to. I thought I had a whole lifetime of baked ham and fried chicken ahead of me. Glass of wine?"

"No, thanks. Did it work, your food plan?"

"Alas. Now almost every time I'm invited to Sunday dinner by a church member, I'm taken to the café attached to the motel at the edge of Hopwood. It's no sort of life. Oh Lord, this is good. It's still *warm*."

"Thanks. I thought you became a minister because of Kierkegaard."

"That's just a vicious rumor. I saw your daughter out walking her dog the other night."

"Langston."

"Langston. Yes. How's it going?"

AnnaLee made a noncommittal sound and looked out at the garden a moment, chewing a piece of bread and considering her answer.

In the two years Amos had known AnnaLee, her children had been nothing more than shadows on her face. There were things he knew; some he heard from AnnaLee herself and some he picked up from people in the church. He knew there was a son, and legal troubles? what was it? and that he'd been gone a long time, ten years or longer. Amos hadn't paid close enough attention to the gossip. He knew Langston had suffered a breakdown of sorts her senior year in high school. There were no pictures of the children in the house; Taos was virtually never mentioned. While Langston was still away, in school, her relationship with her parents seemed undefined. Amos suspected that AnnaLee's public distance from her daughter actually belied something unmanageable, and so he never pushed her.

"I don't know how it's going," AnnaLee said. "We still don't know why she left school, and I don't dare ask. I'm amazed she made it as long as she did, honestly. When she first left for college I told Walt, could you hand me a napkin, Amos? she'd be back within the year, and there were some touch-and-go moments, but mostly she just breezed right through. Then when she started graduate school I knew the pressure would be too much. I was really afraid for her those first two years. And it seems like I'd just gotten good and worked up about getting her some help and keeping her together and the next thing I knew she'd finished her M.A. and was going straight on for her Ph.D. She had a setback a couple of years ago, but we thought she'd bounced back just fine, and now this. And she was so close. She walked out of her *orals*, Amos."

"I heard. What do you suppose happened?"

AnnaLee blew a strand of hair off her forehead. "God only knows. She's bright enough, but unbelievably fragile. She looks, I don't know. She appears to be sort of tensile, but in fact she's made of eggshells. And *maddening*. She's the most maddening child, and yet I can't possibly confront her or go head-to-head with her, because I'm afraid every moment, Amos, that she might break. Which makes me furious with her, because I feel like she has this tremendous hold over me. I've already lost one child, and so she's allowed to misbehave or withdraw or refuse to get a job, whatever, and I have no options. She's standing there in front of me, defiant, a know-it-all, quoting depth psychiatry and change philosophers, and I can't say a word about the contradictions in her own life. Because I couldn't live with myself if I hurt her. I couldn't live if anyone hurt her. Listen to me."

Amos sat up straighter. "I am listening to you."

"No, I mean listen to me. I brought this bread over because I wanted to check on *you*. I didn't mean to deliver the Langston treatise. Not yet, anyway."

"No, no, it's interesting, really. Has she ever seen a—anyone?"

"Just that first year, after. But I've always thought that what was . . . I don't know. Fixed in her? Her temperament was decided at the very beginning. Delicate. When you have a child like that you just pray they're never deeply hurt."

Amos said nothing, but thought: good luck.

"And how are you, actually?"

"I'm fine, AnnaLee." Amos took a drink of wine, looked away.

"You don't seem fine. There's no reason for you to be fine."

"I," he began, "well, the children are coming on Friday, right? That's a reason to pull oneself together. This is also my job."

AnnaLee's eyes filled with tears, but she blinked against them.

"It appears," Amos continued, "that the aunt—Gail? correct?—has had some sort of breakdown, and feels unfit to keep them. A breakdown of the religious variety. Or at least the symptoms involve sacramental symbols. Father Leo called me; I probably shouldn't say more than that."

"No. It's okay—I already know."

Amos laughed. These *towns*. They simply smoked with gossip.

"I don't understand," AnnaLee said, "how Beulah will care for them, as frail as she is."

"Beulah's all they have. There's no other family—well, there's Jack's mother, but she has Alzheimer's and is in a nursing home—and the only option is to make them wards of the state. Gail was the godmother of both girls. Beulah won't allow them to be taken away from her, and rightly so." Amos lifted his glasses, pinched the bridge of his nose. "We'll just have to take care of them—I—the church will have to step in. I don't know anything about children, AnnaLee. I mean to say I know more about small engine repair than I know about children. I'm scared out of my wits. Their damage? Their hearts? How to educate them? I know *a lot* about old people, but . . ." Amos swallowed hard, and didn't dare go on. He watched AnnaLee lean forward as if she wanted to take his hand—he could almost hear what she wanted to say, that she knew something about children, and would help him—but she seemed to think better of it, and sat back.

"I've been thinking about something tonight, Anna. Do you ever feel like you're home? Because I never have that feeling, which led me to wonder about place, the pull of a particular geography or lifestyle, do you know what I mean? Like Haddington, for instance. There must be a million people, maybe a few million people right this minute, living in cities, or in those wretched, isolated suburbs, who dream of a place like this, these streets and alleys, the way we wander around so freely and know each other and can get from place to place without a car. And the county fair—the parade—all that, the fresh produce and honey all summer. They think they would love to live in this town."

"And? But?"

"But. But you can't ever live in the place you dream about, the town you long for. You can't go there, and I don't mean like Thomas Wolfe or whatever, I mean the moment you become conscious of your desire, and then fulfill it, it evaporates. Like think of that bluegrass band that plays at the fair every year."

"The Kitchen Band."

"Now someone from outside would look at that, at those rustic people, some of them playing washboards or brooms, I don't understand what they're doing, plunked down in the middle of a county fair, and they'd see something wonderful, something to be devoutly wished for. But if they moved here and were part of this community, they'd begin to see that band ironically, because really there's no other way to see it, right?"

"Irony is our best hope, yes."

"And the moment you see something ironically, you're neither in it nor is it in you. You don't belong to the town and nothing in the town belongs to you. One is either perfectly present and entirely innocent of one's own contentment (which is remarkably like not being content) or one is aware, and thus distanced, and no longer at home or happy. Am I wrong?"

AnnaLee stood and picked up her basket. "I'll have to think about it. But you'll stay, right? You're not going to flee because your vision is ironic? Because I can see you moving from place to place, each one more isolated or bizarre than the last, in some desperate attempt to meet what is ultimately more real than your ability to perceive it."

Amos opened the door for her, smiling his closed-mouth smile. "We're all doing the best we can, aren't we?" he asked AnnaLee, as she stepped down onto the slate flagstones.

"Yes, we are," she said, and walked into the darkness of the alley.

Chapter 6

LANGSTON AT WORK

The streets of Haddington were so deeply imprinted on Langston's consciousness she could have conducted her morning constitutional if suddenly stricken by blindness. Some days she spent her walk in a cloud of wonder about the people and the lives behind their doors. She tried to imagine penetrating any one of the houses—Clara Lodge's house, for instance—and making her way first into the living room, and then into the deeper sanctuary of the house, and then into the secret places, like the hope chest where Clara kept, perhaps, old letters and moth-eaten baby blankets, and then into Clara's head and heart, her knowledge of herself. Clara was patrician and widowed, her one daughter dead of cancer, and she stood quite elegantly and kept her hair dyed blue-black.

Langston admitted to herself she knew nothing of Clara, and she nothing of Langston, and yet Langston was sometimes able to stand in front of this modest home and picture herself flying like an arrow through Clara's life and into her very body, where Langston felt she might understand the manifold resonances of Clara's life.

Mostly Langston didn't wonder about her neighbors. Mostly she suspected there was little to know, and so she spent her walk engaged in more fruitful enterprises. On this particular day she was pondering the question of faith, religious faith, and where it was located and how one approached it. There were many theories, some erudite and some homespun, about how one arrived at a position of faith, but for Langston there was only one: Kierkegaard's. The Leap. Kierkegaard's *infinite qualitative difference between time and eternity* eliminated the possibility of a gradual approach. The leap of faith was an existential act that contained in its very execution, perhaps, an apprehension of eternity? Langston wondered. She tried to consider the other approach, the way it might happen in a life that one could spend years weaving toward a miracle, moving forward then dropping away with a little sideways feint, as if being watched by a man-eating beast, and how finally, with just a few steps to go, one would leap into the jaws and be changed forever. *Sola fide,* Luther said. The question of faith plagued her because literature was her religion, and she was curious about the reader's relationship to a text. It struck her that we come to texts in the same way we come to God, either as leapers or tremblers, and that such a decision affected the way we . . .

Langston came to her senses just in time to realize she was about to trip on the broken sidewalk in front of her own house. In heaven she would ponder a thing as long as she pleased, and she would eliminate these sidewalks. As she stepped up on the front porch she could sense a sort of urgency in the air, not an atmosphere she ordinarily associated with her childhood home. The minute she walked in the door she knew her mama had taken some of Jolene Fletcher's diet pills, because AnnaLee had set up the ironing board and was pressing Walt's underwear, and all the lamp shades were off the lamps and piled next to the vacuum cleaner.

"Grandma Wilkey is coming, isn't she?" Langston asked, adopting a tone both knowing and sympathetic, like one might use with a frightened child. One thing Langston wanted her mother to understand was that she understood the whole scenario, rich with human pathos, for what it was.

AnnaLee nodded but didn't look up. She continued to iron the boxers with a strange ferocity. Walt would put them on the next day or the day after and never see or feel or recognize that she'd ironed them, and then he'd slide on his blue work pants and head off to work.

"And may I also assume Jolene gave you two of those blue pills and that you took them both?" Jolene lived in the house behind them, on Plum Street, and was a registered nurse at a small clinic in Hopwood. She was a generous soul, and stole samples of whatever was needed to keep her community running smoothly.

"May I ask what Grandma Wilkey wants of us today?" Langston was referring to AnnaLee's own mother, her flesh and blood, although the way her mother panicked whenever Grandma Wilkey came to town would have caused anyone to think they were discussing a mother-in-law.

AnnaLee straightened up and blew a strand of hair out of her face, then returned to the boxers, ironing as if the Devil were on the case. "Well, Langston, she is coming to inspect. She's coming to see if there is dust in the pineapples on the posts at the end of the bed she gave me when I left home because she doesn't give anything away with a free heart and clearly that bed still belongs to her. She's coming to say, 'What on earth have you done with Mother's teapot,' and I'll say, 'There it is, where it always is, inside the china cupboard,' and she'll say, 'Isn't it a shame it can't be in a more graceful spot and what a shame people no longer take tea.' And then I'll offer her a cup of tea and all I'll have is Constant Comment and she'll make a face but drink it and treat me like I'm a brave soul, having failed so completely after all."

"Oh, dear; you are speaking rapidly."

"I don't have much time."

"Mama," Langston said, approaching the ironing board, then thinking better of it. "Grandma Wilkey is yet another type of person overrepresented in literature, in my opinion . . . can you hear me in your current state? . . . which she would never of course know because one would be hard-pressed to name a single book she'd ever read. I don't know that she'd read a novel even under threat of death." Speaking of death, Langston nearly confessed that she was waiting for her grandmother to die, because rumors abounded that Grandma Wilkey had over the years tucked away hoards of cash in picturesque receptacles like coffee cans, mostly under the floorboards of her bedroom. Langston didn't want the money—she had no use for it—but she did want to know if the story was true. Her grandmother lived in a Civil War–era brick farmhouse west of Hopwood, between Hopwood and Jonah, on three hundred acres she oversaw when Langston's grandfather was alive and which she continued to cash-rent to farmers who used pesticides with abandon. When the farmers market opened every summer, Grandma Wilkey's land produced the most robust and photogenic fruits and vegetables in three counties.

"I say overrepresented in literature because she's shallow and has a misplaced sense of aristocracy. She is wealthy but miserly, and is a woman who takes pleasure in devastating other women. She heaves her metaphoric weight around with an imperiousness that causes my own mother to resort to drugs, of which I heartily disapprove."

AnnaLee switched from the boxers to handkerchiefs, the use of which Langston found horrifying, but concluded that was a lecture best saved for a day when there weren't more pressing disapprovals at hand.

"I heartily disapprove of you taking drugs, Mama."

"They aren't drugs, Langston," AnnaLee said, quite speedily for a usually relaxed woman. "Jolene calls them 'pep pills' and I believe they are used entirely in the aid of dieting."

"Are you 'dieting'?" Langston asked. It was a sham, this weight loss excuse. The women of Haddington were universally chunky and none of them seemed to notice. But when the occasion demanded it, such as a graduation party or in order to rev up for a parade, they suddenly found themselves in need of weight loss pharmaceuticals.

"I am today." AnnaLee put an end to Langston's attempt at her reformation, and for a moment Langston was so disoriented she saw stars. She took shallow breaths and rubbed the palms of her hands against her blue jeans. Still? It was still okay, she thought, to find a way around (*the way through the world is harder than the way around it*, Wallace Stevens said) the most intractable elements of their life there in Haddington, around their history? The tranquilizers, the fertilizers, the diet pills . . .

"Well," Langston said, swallowing hard. "How much time do I have before she arrives?" Of course she had plans for a sunny day in May, but she would have to sacrifice them for the sake of her mother's mental health, such as it was.

"At four o'clock."

"Okay. It's eleven now. What are you going to do for five hours, what is your plan? Because if you choose to straighten the crawl spaces you're on your own. I absolutely will not retrieve you from under the house again." She tried to sound firm. "And where is my father?"

"He's at work, but he came home and got that lamp, the one that belonged to Aunt Tilda, it shorted out again and he's trying to fix it in the shop. If Mother finds out it's not working, she'll—"

Langston walked toward her mother, bravely risking AnnaLee's frenzied use of an extremely hot, weapon-shaped implement. The whole situation moved Langston to a fit of compassion she could barely negotiate. "Grandma Wilkey will do nothing, she can do nothing." AnnaLee no longer allowed Langston to read to her from Freud and Jung, and so Langston had, of late, begged her mother to delve into popular psychology. As much as it pained her, the pandering and imprecise language of Personal Growth, Langston believed her mother could do with some *empowering* where Grandma Wilkey was concerned. "Grandma is an old and bitter woman. Picture this with me, if you will. Picture the day she dies, and after the funeral procession has wound out of the cemetery like a black ribbon, stay with me, Mama, we shall all go back to her house and have a picnic on her big front yard. There will be lemonade and molasses cookies and little diamond-shaped ham salad sandwiches and everyone will be both happier and richer. And then when we all get to heaven we'll be reunited with her and she'll be greatly improved."

AnnaLee sighed and looked up. Langston gently covered her mother's hand with her own and lifted the iron from the already singed handkerchief. AnnaLee had been known to set clothes aflame. "How is that supposed to make me feel better? Thinking of my mother's funeral? What is wrong with you, Langston?"

"It's supposed to comfort you for a variety of reasons. One. Grandma Wilkey is mortal, and in front of you at Death's ticket window. Two. Her calculating and graceless use of her riches, which cause you so much pain now, will entirely profit you upon her death. Three. The nicest thing I could think to say about her is that she will eventually die."

"But sweetheart, that's your failing, not hers. Don't you see? in this equation you're drawing you've left out the principal variables; namely, that she loved only three people in her life—her husband, her son, and her grandson—and she lost them all. It's her losses, Langston, that's what we're left with. That's why she's so, I don't know. Hatchetlike."

"But that is . . . I'm sorry, but is that not the human condition? Are we not all left with our losses?" Langston didn't dare mention her mother's own. "All I'm trying to say is that Grandma has no power over you. She has no power because she has no strength, and she has no strength because she has no gentleness, and therefore you must not fear her, but face her as the desperate and lonely old woman she really is."

AnnaLee looked at Langston a long blank time. "I thought I might get through the day without a sermonette, but I see it was not to be." She cast aside the ruined handkerchief, then walked over and dropped down onto the old brown sofa, causing clouds of dust to rise around her like smoke. "Your grandma is not old, not really. She's only seventy-seven, and her own mother lived to be nearly a hundred. And she is anything but lonely. She has her Flower Club, her quilting circle, and the Ladies' Auxiliary at the Presbyterian church in Jonah. She has no need for more friends or more activity."

"Yes, Mom! But consider what Paul Tillich says. He tells us that—"

Instead of seeing in her mother's eyes that long-dreamed-of glint of intellectual recognition, the one that would signal, finally, that AnnaLee had returned to herself after such a long absence, she just tilted her head back against the couch and blew air out of her cheeks, staring at the ceiling, which was peeling and cracked, and said, "For the love of God, how many times will I have to hear that Paul Tillich lecture? How many? Would you read someone else for a while and abuse me with him?"

Langston squinted at her coolly. She could, in fact, and her mother perfectly well knew it, abuse her with Kierkegaard and Schopenhauer and Niebuhr and Buber and Meister Eckhart, Nietzsche and Hume and Hegel, to name a scant few. AnnaLee was getting off lightly because she was drugged.

"Besides," AnnaLee continued, "and I've said this many times, Grandma Wilkey doesn't seem to be affected by her hypothetical brokenness, Lan, and I can't see as how anything else really matters."

"No, you're right. I acquiesce." Langston knelt before her mother, resting her hands on AnnaLee's knees. AnnaLee looked at her with interest. Her pupils were quite small.

"But!" Langston said, raising a finger. "The fact of her brokenness might matter in the way you look at and deal with her. The fact of it, your knowing of it, might lessen her power over you, and voilà! What is only imagined—her powerlessness—becomes manifest. Remember the words of the Gnostic Jesus, I forget which book: 'If you bring forth what is within you, what you bring forth will save you. If you do not bring forth what is within you, what you do not bring forth will destroy you.' "

"It was Thomas."

"Yes, the Book of Thomas."

"And anyway, the Gnostic Jesus? From a girl who refuses to go to church with her mother?"

"As if church has anything to do with Jesus." Langston stood and held out her hand to her mother. "Off your haunches woman. Those drugs won't last forever and there are rugs to beat."

AnnaLee took Langston's hand but didn't rise. "Sweetheart, sometimes I feel, well, *often* I feel that you're talking to me as honestly as you know how, and yet everything you say is in code. Or maybe it's more like you're trying to say something to me as you pass by in a speeding car."

Langston frowned. "I don't know what you mean."

"I've begun to feel," AnnaLee rubbed her forehead vigorously, as if she had a headache, "that we'll never get it said, is all, that we'll continue to just skim past each other, that everything is impossible and time is too short."

Langston looked around the room as if she might be able to find the thing she seemed to be missing. "I still don't know what you mean."

A look of pain crossed her mother's face, just faintly. "Okay. Okay," she said, patting Langston's hand. "One hill at a time. Today it's Grandma Wilkey."

"Yes! Today it's Grandma Wilkey." Langston was relieved, without knowing why. For the next hour she helped her mother vacuum the lamp shades and pound the arms of the sofa and chairs, which sent her into a nearly asthmatic fit of wheezing. Then she left AnnaLee to her panic, and went up to the attic to her own work.

*

The attic was too hot. The windows were all open, the fan was on and complaining mightily, and the room was too hot. Langston took some time to study the fan, the brand name of which was Tornado, and then she took some time to consider how Hoosiers are virtually free of irony. When she was in kindergarten a tornado had killed twenty-six people in a town of five hundred just a few miles down the road. Violent storms were a constant threat, and thus her father had given her a fan by the same name.

Her bed looked a bit untidy, and so she straightened the counterpane made by her paternal grandmother, the sweet and dead Nan Braverman. Then she studied the stitching, trying to discern how Nan had found the patience to finish it. She could not. Langston's pencils were all slightly too dull, so she sharpened them in the old-fashioned sharpener her daddy had hung on the wall for her, and a tag in the back of her T-shirt was causing her a bit of a rash, so she removed the shirt and cut out the tag. Her braid lay heavily on the back of her neck, so she lifted it and stood a few moments in front of the grinding Tornado fan, then let the braid fall. Lifted it. Let it fall.

She lay down on her bed and thought of Mrs. Dalloway throwing open her windows on the morning of her party *(What a lark! What a plunge!)*, the cool dampness of London, and lovers lost, and the stones in Woolf's pockets, the river, which somehow led her to think of the summer all the soldiers were marching and the dust on the leaves, and how could it be that she was left in a world without . . . ? At least there had been Hemingway's sentences, and at least the little boat finally took the children to the lighthouse. Langston sat up with a start, her face damp with sweat, then looked at the clock and saw there was just enough time to take Germane for a quick walk before settling back down to more neurotic housecleaning with her mama. She stood and stretched and Germane instantly stood, too, and then they descended the stairs, quietly, so as not to make AnnaLee think they were making unnecessary dirt, and snuck out into the day.

*

When they returned home, the house was very quiet, which seemed ominous. Langston and Germane walked in on tiptoes. The living room seemed finished, in more ways than one. AnnaLee had cleaned and polished it as far as it could go, which was about an inch from threadbare and inexpensive to begin with. Langston had often mentioned to her mother that it seemed preferable to have no furnishings at all—to live a life of austere beauty—than to live with "things" that assaulted the eye and battered the aesthetic conscience. AnnaLee ignored her.

Langston took in her surroundings as if she were her Grandma Wilkey. It was painful. Her grandmother was inordinately proud of her ability to hold on to items of quality, and critical of everything other people owned or did. She was possessed of the instinct to zero in on the sorest place in AnnaLee's life and grind her heel into it. And in addition to all that, Grandma Wilkey's house was genuinely beautiful, and she had, in fact, held on to every lovely thing she'd ever owned, including gifts from her wedding to Langston's grandfather, almost sixty years earlier.

The carpet in AnnaLee's living room was dark brown, worn down to the nap in many places, and stained. Grandma Wilkey had hardwood floors throughout her house (except in the bathrooms, which were porcelain tiled), accented with oriental rugs. The walls of the Braverman living room were covered with fake wood paneling, in dark wood halfway up the wall, and then in sheets of decorated panels the rest of the way to the ceiling. The upper panels had originally been white, and were now ivory colored, with a pattern of Civil War bugles and drums, and something that looked like scrolls, in avocado green. The original ceiling had been tin, but Walt had taken the tin down and thrown it away, probably in the early sixties, when people all over the place, in Haddingtons around the world, had believed they could do without the outré, and destroyed it. Now the ceiling plaster was mottled and water-stained. It had never really recovered from the violence done to it. AnnaLee had recently talked about installing a ceiling fan in the center of the room, where currently three forty-watt bulbs were covered by a frosted glass dome filled with dead bugs. The Wilkey walls were, in some cases, paneled with sheets of oak taken from Wilkey land. The hearth in her parlor was carved of native sycamore. Her tin ceilings remained where they had always been—on her ceilings.

Langston walked through the parlor (which she avoided looking at; one could only take in so much) and back into the kitchen, where she found her mother sitting on the floor, sobbing. AnnaLee had, apparently, tried to bake an apple pie from scratch. It had been an unwise ambition, not least because of the amphetamines, which probably hadn't allowed her to recognize when the crust was ready. Langston sat down in front of her.

"Have I ever told you about the time I asked Ja—... one of my professors why it would be that I kept dropping things? I was having a terrible week, running late everywhere. In one day I spilled coffee on my pants just before I was about to leave for school, and then dropped my car keys in such a way that for a few minutes I couldn't see them, and then got out the door and dropped a pile of papers I was carrying and they scattered all over the porch. I thought I might weep. I got to school and saw my professor and I said to him, 'Why? Why is this happening to me?' And you know what his answer was? He looked at me as if he couldn't imagine how I had missed it. 'Gravity,' he said. Gravity."

AnnaLee covered her face with her hands, then tipped over and bonked her head against the cabinets under the sink. They had originally been cherry, but Walt painted them avocado green. "Sweetheart, please." She cried harder.

Langston searched her mind for another way to say it, but she knew she was up against not just intellectual resistance, but substance abuse and decades-old wounds. Taoism, perhaps? But how to say "The Pie that can be made is not the true and eternal Pie" in such a way that wouldn't cause AnnaLee to chase her with a broom?

"Mama, it's just gravity. It's just a pie." That seemed a fair compromise.

"It is not just a pie," AnnaLee answered, snuffling behind her hands.

"Then what is it? Tell me straight out."

Her mother lifted up the hem of her dress and wiped her face. Langston politely looked at the stove.

"How could you ever possibly understand it, loved as you are?"

"I don't think it's love you weep for."

"Oh, good God. Obviously." AnnaLee straightened up and began to breathe deeply, a sign that she was trying to regain control. And a good thing, too, as the grease-stained clock on the kitchen wall read 3:00, which meant that Grandma Wilkey was due in an hour and would actually arrive in forty-five minutes, in the hopes that she might catch her daughter further compromised.

"Would you like for me to walk down to Lu's Diner, onerous though it would be for me, and see if I could buy a pie?" Langston asked.

"No, no. It's too late for that."

They sat still a moment. Langston waited for an opening.

"Do you understand, Lan, that I just wish I might once be above criticism? That I might arrange things in a way that she couldn't find anything to say?"

"Yes! Yes, I do understand it, and what that means is that you are on the defensive. You are trying to eliminate Grandma's ability to harm you, right? But there's another way!"

AnnaLee rested her head in her hands.

"Do you know anything about the martial arts? Because I don't really, but from what I understand, part of the principle around, say, tae kwon do, or whatever you call it, is that one deflects blows by eliminating the force of the opponent's foot or fist or something. Whatever they hit you with. So the principle of fighting is that my fist contains a

69

certain amount of momentum, and pain occurs when my fist encounters an immovable object—in this case your face. But let's say that I swing at you with all my strength and put behind my punch the whole of my weight and *you simply step out of the way*. What will happen to me?"

"I can only guess," AnnaLee said.

"That's exactly right. I'd simply fall down. And that's what would happen to Grandma as well, if you simply stepped out of the way of her blows."

"All right, Langston." AnnaLee smoothed her hair back, ineffectually, and tried to gather herself up enough to stand.

"What do you mean, 'all right'?"

"I mean I'm stepping out of your way. Now if you want to help me, take some Comet cleanser to that downstairs bathroom sink."

"Mama, Grandma Wilkey will *never* go into our bathroom, not ever."

"She will if you don't clean it."

*

The bathroom was worse than Langston had expected; more porcelain had chipped away from the sink and the toilet seemed to be listing toward the basement. Langston pulled the shower curtain closed on the invincible black mold that grew in the tiles, and straightened up the tragic little throw rug in front of the tub. It had once been an expensive rug, but the edges of it had been shredded by generations of cats, all currently deceased. The sink was just a small basin attached to the wall with nothing hiding the pipes beneath it. In the corner under the sink AnnaLee kept a bucket of cleaning supplies, and even they weren't glamorous. There were no fancy nozzles or interesting bubbles or surgeon general's warnings: just Comet cleanser and the kind of toilet bowl cleaner desperate criminals tended to drink in prison. Langston scrubbed the porcelain and the fixtures, which were reversed, so that when one turned the tap that said hot, one actually got cold. She scrubbed with an energy she preferred not to examine, because it contained a protective pity for her mother that made her wretched.

The mirror was the door of a white metal medicine cabinet from the fifties, covered with toothpaste splotches and beginning to lose its silver at the edges. Langston used the old hand towel that hung on a hook above the sink to clean the mirror, then dug through the little cabinet next to the toilet where AnnaLee kept linens, looking for a more attractive towel. She found a lovely red one, clearly intended for Christmas, and draped it so the holly didn't show.

There was a knock at the door. Langston glanced at her watch; it was three fifteen.

*

Grandma Wilkey sat on the very edge of the couch, so that as little as possible of her person touched the nubbly brown upholstery. Langston could tell her grandmother didn't want to lean back against the afghan AnnaLee had placed on the back of couch, which was made from little knitted squares, put together by Nan Braverman. Nan had chosen colors she thought would match AnnaLee and Walt's furniture, and unfortunately, she had been correct. The army green, red, brown, and yellow squares, mixed together in the most frantic ways, resembled nothing more than a terrible gastric event involving a pizza. The afghan threw Langston into a tailspin, too, but her grandmother's all too obvious disdain was irritating.

"Perhaps you've noticed the lovely afghan behind you, Grandma."

"Where's your mother?" Grandma Wilkey demanded, smoothing out the cream-colored linen skirt over her knees.

"Nan Braverman made it just a year before she passed away. She was a fine woman. Salt of the earth."

"She knew I was coming, didn't she?"

"Mama's just getting dressed, I think. You are quite, quite early."

They sat in silence for a moment, and then Grandma Wilkey twisted around and looked at the stairway. "Where's your mother?" Her voice was growing progressively shriller as she aged, and she spoke more loudly as her hearing deteriorated. Langston could imagine small animals taking flight in terror every time her grandmother spoke. Germane lay at Langston's feet with his head on his paws, worried.

"She's upstairs getting dressed, Grandma. You are quite early."

"She knew I was coming, didn't she."

"Oh, yes. We all did. Can I get you some tea while you're waiting?"

"No. I'll wait for your mother."

Langston allowed her to stew for three minutes or so, a painfully long time to sit in a silent room with someone.

"That's a lovely suit you're wearing. Linen, isn't it?"

Her grandmother held out one arm and admired the cut of her summer jacket. "Yes, yes it is. I bought this suit from Jacob Taylor's, an excellent women's clothier, in nineteen and fifty-six. Your grandfather was taken aback by the cost, but I just told him: this suit will outlive *you*. And it certainly has. I store my seasonal clothes in mothballs in my attic and have them dry-cleaned once a year. I still have a number of fine pieces from when I was in high school, if you can imagine."

"I can imagine."

"They mostly still fit me, but of course are completely out of style. If you buy fine things and take care of them they'll last you a lifetime and people will always know you're that sort of person. What is it you're wearing, by the way?"

"Oh. Well, this is a white cotton T-shirt made, I believe, by the Gap. An excellent shirt. And these are blue jeans—dungarees, I think they used to be called. I dress very simply, because I read that Albert Einstein owned something like seven white shirts and seven pairs of black pants, and then he never had to think—"

"Where's your mother?" Grandma Wilkey twisted again and looked at the stairs.

"She's getting dressed in her room. You're still quite a bit early."

"I have a number of things to do today! I have to see John Warden at the bank, and I have an appointment to get my hair done at five-thirty. I can't just sit here and waste the entire day."

"Your hair already looks quite nice." Her hair looked like it belonged on a Mrs. Beasley doll, but Langston would never say so.

"Yes, this is a new rinse. I'm pleased with it."

"And your jewelry is very becoming today."

"This is my mother's strand of pearls and matching earrings. Cultured pearls, of course, none of those freshwater counterfeits everyone is so mad about. Some women won't wear pearls after Memorial

Day but I think that's ridiculous. If you have them, wear them, I say. There's never an occasion that can't be improved with lovely jewelry. I see you still don't wear jewelry."

"No, no. I'm not much interested in adornments. Would you like to know why?"

"Where is your mother?" Grandma Wilkey reached up and smoothed her brow with her hands. She still had a manicure once a week in Jonah, and now her fingernails were painted the same color as her pearls. Her hands were lovely, the fingers long and tapered, and Langston could tell that she was accustomed to gesturing in ways that flattered them. A delicate chain hung from her platinum watch. After she had completed her gesture of impatience, she looked Langston in the eye and gave her a pursed-lip smile. Her eyes were even bluer than her hair.

Langston felt like laughing. "Grandma, you are a *beautiful* woman."

Her grandmother sat up even straighter and smoothed her skirt again. "Well, I try. I've done the most with what God gave me and I always say—"

AnnaLee turned the corner of the staircase and made herself available to her mother. She was wearing her favorite housedress, a light brown with yellow flowers that gathered under her ample breasts and hung in folds almost to the floor. It was sleeveless, and her large, tan, muscular arms seemed to go on forever. She was barefoot, and she had gathered her hair up into a twist that was already collapsing. Langston sighed. Her mother held her hand out toward Grandma Wilkey and Langston noticed again her mother's flat, blunt nails. Her hands were so strong they could have belonged to a man.

"Mother, it's so nice—"

"Now AnnaLee, I would advise you to become more punctual. I've been sitting here for almost twenty minutes."

"But you said you'd be here—"

"I know what I said, and I thought I taught you better than to keep your guests waiting."

"Grandma, I think Mother is trying to say that if *you* had been on time—"

AnnaLee said, "Langston!"

Her grandmother said, "Langston!"

Langston rose. "Shall I start the tea?"

Her grandmother sniffed and looked at the floor. "Your mother hasn't even offered me any tea."

"Would you like some tea, Mother?"

"I don't know. What kind do you have?"

"We have Constant Comment. Would that be all right?"

Grandma Wilkey took a deep breath. "That's what we drank during the Depression, if memory serves. Well, you make do with what you have."

AnnaLee turned and began to take cups and saucers out of the china cupboard.

"Is that my mother's teapot in there, AnnaLee?" her mother asked. As she stood to her full height, Langston realized her grandmother was at least an inch and maybe two taller than she, which made her tall indeed for a woman in her seventies.

AnnaLee turned and looked at Langston, who gave a small shrug.

"Grandma, isn't it a shame that Mama has to keep it in such a humble cabinet?"

Her grandmother tugged at the corners of her linen jacket, straightening the lines. "That dog isn't coming near the table, is it? I have never in my life allowed an animal in my house."

＊

With their tea AnnaLee served small ham salad sandwiches and cantaloupe, which Langston thought was lovely, but her grandmother didn't eat much of anything. She claimed to be feeling peckish at odd hours of the day and night, but never at mealtimes.

Their visit was winding down; Grandma Wilkey had exhausted her inventory of criticism and was about to start asking very pointed questions about Walt and his potential for better employment, so Langston leapt in.

"Grandma, Mama thinks this new minister, Amos Townsend, is all the rage."

"Has anyone seen my keys?"

"I think they're on the coffee table, Mother."

"What do you think, Grandma? Have you met him?"

"I don't see them on the coffee table."

"Well, I do. That's your Daughters of Job key chain, isn't it?"

"I can see perfectly well! And I do not see them on the coffee table!"

"And isn't it a shame about Alice Baker? Did you attend the funeral, Grandma?"

Her grandmother folded her napkin and slid it under her plate. "It's a *horrible* thing. Never would have happened in my day. Oh, I imagine if your granddad were alive, what he'd think."

"It never would have happened in your day? I've always assumed death was general over Indiana."

AnnaLee walked over and picked up her mother's keys off the coffee table. "Here they are."

Grandma Wilkey pushed her chair out and stood up impatiently. "Where were they?"

"They were on the coffee table, Gran—"

"They were on the floor, Mother, where you couldn't see them."

"That dog probably got ahold of them," Grandma Wilkey said, snapping her purse shut. "I'm going to have to have this suit cleaned."

"Oh, for heaven's sake, Grandma, Germane is the most intelligent, noble—"

"Langston," AnnaLee said, raising her hands to heaven, "does this have to happen *every single time* my mother visits?"

"No, it certainly does not," Langston said, more archly than she intended. "Grandma could simply learn to behave herself and then none of—"

"I'm going." Her grandmother strode toward the door. She stopped with her hand on the doorknob. "Well. Come kiss me, you two."

AnnaLee walked over and kissed her mother on the cheek and then Langston did the same. She didn't kiss them back, but she slipped a twenty-dollar bill into Langston's hand. "Buy yourself some nice clothes, dear. You're a very pretty girl. Don't slouch."

Langston stood straighter.

"And AnnaLee, I assume the minute there's word, any word, you'll—"

"Mother, of course—"

Langston stood frozen, watching her mother and grandmother in the complicated dance of opening the door. So much was being said so quickly, and so late in the afternoon. Her grandmother seemed to be grimacing, and her hand slipped from the doorknob. Langston involuntarily thought of Cubism—and it was a comfort to her, to be reminded of such a construction—the way we perceive in an instant the table from every possible angle, even what lies beneath. Because the whole story was right there in front of her and had been so the whole worried day: all her grandmother's loved ones *(all my pretty ones? Did you say all?)*, the truly loved—her husband dead of a stroke at sixty; her son, the beautiful Jesse, choked in his high chair; and Taos, the one she maybe held most dear of all—were taken from her and she was left with just this *rind*. And she would never forgive them. AnnaLee, the pale replacement, and Langston, the invisible. And Walt? His was a life sentence.

Langston and her mother watched Grandma Wilkey walk down the front steps, taking them slowly, and climb into her 1978 Lincoln Town Car, which had been and remained snow white. Langston had once heard her father comment to her mother that Grandma's car was bigger than the trailer they and Taos lived in before they bought the house in Haddington. The Lincoln started with a heavy purr, and they watched as Grandma Wilkey very carefully negotiated her way out. It took a long time, even though there were absolutely no obstacles in her path. She could have just driven away.

Chapter 7

FLIGHT

After his first meeting with Jack alone, Amos wrote: "Hyperabundant attachment formation; boundary disorder; abandonment," all of which had been just shorthand, a way for Amos to remember his first impressions without transcribing the taped recordings he made of counseling sessions. Jack was neither simple nor stupid, and Amos could see why Alice would have chosen him, especially at so young an age. Who better to marry than someone who believed in marriage more than he believed in anything else?

Jack could remember, or thought he could remember, the genesis of his desire for a family: he was nineteen, working on a dairy farm, still living at home with his parents, Max and Edna Maloney. Like Alice,

Jack had been an only child born late in his parents' life, and he'd grown up in the particular silence of preestablished routines. The ghost of Max and Edna's childless years seemed to follow Jack everywhere: vacations they'd taken before he was born; aunts and uncles who died before he'd met them; the dogs his parents, thinking they'd never have a baby, raised and loved and buried. Max worked in a tool-and-die for thirty-five years (when he retired they gave him a windbreaker), and Edna was a homemaker, very devoted to inspirational verse. She took up counted cross stitch as a way to incorporate verses into wall hangings, and later she learned needlepoint.

Jack often felt there simply wasn't room for him in his parents' history, and they must have felt that way, too, because they compensated with too intense a devotion. Edna saved every piece of paper Jack doodled on as a child, every ribbon he won in track, all of his outgrown clothes and shoes. Each room in their small house contained a shrine to Jack: a cluster of school pictures around his bronzed baby shoes, his trophies in a frozen row on top of the piano. Rather than making him feel secure, as they had hoped, his parents' efforts only made Jack feel more alone, as if his life were not his own but a testimony to Max and Edna's remarkable good luck, their ability to succeed at having a family.

Then, at nineteen, he volunteered to help his young neighbors, Chris and Becky Duncan, move from the small house they rented next to his parents to a larger house on the other side of town. Becky was pregnant and they needed more room, they told him, when he arrived at eight in the morning on a Saturday. Chris said, "We've been up since six, packing the rest of the stuff we didn't get finished last night." Becky told Jack, "We can't tell you how much we appreciate your help." Jack said he didn't mind, and started carrying boxes out to his truck. The first was labeled: Kitchen, Silverware, Dish Towels, and Junk Drawer. Something stirred in Jack, an unrecognizable feeling. After a few trips to the truck he walked back into the living room and simply stopped moving. What was wrong with him? Was he too hot, too thirsty, had he slept poorly? And then he heard Becky say, "Sweetheart? Are we taking this little nightstand the previous people left here?" And he knew, just like that (or so he told Amos), that he had fallen in love. What he'd fallen in love with was the idea of an adult life, the strange notion that the articles in a box marked "Kitchen, Silverware," contained not someone else's life (like his parents') and not Jack's life alone, but Jack's whole heart in combination with the heart of another, no dividing line between what he owned and what she owned. Their house. Their baby. Their Junk Drawer.

"Would you say," Amos asked him, "that you'd been particularly intense or romantic as a younger man? In high school?"

He was intense, maybe, but Jack assured Amos he had not been romantic. He'd been an athlete, had lettered in four varsity sports, and so had not had much time for girls. He'd dated, but very casually, and usually in a group.

"So you'd never been in love when you had this insight?"

Not only had Jack never been in love, girls had seemed completely foreign to him, impossibly far away. In the mid to late seventies girls still had secrets, he told Amos. They hadn't learned to completely expose themselves, and no one had taught him how to see them, or else it just wasn't in him to see.

"You fell in love with the concept of marriage before you'd ever loved a girl?"

Jack nodded. That was about the size of it.

*

It had taken him another eleven years to find Alice (all through the eighties, a ridiculous time for a man like Jack to look for a bride) and by then he was nearly out of his head with longing and worry. In that time he'd bought the Masons' dairy farm, where he'd worked since high school, after the bank foreclosed. His father had been killed in a car accident; his mother was showing signs of dementia, and had moved in with her sister, Gail, and Jack had inherited their house in Haddington, which he sold to buy a farmhouse on the Crooked Tree Pike. By the age of thirty he owned a home on ten acres of land, a dairy farm, a brand-new truck, and had ten thousand dollars in a savings account.

"For what?" Amos asked. "What were you saving the money for?"

Jack looked puzzled. "For my children's college fund. Oh, I forgot," he'd said, laughing, "you don't have kids."

"Neither did you."

*

A breeze blew in the open study window facing Plum Street; Amos had been able to sit without moving for long periods, many days now. Already today he had lost more than an hour of the afternoon, just dropped it, his body completely still, his heart beating without any consent from him.

Amos can reconstruct the day Jack met Alice as if he'd been there. He heard it from both of them, and their stories were consistent: how Jack was in church (Amos's church, before Jack converted to Catholicism), bored, restless as if he had a grievance, how Alice, nineteen years old and home for the weekend from art school in Indianapolis, had walked in with Beulah. Alice, Jack said, had been wearing a pink sweater with short sleeves, and a black skirt. She was wearing a black headband and pink lipstick and just the slightest trace of makeup on those beautiful brown eyes, and she and Beulah sat down in front of him. He fell half in love with her from behind, he said, just looking at the curve of her neck, and then, out of the blue, she'd turned around and smiled at him.

Amos pictured that heartbreaking overbite, those dimples, a flock of white birds taking flight. "And your world shifted? Is that it?"

"She was just the one," Jack said, looking miserable.

*

Amos had his top desk drawer open and his hand on the small cassette tape before he realized what he was doing. Just to hear her voice. Just to check his memory. His hand shook as he slipped the tape into the micro-recorder he used for pastoral counseling sessions. He hesitated before pushing play, a moment the length of a monkey's paw, imagining Alice limping up his darkened staircase, returned to Amos from her civil war, not quite whole. Then he pushed play anyway.

THE SOLACE *of* LEAVING EARLY

"I went to church with Mom, I saw him when we first walked into church, the back of his head is sort of broad and flat and his hair is straight and honey-colored, that's what I noticed first. He was tanned and wearing a white shirt and he took up a lot of the pew with his, I'm not sure what to call it, his maleness. He looked more like a man than anyone I'd ever met, I can't remember my own father. We sat down in the pew in front of him and I could hear him breathing and then I could sense that he'd stopped breathing? stopped making some essential movement? and for a moment I thought, well, there goes that one, I've killed him. It was the pink sweater. All girls should have one. And I wasn't looking for him at all, I didn't want a boyfriend. I wanted to go to art school and then out into the world, and I wasn't used to having any power, I'd been a plain girl. Inside I felt like a plain girl. And my mom suddenly seemed very nervous, sitting there, looking at me like I should do something, I don't know what she thought was happening, but the look on her face was really dramatic, it struck me as funny. That's what was going through my head when I turned around: that I'd killed him and ought to turn around and apologize, and then wondering if he could see Mom's face, all anxious like she was standing at the edge of fate, and I was going to say something funny, I can't remember what, but when I turned around he was looking at me in an amazing way, his beautiful face, the curve of his mouth, I felt like I was looking at my own sweet, sweet children. That's what happened. I saw my children, and I smiled at them."

Amos pushed stop, then sat back in his chair and waited for the afternoon to let go of him, these days he was living in.

Chapter 8

THAT SOLITARY INDIVIDUAL

Even with the breeze the attic was too hot to work; Langston tapped her

pencil on her desk, then smoothed the yellow, lined paper she preferred

for writing, tapped and smoothed. Every day Germane followed her

up the stairs loyally, even though she had explained to him upward of

eleven times how much cooler he would be on the front porch. He lay

beneath her desk, close to her feet. She absentmindedly rubbed his belly

with her foot, smoothed the paper, stared out the window at Chimney

Street.

She was so hot her skin felt itchy, so she slipped off her blue jeans

and her T-shirt and lay down on her bed to read. She had embarked on

Kierkegaard's *Purity of Heart Is to Will One Thing,* which had somehow escaped her during all her years of study. She had only gotten through the translator's notes over the past two evenings, because the day's accumulated heat made study difficult. The pillows, the cool, white cotton pillowcases, felt divine against her skin. She lifted her braid and leaned farther in. *Something has come in between,* she read. *The separation of sin lies between. Each day, and day after day something is being placed in between: delay, blockage, interruption, delusion, corruption.* Langston closed her eyes, and her mind filled with images almost immediately, as if she were beginning to dream. She thought of Hermes Psychopompos, who leads us over thresholds: between life and death, between sleeping and waking. As the psychopomp, Hermes carried a staff of intertwining snakes. Snakes. She saw two women, one with her heel on a serpent, and another moving her hands, her fingers like panicked birds. She thought of a verse of the Bible she loved but could hardly remember: *I will return . . . ? I will give back . . . ?* First Kings? Leviticus? She saw her own body as if in a glen, naked, and she looked like her mother, and there were large, flying . . . what were they? flying away from her body, leaving her bare and sleepy. Locusts. *I will restore to you the years the locusts have eaten.* That was it.

*

Every day during May Germane and Langston left for their afternoon walk believing they were experiencing the last perfect day, but every day there was another. Friday following their nap was still bright and hot, but the humidity was low, and there were so many trees and flowers in bloom, Langston felt like she'd stepped into a gorgeous, impressionistic painting: *Girl and Dog Abroad in Flanders.* She had promised AnnaLee she'd pick up a pie for her to take to Beulah's that evening, so they set off for a quick stroll with the diner as their final destination.

The first person they passed, on Taft Street, a short thoroughfare in a state of advanced hopelessness, was a girl (now a woman) Langston had gone to school with, Stinky Williamson, who was sitting on her front porch drinking a Coke. Stinky waved, and Langston waved back. Stinky and her melange of relatives lived in a small house built on and of concrete blocks, and there were always many cars in her yard and around her house elevated on concrete blocks. Indeed, Langston often expected to see the Williamson clan using them as shoes. Stinky was one of Langston didn't imagine even God knew how many children, born perhaps to a mother and perhaps to a sister, sired by one of a number of men so whiskered and reeking they could not be considered by a tender imagination. Her older siblings had earned the names Scratch, Trotter, Dumpy, Tubby, and Weevil (to name a few), and Langston once overhead Stinky tell a curious classmate years earlier that she earned her name for refusing to "potty train," which was how the Williamson clan referred to urinating in the dirt surrounding their house. Taos had concluded from very early on that the Williamson children were named in the Native American way, after an event or a personality glitch had asserted itself firmly, and before that they were probably just called Baby.

Stinky's fate was predictable. She was placed in progressively slower and slower classes in school until she simply dropped out, pregnant at fifteen. She never left her parents' home, and continued to live there now, with no vocation or occupation other than producing more Stinkys. She was quite large and slow-moving, and every time Langston saw her, Stinky acknowledged her in a very friendly way; they had, after all, grown up together.

Farther down Taft they passed the home of the local piano teacher, a strange, tall woman named Hetzebel who had broken away from her Holiness family at eighteen and now lived alone, teaching secular music and periodically setting her house on fire. No one knew how or why, but one in five calls to the volunteer fire department were from her. Langston had once asked her mother what she thought of Hetzebel, and AnnaLee had replied, "She needs to concentrate more on *water*."

They turned onto Main Street at the east end, and headed for the diner. Along the way they came upon Old Frankie Lamotte and his son, Frankie Lamotte. Frankie and Frankie, in order to contribute something lasting to the world, carved statues out of tree stumps with a chain saw. The statues surrounded Frankie Sr.'s backyard like a ghastly wooden zoo. There were eagles in flight, a bulldog, a bear with raised claws, a slinking coyote (which Frankie the elder called a kye-ote), and their latest creation, a squirrel nibbling on a nut.

The Frankies waved their free hands at Langston and Germane and then continued putting the finishing touches on the squirrel. The chain saws whined and died down to a hum, whined again. Apparently the Lamottes' gestures had to be very precise and delicate, or as delicate as one can be with a chain saw. Langston stopped and considered the menagerie. She tried to determine what the single most alarming thing was about the carvings, and then realized that the squirrel was the same size as the eagles, and they were the same size as both the bear and the bulldog which was approximately the height and width of the kye-ote.

The rest of the trip to the diner, another block, was without incident, but when Langston opened the door to the small restaurant her breath was nearly sucked out of her body by the dry blast of the window air conditioner, which was running at full speed and creating a deafening racket. The owner had taped streamers to the top of the unit, which were sailing out horizontally, presumably so her customers could have a visual representation of how cold they were.

The diner was, architecturally, what the locals called a shotgun house. From time to time Langston listened to a call-in radio show, broadcast from the AM station in Hopwood. Bill Linklater was the host's name, but he had taken as his *nom de air* Bumpkin Bill, and considered himself an expert on trivia. Langston had, on occasion, picked up an interesting little tidbit of knowledge from Bumpkin Bill and his callers, and one evening a man called in and asked how shotgun houses got their name. Bill said he believed the name was born of the fact that one could stand in the doorway of such a domicile, fire a shotgun, and the shell would travel straight through to the back door. Langston had been horrified. Who initially realized such a thing? she wondered. Whatever reason would one have for firing a shotgun into a house in the first place? Language evolves, of course—Langston very well knew this, even though she had withdrawn from Transformational Grammar twice in her graduate school career, before completing it her final semester—if it didn't we'd all still be speaking Elizabethan English, or more accurately, painting stick horses like those in the caves at Lascaux. But it seemed to her that some evolutions would be better aborted. The barbarism we have revealed, she thought, in our homely speech.

The bells on the diner door clanged as she pushed it shut, and be-

fore Langston could protect herself, she was forced to take in her surroundings. Some days she was able to ignore the aesthetic travesty of
her hometown; sometimes she felt it acutely.

Four booths lined the wall to her left, with a broken jukebox inter-
secting them. The table tops were cloudy gray Formica trimmed in silver, with silver legs bolted to the floor. The booths were red vinyl.
Most of the seats were sprung, with hollows into which thighs uncomfortably nestled. The middle of the room was taken up by tables for
four made of the same despairing materials, and to her right was a
counter where five or six people could eat facing the kitchen. The vinyl
on the floor, originally white with gold flecks, had yellowed and was
peeling in places, revealing black tar paper underneath. There were two
ceiling fans spinning ineffectually, their blades gummy with old grease
and dust. And hanging randomly about, as if the diner were trying to
be a parody of itself, were old speckled strips of flypaper. Not only was
it repulsive to look at, but Langston was certain it was unhygienic, as
well as unacceptably cruel. A few years before, when she was home
from college for a visit, she had tried to engage the proprietor, a surly
red-haired woman of indeterminate age (she must have been in her
early sixties, but had adopted the style of dress and makeup of a cheer-
leader from the 1950s, which she had never been), named Lu. Lu was a
professional smoker and barely had a word for anyone, so Langston approached her hesitantly at first, and then with more confidence. She
asked Lu if she had ever been introduced to the concept of karma. Lu
didn't reply. Langston briefly defined it for her, and then explained that
many adherents of Eastern religions believed that one's karma was affected by any kind of violence, even against, say, the common house or
diner fly. Lu smoked and stared at Langston, but said nothing. Langston
searched her eyes for any sign that Lu was following the line of reason-
ing, and saw nothing but ashtrays and bowling balls. Her spiritual deso-
lation made Langston breathless for a moment, but also more resolved.

Langston went on to describe the hajj, the sacred pilgrimage every
Muslim must make at least once in his or her lifetime, to the holy cities
of Mecca and Medina. Mecca, Langston said, was surrounded by a
"zone" called the Haram, which had been established by the Prophet
Abraham and sanctified by the Prophet Mohammed. In the Haram not

a single living thing could be harmed, not a blade of grass, not a wild-flower, not even a troublesome bug.

"Do you see where this is leading?" Langston had asked Lu, smiling at her in a way she hoped indicated goodwill.

Lu continued to give Langston an inscrutable gaze. Her short hair was dyed red, but her single eyebrow was black and gray. The skin around her eyes was so wrinkled her eyeliner spidered off in many directions, and her face was riddled with dark brown spots—the archaeological remnants of tanning, Langston guessed. Lu's mouth was permanently puckered from drawing on cigarettes, and her lipstick, probably chosen for her by a sadistic Avon lady, was a ghastly pink.

Finally Lu opened her mouth, and the smell that emerged could have come from the earth's own furnace. "Are you going to pay for that pie, or do I have to call the deputy?"

Langston was grateful to see that Lu was nowhere in evidence today, being a bit uncomfortable around her since the karma colloquium. The diner was almost empty. Herschel Lewis sat at the counter, sipping coffee and reading the farm report in *The Crier*. He was retired, but as Langston understood it, work habits die hard. The top of his bald head was maple-colored from years in the sun, and his gnarled hands made the paper look slight, like the wings of a moth. And here was a thing that had, over the years, impressed Langston about the older residents of her hometown, especially the farmers: Herschel's white T-shirt and bibbed overalls were immaculate. They even looked pressed. She felt her heart sway a bit in her chest. How lovely lovely and fortunate for him that he was able to be happy with the little bit he was afforded in this narrow life! Oh, for a moment, how she yearned to be one of them. The moment passed.

Her thoughts were interrupted by the conversation between Wally Blevins and his constant companion, Larry McCoy, who were sitting at the counter next to Herschel. Both men were in their early forties, wearing old T-shirts and stained blue jeans, along with seed caps: Wally's advertised a fertilizer plant called Sohigro, and Larry's proclaimed his membership in the Nubian Goat Society. Herschel was studiously avoiding them.

"Would you have done it? I mean if you was him."

"Hell yeah!" Larry replied, but not too loudly. "I'd a done it if I was nobody."

Langston cleared her throat. No waitstaff was in evidence.

"Did you read about them things she done? Man oh man."

"I heard about it on the news. Had to send the kids to bed early. I asked Linda would she, you know, if I bought one, and she slugged me upside the head."

"The thing about it is, and this is what the girls at the plant keep saying, is that she's gonna be *famous*. She's gonna be in history books, and all because she—"

"Can you imagine? Can you imagine being famous for doing that?"

Selma Sue appeared behind the counter and raised her eyebrows at Langston. She would be the server for the day, but didn't bother saying so.

"Hi, Selma, hi, I think my mom ordered a sugar-cream pie? Is it ready?" Why was she always so nervous around these people, Langston wondered, as if she'd done something terribly wrong?

Selma studied her, then flipped through the little pad in her apron, giving Langston time to consider her and her idiosyncratic style choices. Over her standard issue, white polyester dress, which looked like it had been purchased at a nurse's yard sale, she was wearing a hot pink apron that bore the legend "Shut Up And Eat." Near the top of the apron she had attached a little metal button that read, *I'm sorry, but you've mistaken me for someone who gives a shit*. Her hair was cut in the most curious style: it was very short on the sides and on top, cut all the way back to her crown, and then long and straight in the back. She was tanned and puffy, and moved with a strange swivel, as if one of her hips were misaligned. Without a word, she turned and headed toward the back of the diner.

"She ain't bad lookin', you know. A little fat."

Larry agreed. "If I was gonna do it, I'd a got me a supermodel. What the hell. I don't need a bunch of thighs at the party. I could stay home and get that."

Wally almost choked on his coffee.

Selma reappeared, walking slowly and carrying a white bakery box, which she sat on the counter in front of Langston.

"That'll be $9.82, altogether. With tax."

Trying to imagine the graduated tax that could produce such a total, Langston pulled a ten-dollar bill from her pocket.

"Whatchoo think, Langston?" Wally asked, startling her so that she nearly dropped the money.

"Pardon me?" she said, glancing his way.

"What do ya think about all this—throw the bum out, or what?"

Langston cleared her throat, stalling for time, then quickly weighed her options: speak and regret it forever, or remain silent and regret it forever. She chose regret.

"I think," she began, uncomfortably, "that none of this is even remotely our business, and that we turn out to be a grossly prurient and insatiable nation. But since we know all the details, and since they are being bandied about even in the depths of Indiana, I will say that I think he must have loved her, and that she loved him. I'll direct you to the evidence: he gave her a copy of *Leaves of Grass*, which is less romantic and seductive than passionate and expansive. He wanted to open the world to her, as Whitman wanted to open the world for his readers, and his lovers. And she clearly adored him. Perhaps she behaved foolishly—who wouldn't have? And as far as that other thing goes, that pressing question down at the plant—yes, she will be famous for a long time for having performed oral sex on the president of the United States, and she ought to be. I daresay that's closer than any of us will ever get to him."

Wally and Larry stared at the coffee cups, stricken. Herschel continued to read his paper, expressionless. Selma squinted at Langston, nodded, then turned and swiveled toward the kitchen. Before she could make any more faux pas, Langston grabbed the bakery box, and left.

*

After she had delivered the sugar-cream pie to Beulah Baker, AnnaLee knocked on the attic door. Langston was about halfway through *Purity of Heart*, and happy to have company.

"Come on up," Langston called, and scooted back on the bed to make room.

"How's it going with that?" AnnaLee asked as she sat down, pointing to the Kierkegaard.

"Well. It's going well. But I wish I'd gone to graduate school in theology or religious studies. I have so many questions and no one to talk to."

"I brought you this present," her mother said, taking a small green book out of her apron pocket.

"What's this?"

"*A Short Life of Kierkegaard*, by Walter Lowrie. I thought you might find it helpful. Lowrie wrote a much, much longer work that contains a formidable amount of Kierkegaard's writing, but this book is pretty condensed, and . . ." She stopped speaking and looked down at the floor.

"And?"

"Nothing. I just thought you'd enjoy it."

"But wherever did you get it? I've never seen it on our bookshelves."

"I had it when I was a teenager. Your Grandma Wilkey had it on that bookcase in the parlor because she never had enough books of her own to fill it up. I drove out there and got it yesterday while she was at her Flower Club. Taos . . ."

Langston let a long moment pass while she pretended to reinspect the counterpane on her bed.

"Taos loved Kierkegaard," AnnaLee continued, with a certain strain in her voice. "He loved his philosophy and his approach to Christianity, but mostly he loved Kierkegaard's story, the very strange man he was and the sad life he lived."

"I can imagine that. Isn't there a, what, a broken engagement? a lost love at the center of his life?"

"Yes, it's tragic. Especially from this distance. Kierkegaard's father had a terrible secret, which he passed along to his son, and Kierkegaard felt he could never marry, because he would *infect*—something like that—his fiancée with the truth. It was a disastrous choice. I've been moved to tears by less than that, by stories with less dramatic endings."

"I'll read it. Thank you," Langston said, sincerely. It had been years since AnnaLee had been willing to talk like this. She sometimes made forays, tender little jaunts toward her daughter, but mostly she seemed too damaged for Langston to approach her.

"Now," AnnaLee said, straightening the bed in a businesslike way, "speaking of marriages. I'd like for you to go with me to a wedding tomorrow."

"Mama! Is this at your church? No. I can't believe you. You are entirely *ruthless;* you have no heart. No."

"Langston, listen. Joannie Johnson and Jim Cross are getting married tomorrow, and they're just in high school—"

"You gave me a present to make me go to church! That's mean!"

AnnaLee took a breath. "I'm not asking you to go to church. I just think it would be a nice thing—"

"I don't even know these people! Why would I want to go to their wedding?"

"I'm trying to tell you that."

"Are you social just for the sake of it? Do you attend things—weddings and funerals and sheep-shearings, or whatever—out of a sense of *form?* In a place like Haddington, where all civilized conventions are eschewed in favor of—"

AnnaLee held up her hand. "Stop. I mean it."

They were silent a few hot moments. Langston could hear her heart beating, and her mother was flushed.

"Joannie and Jim are teenagers. Joannie is six months pregnant and embarrassed, and almost no one she's invited is coming to the wedding, and her mother called me this afternoon and said Joannie will feel awful if the church is empty. This is a matter of simple compassion, Langston. It isn't complicated, and saying yes will not reveal a weakness in your character. Saying no might very well."

"No."

"It's a little ceremony and a cake-and-punch reception in the Fellowship Room after. An hour out of your day."

Langston pulled her knees up and put her head down on them, then gathered her braid around to her chest so she could tug on it until the pain made her feel she could stay inside her body. Her mother was deliberately trying to drive her insane, Langston knew it, she'd been trying for years, and through tactics so seemingly innocent no one would believe Langston if she accused AnnaLee of it. There would be bowls of salted nuts at the wedding reception, nuts in little glass bowls. Langston couldn't even *bear* to think of them. And those buttery homemade mints that were an ungodly combination of flavors, and probably began as pure lard. Everyone there would be so pathetic and lumpy, and some of the dresses would be homemade, and the bride! A pregnant—

"An hour, Langston."

"Oh God! Oh God all right I'll go! Just leave me alone!" she shouted, then threw herself into her pillow and began sobbing. What kind of love is this, Langston wanted to wail at her mother, that pushes and pushes until we break? She couldn't say no, and saying yes enraged her. There was no place to go. There was no place to *be*.

"Sweetheart," AnnaLee said, straightening Langston's braid and rubbing her trembling back. "I know how unhappy you are."

Langston didn't answer. She just lay facedown, unyielding, until her mother got up and went down the stairs. After she heard the attic door close, Langston raised her head for air and there was Germane's face, and the look he was giving her was so naked, so worried, that she buried her face in his neck and cried even harder, and he just stood still and let her do it.

Chapter 9

THE WEDDING

Amos rose on Saturday morning filled with a dread he hadn't felt since
the last year in Mt. Moriah. His reluctance to accept who he was and
what he had to do (and what he had to do was simple, really, nothing
difficult or dramatic) was so crushing it felt like gravity on an uninhabit-
able planet. Didn't he, he wondered now, facing himself in the mirror
after his shower, become a minister partly as a way to balance this iner-
tia? He knew from an early age that he would not survive in a world of
commerce or industry or law or medicine. Profit alone certainly would
not have motivated him to function every day. If his life were purely his
own he might never get up in the morning, and what is working for a
living but taking as a matter of faith that one is due a certain profit?

Amos's first inkling of his calling came not in church or during prayer; there was no conversion experience. In fact, he had never been fully convinced of the truth or efficacy of his vocation. He decided to become a minister while watching television as an undergraduate English major at Ohio State, sitting in a lounge with other boys from his dormitory. He could no longer remember the name of the program, but it featured a detective who was stalking a multiple murderer, and the detective was driven in his work; driven, obviously, because lives depended on him succeeding. If the detective (Dirk, let's say) decided not to get up in the morning (or even in the middle of the night, in the middle of the winter, during an ice storm) because he was *too sad,* innocent people would die and evil would reign victorious. *I could do that job,* Amos thought, feeling a peculiar wave of energy in the region of his stomach. He meant he could do that job except for the part about being a detective, and examining crime scenes and carrying a gun and living in immense danger all the time. And Amos also didn't want to smoke or drink too much coffee or whiskey, and he didn't really want to hang around with other policemen. He just wanted, somehow, to give his life to other people, and not so much to save them as to save himself.

He dressed for the wedding slowly, and hours ahead of time. Joannie and Jim, he reminded himself, Joannie and Jim; he didn't know them at all. They shouldn't have been getting married, they shouldn't have gotten pregnant, they would never make it and lives would be ruined, or at least dramatically altered. Joannie seemed to know nothing about the world and had dropped out of high school altogether too willingly, it seemed to Amos, and Jim, a former football player at the county high school, had just graduated and was working two part-time jobs in Hopwood, neither of which provided health insurance. They were living and would continue to live with Joannie's parents, Ed and Sue Johnson. In premarital counseling Amos had taken one look at them (at Joannie's furious blush, the way she still carried herself like a child; at Jim's military-style haircut and pronounced ears) and thought: *what a long road you have to walk.* But of course he agreed to marry them. He would have married anybody, really, not considering it any of his business, or a stain on his conscience, how people conducted themselves after the ceremony.

Sitting on the back porch with a cup of coffee, Amos thought about Joannie and Jim, about weddings, about his own sense of apprehension. It's just too soon, he nearly said out loud, it's too soon after the funeral. In a movie this wedding would have been a joyous, healing event, and the audience could have pretended that life really was cyclical, and that all things worked together for the good and in their own season, but that was a sentimental lie, and Amos knew it. His hands were shaking. Deep in his heart, what he wished he could do was grab those two stupid teenagers by the hair and and say to them, "You want to see a marriage? I'll show you a marriage."

*

"You had the girls quickly, I guess," Amos had said, in his first meeting with Alice alone.

She laughed. "Well, you could say that. We got married a year after we met, and I got pregnant less than a year after that. I was twenty-two when Madeline was born, and Eloise came two years later."

"Had you wanted children? That young, I mean?"

Alice considered the question. "No. I—I don't know, really. I hadn't actually thought about any of it until I met Jack, and then it was just a whirlwind. I finished out that year of school, and then came home and started planning the wedding, and I thought I'd go back to school but never did. Then I found out I was pregnant, and pregnancy has a peculiar way of . . ."

"What?"

"It forces you to live very, very slowly inside your future. The doctor told me I was pregnant and I thought, 'Ah. So that's what I'm doing now.' And it was all I did. My mind was driven right down into my body, and I put all of my energy into growing the baby. I almost never thought about art school. I didn't think about the life I had been living, because I was just living my life."

Amos didn't say anything for a minute, trying to imagine that feeling. "And what was your marriage like then, in those first years?"

"Oh, it was good," Alice said, smiling. "It was very pure. We were clean people, and we had done this momentous and subtle thing, we'd gotten married and made a baby together, and we just sank into it, it felt like sinking every day. The smells of a home and the smells of a baby and a marriage bed, the intimacy, the familiarity, the safety, all of it. We were succeeding where other people failed, and we thought we'd go on succeeding at it forever, each year added to the last until . . . until we'd what? I don't know. Built up a big scrapbook, or seen the thing through all the way to the end? So we could die? I don't know."

Amos had smiled, thinking of his recent favorite joke: A man and woman go to visit an attorney. The man is ninety-seven and the woman is ninety-five, and they say, after creaking into their chairs: "We want a divorce and we want it right now." The attorney is stunned, and says, "How long have you been married?" The wife says, "Seventy-five years." The attorney says, "But why would you want to throw that all away now, at the end of your life?" The husband says, "We would have done it much sooner, but we were just waiting for the kids to die."

"So when did things start to go wrong, would you say?" Amos asked.

Alice blinked a few times, readjusted herself in her chair. She had worn, for that first meeting, a black turtleneck and black jeans, small, wire-framed glasses, and black shoes that looked hopelessly European.

"I can't say for sure. I mean, I've rewritten our history a little bit by now, haven't I? Isn't that what we do when we're unhappy? He . . . he held me too tight at night, I couldn't sleep, and when I complained he said he just wanted to be close to me. I started taking a mild sleeping pill every night, just to get through it. My skin started to feel achy, like I was raw. This was early on, in the first four years. And he became very angry when other people left their marriages or were unfaithful, anything. Things that didn't even remotely faze me. I've never cared, really, who slept with whom or how someone else's marriage turned out, no one else's relationships make any sense to me, anyway. Why would I care, why did he care? I would say to him, 'Can't we just wish them the best and live our own life?' but he would rant and rave and snub people we'd loved only months before, and then there was that scandal at your church, well, it wasn't your church yet, but the minister who preceded Pastor Schaeffer, Pastor Kilburn. I'm sure you know all this. When

Pastor Kilburn left his wife and took up with, what was her name, Teresa? who used to play the piano? Jack said we couldn't go back, as if the church—the building—and all the people in it were tainted, somehow. We started going to Sacred Heart because Jack's aunt had converted years before—she's *very* religious, you know—and I said to him, 'Jack, you've become medieval.' But he was absolutely determined."

"And you just went along with him?"

"Why not? Catholicism is beautiful, and he found something that was conservative enough and ancient enough to make him happy, and I didn't really care one way or the other. I think I didn't want to fight over small things, I wanted to save up all my strength in case I ever really needed it, in case some disaster ever struck, like if one of the girls got sick or something. I didn't want to be depleted by holding on to petty positions, and I didn't want to be self-protective. I wanted to trust him, and to give him what he needed."

"So what happened?"

"Well. The girls got a little older and I could see I wouldn't be able to go back to art school, so I started just doing little things that interested me. I'd always been good at weaving, and so I decided to make some little baskets, just small things, to practice. And then I thought, well maybe I'll make something no bigger than a cup, and I can make it out of a strange fiber. So I looked around and thought about it, and considered various fibers and what they're good for, and it struck me that it would be very interesting to make some little baskets out of hair."

"Excuse me?"

"Hair, human hair. It's very strong, you know, and beautiful, and it's fairly resistant to the elements and to decay. I went down to the beauty shop and asked Betty if I could start having the hair she swept up at the end of the day, and you know, she said yes without ever asking me what it was for. The people of this town are amazing."

"They certainly are."

"I had this idea that I'd make little braided cables, some dark, some light, and then weave those together, and I got sort of tired of waiting for Betty to call, so I cut off all my own hair. Just to get started. It was really long then."

"A good idea."

"Yes, I thought so. And then when Jack got home he had a fit. I'd never seen him so angry. He shouted at me and had tears in his eyes, he was *shaking*, he was so mad. He told me I didn't have the right to cut my hair off without consulting him, that I was his wife and it was a terrible thing, an unforgivable thing to come home and not recognize me. I asked him, 'Are you saying that this was, in some way, your hair, and that I should not have removed it from my head without your permission?' And believe it or not, he said yes. Then he accused me of being resistant to him, of keeping some part of myself closed, or independent of our family or something. He said I constantly did violence to our oneness, and that he could feel it, and that we would never be truly happy (he would certainly never be happy) or safe and confident until I stopped, until I let go of my need to be an individual."

Amos wrote a sentence in his notebook, tapped his finger against the desk. "Had you done other things, other individual things, before you cut off your hair?"

Alice nodded. "Sometimes I stayed up when Jack wanted to go to bed. Just to read. I took walks. Once in a while I'd say I was going to see my mom, and then I'd drive into Hopwood and see a movie by myself. I love watching movies alone, I don't know why. And sometimes I just wanted to be away from them, you know, not just him, but all of them. And I always told Jack if I'd gone to see a movie, but it made him crazy. He hated for me to have an experience, or a memory? maybe a memory of something? that he didn't have."

"That was about four years ago?"

"Yes, that's right. Four years now. And things have gotten dramatically worse."

*

At one o'clock Amos arrived at the church to check on the arrangements, such as they were. There were two baskets of flowers, lilies, sitting at either end of the altar, and white bows attached to the end of every pew. He could hear the murmuring of the women in the Fellowship Room, where they were setting up for the reception. The pianist, Rhonda Macey, was already there, wearing a plain blue dress with a small corsage, arranging her music on the piano stand. He waved at her on his way back to his office, and she waved back. Rhonda was all business at weddings, which Amos appreciated.

In his office Amos straightened his tie and went over the page of vows he kept tucked into his Bible, the very standard stuff (and which Joannie and Jim had requested—they didn't need poetry, thank you), then looked out the window at the empty parking lot. At one-thirty he would pose for a photograph, and the service would begin at two. He sighed.

*

He saw them together and separately, for six months. Father Leo hadn't helped them, Robert Collins hadn't helped them (the thing Alice didn't say in front of Jack was that she felt those men encouraged Jack, however incidently; that they reaffirmed his growing belief that the family was the single most sacred institution in human history, and that a man's job was to guide it like a ship through a storm), and certainly Jack's mentor in "an organization," as Alice had put it (the organization being Faith In Families, Amos had learned with alarm) hadn't helped them, although he had whipped Jack up into a frenzy of religious zeal and emotional pomposity. In those six months Amos watched Jack slide into a stunning decline: he lost weight, he became more involved in the charismatic renewal movement in his church—once even asking Alice to undergo an exorcism—and finally, out of desperation, he started taking an antidepressant, which made him sleepy and tongue-tied. He was convinced he would lose Alice and the children, and in his fear, clung to them more tightly than ever.

*

Jim Cross had requested permission (and received it from Amos) to play country music on a portable stereo during the reception, but prior to the ceremony Rhonda had been allowed to choose the music she'd play, and Amos was relieved to hear only the standards. If he had had to face, today of all days, some girl trudging up the aisle with a karaoke machine in order to belt out "The Battle Hymn of Love," he would have fled the building.

But everything seemed fine as he preceded the groom and his best man out the side door. Everything was quiet, and Rhonda was playing just the usual processional. There were only about twenty people scattered through the pews, evenly divided between the bride's and groom's sides. Amos took his place at the front of the church, then turned and patted Jim on the shoulder, wishing him luck. Jim gave him a goofy smile, a kid's smile; this was nothing to him, Amos thought. It was just like prom night. The swinging doors at the back of the church were opened by the ushers, and the matron of honor, Joannie's sister, Tracy, took her first steps down the aisle. Tracy was more than a few pounds overweight, and was wearing a tight, pink dress that caused Amos's head to swim. He was so embarrassed by the color and the revelatory nature of the dress that he began to blush, and had to look down at his own shoes. Then Rhonda played the first notes of the bridal march (loudly—why did they always have to be played so *loudly*?), and the pews creaked, indicating that the few witnesses present were rising to watch the bride. Amos looked up just as Joannie took her first steps through the door, clutching her father's arm. Ed Johnson looked flushed and worried (there was the small matter of his daughter's pregnancy), and Joannie was strangely pretty, her hair gathered up, her cheeks pink. Rather than looking puffy, as she had the last few months, she just seemed healthy and young. Amos smiled at her, oh the world and what she'd gotten herself into, she had no idea, and somehow she'd probably survive it and look back on this day, how? what would she see? That was the strangest thing about weddings, from Amos's point of view, that they pretended to be sacred occasions but in fact had no meaning. Because a marriage isn't a marriage until it's over, he thought, until the couple looked back, years later, at the moment they wed and said, "Oh, that's what really happened that day."

"Dearly beloved, we are gathered together here in the sight of God, and in the face of this company, to join together this man and this woman in holy matrimony, which is an honorable estate, instituted of God, signifying the mystical union between Christ and His Church . . ."

Amos began, feeling sweat break out over his upper lip. He glanced over at the windows (they were open) and then up at the ceiling fans (they were on). The church was unbearably hot.

*

He began to behave with increasing desperation: talking to her all night, waking her up if she dozed off. He began letting the children sleep in their bed, something he'd never let them do before, claiming their presence would erode the intimacy of marriage, and those were the only nights Alice got any sleep, with her arms wrapped around one of the girls, the other tucked up against Jack. They were all legs then, the girls, and the bed wasn't nearly big enough. And twice he locked Alice in the house with the new deadbolt he'd applied to the outside of the front door, so she couldn't attend one of her own openings in a gallery two hours away, convinced she'd opened her own checking account with the money from the pieces she'd sold, convinced she was having an affair with the director of the county arts council.

*

". . . which holy estate Christ adorned and beautified with his presence, and with the first miracle at the wedding of Cana in Galilee, and is commended of Saint Paul to be honorable among all men: and therefore is not by any to be entered into unadvisedly or lightly; but reverently, discreetly, advisedly, soberly, and in the fear of God." Amos was openly perspiring, and tried to pull his handkerchief out of his pocket without making a scene. His glasses seemed to be fogged, and were slipping down his nose, and if he didn't do something soon his whole face would melt and he'd have to just excuse himself and give up.

*

And was it five months ago? or was it only four? that Alice showed up at Amos's house in the middle of the night, pounding on the door and begging for his help? He barely recognized her: she was in just her pa-

jamas (flannel, blue, with white clouds), barefoot. Saying Jack had put
the girls to bed, and then asked Alice to sit outside with him (and it was
cold outside—was it January, December?) and he wouldn't let her take
a coat, there was no time, and she didn't even put her shoes on, and
they'd stepped outside and Alice sat down on the swing but Jack stood
above her and said that he wanted her to think about what life would be
like without him and the girls, the howling wasteland of the world
when they were not together, he wanted her to think about it very carefully, and with that knowledge they could go forward and live the rest
of their lives happily, knowing the tragedy they'd avoided, the longing
and the emptiness and the meaninglessness, the *cold*. Then he'd walked
in the back door and closed it, and Alice found herself locked out,
rather than in, and her children in there with him. She'd used the emergency key she kept in her wheel well and driven straight to him, straight
to Amos; he could see she was terrified (and freezing), and after he'd
given her a pair of socks and wrapped her in a blanket and asked if she
wanted him to call the police and she'd said yes, he turned to her and
said the thing he said. And standing there now, in the sight of God and
in the face of this company, why had he really said it? He was worried
about her and about her children and even about Jack, but wasn't there,
if he looked deeply and honestly into his own heart, something else?
Wasn't there her collarbone to consider, visible when the neck of her
pajama top shifted, wasn't there a plain girl inside who had never had
power and wouldn't dream of misusing it? Hadn't she cut off her own
hair to make a little cup, and didn't he feel sort of like that detective, the
one who worked tirelessly to save the innocent and allow righteousness
to prevail? They were standing at the bottom of the staircase, the walnut staircase with the shining rail, under a small, hanging light in a
pewter fixture, and he'd taken her by the shoulders and looked her
in the eye and said, *"You must take your children, and leave him."*

*

"Into this holy estate these two persons present come now to be joined.
If any man can show just cause why they may not lawfully be joined to-

gether, let him speak now, or forever hold his peace." Amos wiped his forehead with his handkerchief and waited to see if anyone would stand. Joannie's mother was weeping into a battered tissue; Jim's parents were staring stoically at the lilies on the altar. Amos saw Walt and AnnaLee Braverman in the middle of the church, and someone sitting beside Walt—was that Langston? staring at Amos with a furious concentration. Her whole body seemed coiled, about to spring. For one dreadful, thrilling moment Amos believed Langston would interrupt the ceremony, would actually, for the first time in his professional life, proclaim a reason that two people should not be married. But she didn't rise.

"If there are no impediments, who gives this woman in marriage to this man?"

"Her mother and I," Ed said, his voice cracking, then leaned over and kissed Joannie on the cheek before turning to sit down with Sue. But Joannie wouldn't let him go, she clung to her father too long and Amos felt his eyes start to burn with tears, how wretched this suddenly seemed, that Ed should be losing his daughter this way, to a stupid, truck-driving, country-music-loving, football-playing idiot like Jim Cross. An *animal*. She was someone's *daughter*. Amos felt his stomach flip over once, just a warning of imminent danger, but not the disaster itself.

*

They moved to a small, rented house outside Haddington, toward the bigger town of Jonah. Beulah had helped Alice pay the rent until she was on her feet, and had helped with the girls, because by then Jack had started calling Alice every hour and sending her three or four letters every day, and showing up outside at odd hours. And she had done everything she could, no one could argue with that, *the full extent of the law* was how one of the deputies had described it to Amos.

Amos knew what the letters said because he'd gotten them, too, almost fifty of them. They were in a file folder in his study at home marked "Baker-Maloney." In it were the notes from his counseling sessions, three postcards of Alice's baskets, a log of their appointments, photocopies of letters Amos wrote to the county sheriff, and the letters Jack had written Amos.

It is God's dearest wish that our family be together on earth as we will be together in heaven. I am so depressed I can't think. The doctor has increased the dosage of my medicine to 75 mg a day and I am shaking all the time. Something terrible is going to happen. Alice has cut her hair again and is wearing a new pair of pants, green corduroy, and I am sure these two things are designed to attract men. She will have men in the house with my children. If she doesn't come home to me we are all damned the evidence clearly states that children can recover from the death of a parent easier than from a divorce.

✳

"Will you, Jim, take this woman to be your wedded wife, to live together after God's ordinance in the holy estate of matrimony? Will you love her, comfort her, honor and keep her in sickness and in health, and forsaking all others, keep only unto her as long as you both shall live?" Amos's palms were slick with sweat; he fumbled with his Bible, caught it just in time.

✳

At the end of the full extent of the law, Alice bought a handgun, legal, authorized, having endured the requisite waiting period and background check, a used Colt .45 semiautomatic, the sort of gun that would cause a grown man to panic and run. She practiced with the gun at a shooting range in Hopwood. Amos couldn't help but marvel at Alice, here, in this part of the story. How she brought the gun home and explained to her children that it was profoundly dangerous, and she couldn't hide it, she needed to keep it close, and how they never touched it, but knew it was there. How Alice sent only one reply to the two hundred or so letters she received from Jack: "If you come near me, or near my children, I'll kill you, and *then* you'll know something about tragedy. *Then* we can test your theory about whether children recover faster from death than from divorce."

∗

"I will," Jim said, without any discernible conviction, but nervously, as if he'd suddenly realized where he was.

"And will you, Joannie, take this man to be your wedded husband?"

∗

She had just picked the girls up from school, the girls were carrying bags with the costumes from a little Renaissance drama they'd been in at school, Alice had made the costumes, and they'd walked in the front door and let the screen close, and no one closed and locked the storm door, she wasn't barricaded in there, it wasn't a fortress, after all.

∗

"Repeat after me."

∗

Alice had seen him drive up, and get out of the truck, walking with a terrifying purpose, Amos imagined, although all he could do was imagine. He knew she picked up the phone and dialed 911, then said to the dispatcher, "This is Alice Baker-Maloney, I live at 1411 Pettigrew Road, and I believe my husband is going to try to harm me." Then she lay the phone down on the table so the dispatcher could hear what happened.

∗

"Repeat after me."

∗

He was going to kill the children, kill Alice, and then himself, or so said
the note he left, but by the time he burst through the front door, his
own gun already raised (a 9mm, borrowed from a man who worked for
him at the dairy), Alice was standing between him and the children.
(You could hear the children on the 911 tape, the sheriff's deputy said
to Amos later.) Things happened very quickly after that.

*

"Bless O Lord this ring, that he who gives it and she who wears it may
abide in thy peace, and continue in thy favor, until their life's end."

*

Robbie Ballenger, the local funeral director and county coroner, had
spent an hour with Amos at the funeral home, patiently explaining to
him what had happened, the sequence of events, all of which were visible at the scene and validated by the taped phone call, and by the witnesses. Witnesses? Amos asked, stunned. The children, Robbie meant.

*

"Forasmuch as Joannie and Jim have consented together in holy wedlock, and have witnessed the same before God and this company, and
theretofore have given and pledged their faithfulness, each to the other,
and have declared the same by giving and receiving a ring and by join-
ing hands, I pronounce that they are Husband and Wife. Welcome
them, please."

*

Without a word, Jack raised his gun and shot Alice twice, once in the
neck (just grazed her, that one), and once low in the left shoulder, and
Alice raised her gun and fired it only once. "Hit him right between the
eyes, Amos," Robbie had said, shocked. Amos had nodded, "She had a

steady hand." By the time the police arrived, the children were standing in the front yard, wailing and pointing at the house, and it was all over.

*

"Congratulations, you two," Amos said, shaking Jim's hand and kissing Joannie on the cheek. "Best of luck to you," he said, and he meant it, he meant it.

PART TWO

Go tell court-huntsmen, that the King will ride,

Call country ants to harvest offices;

Love, all alike, no season knows, nor clime,

Nor hours, days, months, which are the rags of time.

JOHN DONNE

Chapter 10

AT THE CORNER OF
PLUM AND CHIMNEY

Her mother told her she didn't have to stay for the cake-and-punch reception, for which Langston was greatly appreciative. She stood and slipped out of the church before the receiving line formed, and as she walked down the street toward home she tried to figure out what had happened.

There had been a woman at the wedding and Langston had seen her first, Miss Grogan, who used to be the secretary at the high school; retired now. Langston hadn't thought of Miss Grogan for years, but recognized her right away, and when Miss Grogan saw Langston she tried to stand up and hug her, but she was a large woman and none too steady on her feet. After she'd pulled herself up (holding on to the pew in front of her), she took a moment to tug on the hem of her fuchsia blouse, a delicate gesture that aligned the shoulder pads and made her appear better ordered. There was something in the scene, the struggle to stand, the automatic straightening of the hem, which caused Langston pain, and frightened her, as well. She saw something in it, a terrible thing, akin to how Nan Braverman, God rest her soul, used to eat her dinner. At the end of her life, Langston's parents took every meal to Nan, and Langston was sometimes forced to help feed her; Langston's consistent pleas that her sensibilities were being violated fell on deaf ears, AnnaLee's argument being that if Nan could manage to die, Langston could probably afford to watch.

Langston hugged Miss Grogan and asked her how she was enjoying her retirement. She said she was looking forward to a trip to the Holy Lands with her church. Langston patted her on the hand, remembering Nan sitting at her round, gray Formica table, how AnnaLee used to move around the kitchen, putting soup in a bowl, cutting bread into bite-size pieces, pouring a glass of prune juice, and all the while Nan sat without moving. Her patience was a horror. She was just sitting, waiting for AnnaLee to put her food on the table, waiting for Langston to begin spooning it into her mouth. And Nan wasn't dead yet, she wasn't without feeling; something quick moved yet in her eyes. What was it? What connected that posture of her grandmother, the childlike faith that the necessary thing would arrive and move her into another day, with Miss Grogan's agonized rising?

And then Amos Townsend walked out, and Langston had to admit to being taken aback by his appearance. For one thing, he was far more graceful and old-world than she thought the first time she saw him (although Ichabod Crane was *barely* American), going gray at the temples and wearing very stylish eyeglasses. His fingers looked as if they had been carved by a puppet-maker, and he wore a spring tan. AnnaLee reported that he gardened. But mostly he looked stricken, haunted by something, and Langston wondered what. What was causing him to suffer so? And then when the service began it appeared he might faint or otherwise revolt, and she studied him very carefully, trying to discern some clue from the ceremony itself, but of course, it was just the standard fare, nothing of his or anyone else's condition in it. By the time the poor couple were actually joined in holy wedlock, Langston was afraid for the minister, who was pale and perspiring and once almost dropped his Bible.

As she was leaving the church she glanced one last time at Miss Grogan. It was something simple, probably. She and Nan were both perfectly familiar with the limitations of their bodies, both beyond the point of hoping for a certain kind of change. Langston couldn't see it all, sitting there in the wedding, and she couldn't have said it, but she knew for just a moment that there are so many ways to go—an infinite number of ways to go as we spiral out from our genesis. Some fight against any measure of grace, and some decide to sit very still at the table and linger. Some stand right inside their impossible weight, tug at the edge of a blouse. Fuchsia. However did people manage?

*

Before she left graduate school, Langston had embarked on three projects, all of them intricate and time-consuming. She had written every day, sometimes for six-hour stretches; most of that work was rejected upon rereading, inasmuch as she considered herself a person of exacting standards. She had tried (with little fruit) to keep up the practice after she moved back home to Haddington.

For many years Langston was a student of literature who was secretly attracted to philosophy and religion, but she always believed she would finish her Ph.D. and become a university professor in an English department. The life was deeply attractive to her, for a variety of reasons, and she could easily picture herself taking a tenure-track position at a small, affluent liberal arts college and staying there until she retired. Germane and she would live quietly in a small cottage at the edge of campus, where she would tend to her lovely English-style garden (the details here were foggy, since gardening wasn't so much in her nature) and write her scholarly books on the American Romantic period. Her students and a few well-chosen colleagues would come a few times a week for tea. Perhaps the college would be somewhere in New York state, or in New England, thus allowing her to spend some weekends in the city, pursuing cultural objectives and occasionally indulging herself in a . . .

There was no use considering it now. She had closed that particular door, and so would have to make her way in the world in some other fashion. She felt, again, that odd creeping grief come over her when she considered that she had given up the life she had planned; she saw, as if from a great distance, the flowers in the garden at the back of her cottage, the front door with its brass mail slot (which made the house appear to be smiling), the vines around the windows with their many panes of glass. And what was this? She seemed to be endowing the scene with some stolen light, so clear to her was every lost aspect. Through the kitchen window she could see peppers drying on a string, a bouquet of flowers hung upside down on a nail, and something else. A small blue bottle, small enough to fit in the palm of her hand (if she had been able to touch it). A cork was broken off deep in the neck of the bottle, as if someone tried first to pull it out, and then to push it all the way in. There was an image embossed on the side of the bottle: a goat, or a horse with a wreath of flowers around his neck. Langston remembered, or thought she remembered, what the bottle had once contained: medicine. A sticky-sweet cure for—

She came to her senses with a slight jump. Where had she been? *And where was that house?* Her heart was pounding, and she noticed, for the first time, that Germane was chewing obsessively on one of his paws.

"Stop that," she said, a bit harshly, hurting his feelings. Only a dog could drag a person so mercilessly back into the present. She rubbed his ears, assuaging him. It was hot in the attic, and a storm seemed to be gathering in the west.

*

The only fate left to her was writing. She had thought at first that she would do something very edgy, risky. She'd imagined some postmodern/noir/urban setting in which the fate of the characters (and the revelation of the metaphorical intent on the author's part) developed through an accident, a slip of the tongue, a wrong number, something like that. A typographical error. A failure to listen. The book would take place almost entirely in basements, subways, and dark rooms. The fact that she'd never lived in a city might have been considered a limitation, but she had great faith in Henry James's position: *a writer is a person on whom nothing is lost.* She would simply combine what she knew about "the city" (the city of the psyche, that is) with images she had gathered over the years from other novels, and from movies.

That novel (working title: *Tunnel*) began promisingly enough, Langston thought. Our protagonist, who is without either a name or a gender, is riding the subway from one end of the city to the other. He/she is minding his/her own business, when a homeless man (definitely a man) approaches the—let's just call him/her The Protagonist—and says: "I have a message for you." The Protagonist is sublimely disinterested in the machinations of the plot; in fact, The Protagonist will do everything in his/her power to thwart the plot, in a postmodern fashion. The Protagonist neither answers nor fails to answer, but spends quite a long time considering the attire of the homeless person, some of which seems genuine and some of which lacks verisimilitude. The "homeless" man, less confident now, says, "Aren't you the one? Did you see the V of geese this morning?" (Are there geese in the city? Langston felt certain there were.) The Protagonist says nothing, but reaches in his/her pocket and pulls out a deck of cards, extracts the jack of diamonds, and reveals it to the "bum," which causes him to back away from The Protagonist in a state of great fear and respect.

That was as far as she'd gotten on *Tunnel* before she lost interest in it. Even though it was clearly headed in the right direction, she couldn't seem to work up any excitement over it. Some essential heart was lacking in the postmodern novel of the subway.

Since she couldn't be an academic, she'd decided to continue working on the academic novel she'd begun in Bloomington, and to that end had been compiling descriptions of English Department Types. So far she had no plot, setting, or conflict, but she did have sixty pages of character description she was sure would stand her in good stead when she entered the actual writing of the book. Today she was considering three types:

1. *The Sage*. The Sage is almost always a man of great maturity and academic rank, a man who saw himself from an early age as possessed of a certain tender erudition that needed to be shared with the young. His ambition is so subtle as to appear nonexistent, and so he has seemingly floated into his full-professorship without incurring the disdain of any campus radicals or poets. He is soft-spoken; does not hold with punitive grading; sometimes breaks into song during a lecture on the American folk tradition. The Sage has a predilection for the Good Life, and so is a lover of red wine, Italian opera, old maps, and European travel. The Sage is an elusive creature, and is rarely present for office hours. Over the course of his career he will perfect the syllabi in the four or five courses he will be asked to teach in the fifteen years approaching retirement, and he will deliver the memorized lectures again and again, as if extemporizing, never picking up a text, but quoting it at length. (Indeed, The Sage often stops reading altogether somewhere in his late forties.) His students will find themselves agog at the breadth and depth of his knowledge. Many dewy-eyed young women will approach him after class, all to be turned away kindly. The Sage is no predator, although he may have many wives. He is after, if Langston may be so crass, a certain level of income in a woman, enough to supplement his salary (including merit pay, honoraria, the occasional fellowship, etc.) all toward the goal of allowing him to *cease teaching altogether*. The perfect life for The Sage is one in which he is known and honored as a Professor; paid as a Professor, but not required to Profess. He wants to write, he wants to paint, he wants to build a harpsichord. His wife (first, second, third—no matter) briefly takes up yoga in a serious way, or photography, or puppeteering. Their love is deeply civilized. Perhaps they drag a communal rake through their Zen garden. The Sage (and his wife) can often be found either departing for or returning from Paris (wherever geographically the Paris-of-the-moment happens to be: Prague, Tuscany, Venice, etc.). The most common statement of The Sage (if he can ever be found), is, "I miss my students, of course, and our rigorous interaction, but my work is going well. The northern Italian landscape is more conducive to creativity than any other in the world."

2. *The Wasted Genius*. Usually a man, the Wasted Genius is (maybe)

the most brilliant human being academia has ever encountered, but it's
impossible to say for certain. His poetry is written in cantos; his lexicon
is entirely idiosyncratic; his wild-eyed lectures often include references
to the most obscure elements of sixteen other disciplines. Stranded for
vague historical reasons (all tragic) at a third-rate state institution, the
WG usually takes up alcohol and drugs in copious amounts. He witnesses a murder in a darkened bar on the wrong side of town. Visiting
poets try to match his wildness, his brokenhearted edginess, drink for
drink, and end up blinded or in fistfights. By the end of his career
(which is usually marked by the presence of a large-caliber handgun in
or near a classroom) his lectures have become so cryptic that his follow-
ers must write down everything he says in order to remember the life-
altering experience of hearing him the first time. He retires to a vast
western state and is never heard from again, although there are many
sightings of him, all apocryphal. The favored statement of the WG:
"Why do the voices of the dragon tell us we must kill our families?
Because we awaken unto death, the fire in the attic, the swamp in the
basement. In the end, Macbeth is unable to sit in his own chair, at his
own table—and that, *that* is what the dragon means. I'll kill your family
for you if you're too chickenshit to do it yourself."

3. *The Grown-up Nerd.* The Grown-up Nerd can be either a man or
a woman. If the GUN takes the male form, he can go one of two ways:
He can become the purveyor of strange and arcane information, usually
from seventeenth-century England, which he will toss about as if he
were gossiping in the most clever way, and as if everyone finds inside
humor about Jacobean theater funny. This man has the potential to
paint his garage floor, and listens solely to the chants of Hildegard of
Bingen, typically wearing an expression of abandon. He is deeply eccle-
siastical and hierarchical, and makes for a grand administrator. The first
type is harmless, and indeed, can be benevolent. The other male GUN
is one of the most dangerous men in the department, because he is
driven to use his newfound status to attain the attention (if not the affections) of all the people who might have ignored him in junior high
and high school. He will collect the prettiest, smartest undergraduate
women—those who are moved by insightful explications of Wittgen-
stein, for instance—eventually breaking their hearts, and will under-

mine in subtle ways all the undergraduate men, especially those who remind him of himself.

The female GUN causes no one any harm. She is quite tall and splayfooted, and is prone to wearing ghastly combinations of polyesters in primary colors, along with the omnipresent Sensible Shoes. If she has moles, she doesn't remove them. Her work is often brilliant, but overlooked, owing to her general demeanor and lack of star-quality, but she never engages in bitterness or regret, partly because she spends most of her energy on her cats. (Cat hair is a problem for the female GUN, along with her own hair and the hair that springs up from various growths, all of which elude her observation.) Her students find her to be smart and lively, but weird, and she is not especially close to anyone, either students or colleagues. She needs no approbation—which is good, because the male GUN (of the predatory variety) often receives her share of merit pay, while abdicating service on various committees to her superior organizational ability.

Langston sat back and reviewed her work. It was accurate, detailed, precise. But she kept hearing her Grandma Wilkey's voice in her head, saying, just before she skewered someone, "Mind you, this isn't a criticism—just an observation." Langston rested her chin on her fists and stared at the pages. In Bloomington she had felt no conflict over this project; she had, in fact, felt justified, clever, as if she were in the grips of a small, social revelation. She had meant to say, from her solitary position in the minefield of graduate school, *I see you; you have been witnessed.* Now it was beginning to look to her as if she could title the work *Just an Observation.*

She paced the length of the attic. What was happening to her? How had this occurred so quickly, this slide into mediocrity? Two months ago she would have been sitting at her desk in her apartment, completing the description of the one of the Types from the list she'd made, but not yet vanquished: *The Man with the Wide Bottom;* or *The Connoisseur of Pulp Mysteries;* or *Gunther: The Protofeminist.* Had she become one of them, one of the bland townspeople, uncritical, afraid to speak?

Vocatus atque non vocatus: bidden or unbidden, called or not called, there he was again, suddenly, his face so clear in Langston's mind she stopped pacing and closed her eyes, at once trying to shake and to preserve the vision. Her Perfect Reader. How could she have ever considered working without him? For two years she had kept at bay the certainty that all was lost when she lost him; now a bead of sweat coursed down her spine like a snake. Everything that had happened over the past month had contained the same message. She lay down on her bed, her breathing shallow, and waited for the feeling to pass.

*

The one who is conscious of himself as an individual has his vision trained to look upon everything as inverted. His sense becomes familiar with eternity's true thought: that everything in this life appears in inverted form. Langston had just finished reading this sentence in Kierkegaard, sitting in her attic window, hoping the rain would come and break the heat. The afternoon light on Chimney Street was beautiful, dappled, she had even begun to feel a bit sleepy when she saw them turn the corner and emerge from the shadows off Plum Street. *What am I seeing?* she thought, squinting. And then, *Are those* children *on the corner?*

Chapter 11

THE TRINITY

"There are a great many ways we may relocate ourselves," Amos wrote in his notebook, working again on the question of Christ's immediacy, and what it might mean in daily life. He had been pondering the notion of shaking the dust off one's sandals and leaving the village (three of the four Gospels advise it). No. Not relocation, that wasn't what he meant. He wanted to suggest space and relocation, but of the internal variety. Perspective, that's it, that's all. One's perspective is the village one occupies, and if one is treated badly in one's own home, if one is denied comfort and wisdom, fleeing is an option. "And don't take the dirt

with you," he wrote. "You won't need it where you're going." He
crossed it out.

*

He was a terrible writer, Amos knew; he couldn't possibly construct an
adequate or coherent sermon; and he was sick to death of the people in
his church. These feelings astonished him, but he couldn't deny them.
The length of time since Alice's funeral could still be measured in days,
and the night before, Buck Gossage had called him and asked if Amos
could come over right away. Buck's wife, Lucy, was in trouble, he said.
Amos, fearing the worst, fearing that marriage isn't merely the death of
hope (as Woody Allen put it), but literal annihilation, jumped in his old
Volkswagen Rabbit, inside which the roof-covering had come
unattached such that Amos had to shift gears while somehow keeping
the sticky black vinyl off his face, and drove dangerously fast out to the
Gossages, taking curves like a teenager and once nearly hitting a pos-
sum that was doing nothing but lying in the road. When he arrived at
their double-wide, Lucy had her head down on the kitchen table sobbing, while a rottweiler in a kennel outside barked hysterically.

And what was wrong with Lucy? She had wasted her life, as it
turned out, married to Buck and raising kids (and now grandkids). She
didn't know herself, she was never given the time to discover her true
loves in the world. Maybe she was destined to be someone, to do something, but never got the chance. And what would her obituary say,
should she die in the next week: "She kept a clean bathroom"? or "Her
brownies were quite moist"?

"What is it you wish you had done?" Amos asked, a bit gobstopped.

Lucy wailed, "I don't know, I don't know, that's the *point*."

Buck, standing behind Lucy and rubbing her shoulders, shook his
head at Amos. "No, now see, that's—don't ask that question. 'Cause I
already did and nothin' good comes of it."

"I don't know what I should have done, and now it's too late! I'm
too old, I'm forty-eight and I'm not pretty anymore and never will be
again. Have I traveled? No. Have I seen Paris, France? No. Will I ever?

We took back a second mortgage on this house to buy him a boat," Lucy said, raising her tear-streaked face and hitching her thumb at Buck, who continued to stand behind her, miserable. "A *boat*. In *Indiana*. I had three daughters and now I've got six grandkids and every damn one of them takes their meals out of my kitchen. And I've got to be on call to babysit night and day, never a day off, or else the grandbabies might get left alone or with strangers or strapped in their car seats outside a bar, there's no telling. And now I have made up my mind, Buck Gossage, and I'll say it again: I am not leaving this table until my life changes, come hell or high water. Y'all ruined it, you can fix it."

For a moment Amos had been tempted to look around for a camera. Surely this was a joke. Lucy and Buck Gossage had been in church nearly every Sunday Amos had been in Haddington. They had known Beulah Baker their whole lives, and had seen Beulah standing at the Sycamore Grove Cemetery on her arthritic hip, and Lucy was going on strike because years before she'd chosen to get married and have kids, rather than listen for her vocation?

"How should Buck go about changing your life, Lucy? I mean really, seriously, I'd like to know, and I'm sure he would, too."

Buck shook his head again, *wrong tactic*, and Lucy stared at Amos, chin quivering, as if her last hope had betrayed her.

"I don't know," she whispered, swallowing. "But it's all his fault, somehow."

Amos leaned back in his chair. "Yes, I'm sure it is. I've come to believe the marriage vows should include, in the 'Will you love him, honor him, etc.' section, a simple question: 'Will you love him when he stands in the way of your heart's deepest desire?' or 'Will you love him when the fact of him absolutely ruins your joy?' Something like that."

Lucy wiped her face with a napkin. She and Buck were silent.

"Buck, best of luck, here," Amos said, rising. "Lucy, I think you need to shift your perspective a bit. That's the only advice I can give you." And he'd walked out the door (no one offered him a thank-you) into the hot, delirious barking of the caged dog.

*

"Finitude," he wrote, "is the contradiction of the infinite, or anything which is subject to the laws of entropy, decay, and extinction. And for us, for human beings, I would include in the definition a consciousness of the perishing of each moment of existence. Or, more simply: the demand made upon us, as a species, at every moment, to choose one thing instead of another. We might imagine that we are on a boat, and that the prow of the boat penetrating the water is the choice made, or the present thing, and that the wake following the boat is what is *not* chosen, the absent thing: tiny wave upon wave, a body growing wider and wider, finally dissolving into the universe in ways we cannot fully perceive. What is present is finite; what is absent is infinite." He crossed it out.

*

Just a little perspective, that was all he was asking of the world. Consider this, he would say: one bullet hole and one flesh wound (the wound matters, don't think it doesn't) in a woman. A tall man, a lovely man with a flat place on the back of his head. The back of the man's head separates from the front in an egregious physical event. The man and woman fall. Their children are watching. Blood (their mother's, of course) has hit the children. The setting for this drama is a rented house, a house that belongs to someone else, a third party. Said third party (Nathan Leander, one of the wealthiest landowners in two counties) wants to rent the house to someone else, and *there*. There is the place one could achieve a bit of perspective, if one were so inclined, because imagine there are few, maybe only two, left to tidy up this affair. One is an aunt, Jack's mother's younger sister (but not a young woman, not at all), and Alice's mother. Beulah's qualifications are scant. Here is something they must face: after the bodies are removed, who will clean the carpets and walls, so the house can be rented again? Robbie Ballenger called Amos and asked if he thought it appropriate to just hire the firm who did such things without mentioning it to either Gail or Beulah, although the cost would appear in the itemized bill.

"It's a franchise, like a maid service," Robbie explained. "Mostly migrant women happy for the work. Pays well."

Migrant women? "Do you mean Hispanic women, immigrants?"

"Yeah, used to be migrants. They used to pick tomatoes for Nathan Leander, seasonal people. You know. Now they live here year-round."

Amos had closed his eyes and tried to imagine it, living in a foreign country, either uncomfortable with the language or completely mute, no extended family. Rural Indiana is a hard place not to be white and Protestant, with a reliable history and pedigree. And here you are, a woman with children to support, unable to find work except on a cleaning crew.

It was a small house. One level: a small vestibule, a living room/dining room with windows that looked out on a cornfield. Everything painted white, walls and trim, by Nathan, for convenience. A kitchen, and next to the kitchen, the one bathroom. A hallway, two bedrooms, side by side. Amos had been there once, just to talk.

"Amos, that house is a mess," Robbie said.

"Yes. Yes, just go ahead and hire them. And leave it off the bill; the church will pay."

*

Or this: a moving truck. Who hires it, who moves her things out, where do they go? Without parents, who says, "The children must have this _____ every single night, or they can't sleep. Take it first." Where are her nightgowns, her blue pajamas with the white clouds, her hairbrush, the book she was reading? Where is the wedding album, the baby books, who will store them for Madeline and Eloise, who could bear it? And where is *it*? Where is that little cup made of hair? Because it had become, for Amos, the one thing in the world he would steal. (Hair is strong and beautiful, and mostly resistant to the elements and to decay.)

*

One of the first things Amos did after finishing his M.Div. was buy the DSM-III, the *Diagnostic and Statistical Manual, Third Edition*, in hardcover. (There had been a fourth published since—he didn't want it.) He was full of hope, and believed he'd run into, in his work as a pastor, all sorts of interesting maladies. Morbid narcissism, malingering, phobias, severe anxiety disorders, sexual fetishes—he was ready for all of them. And over the years his pastorate had been a little sick, maybe, yes; some were anxious and most were afraid of something, and a few had sexual proclivities best not discussed. There were thin people and fat people, and no place he lived escaped the ironclad rule of social work or social ministry: if you can imagine it, it's happening in your town. But by and large the people who came to him had the most mundane ailments. They were bored or stuck, they had gum diseases, or were victims of the Trinity, as Amos once referred to it in his journal: Lonely, Heartbroken, and Afraid to Die.

Amos hadn't had much call to look at the DSM-III in the past few years (it was heavy, for one thing, and there was almost nothing of substance in it), but a few days ago he took it down. Suddenly, he was faced with an actual condition, a diagnosis of real gravity: post-traumatic stress syndrome, pediatric. He read the entry many times. He copied it into his notebook for good measure, then memorized it. The girls would have to be watched for a month to be certain, but they seemed to have every symptom. He, AnnaLee, Beulah, Lillian Poe (the therapist in Jonah who was treating the girls)—they were all hopelessly out of their depth.

He stood, stretched his back and walked downstairs, then outside for air, and the mountain cur pups next door began to whine and jump against the chicken wire fence his neighbor Vicky had constructed to keep them contained. Amos walked over to the fence, leaned over and rubbed their heads. They were fat and spotted, with hard, smart little faces. Amos was attached to all of them; they had a spirit he admired. But he was too old and had lived too long not to see dogs when he looked at them—desperate dogs and dogs at the ends of chains, hysterical, barking dogs, caged—and then it occurred to him. It wasn't the dog at the end of the chain that told the story, it was the one that broke free, the one barreling full-tilt down the dark street, just about to turn the corner where an innocent person was making her way home. That dog would find us come hell or high water. Alice heard it, didn't she? She had just enough time to look it in the eye, and raise her gun, and leave her children, God help them, to Amos.

"Hush," he said to the pups. "It's late."

*

The next day Beulah opened the door of the mobile home and stepped back, inviting him in. Amos blinked, adjusting to the darkness inside. He'd known her since his first days in Haddington, but had never been in Beulah's house before. It looked exactly like the home of a woman long-widowed, someone serious but not excessively so. To his right was an eat-in kitchen; yellow walls, white linoleum, dark cabinets. This end of the mobile home had many windows, and the light on the kitchen table was so bright he could see swirls of water drying on the surface. The living room walls were covered in pressed-wood paneling, and the combination of that with the dark green carpeting made the room feel like a cave. A sofa, covered in a rough tweed, a glider rocker, an antique coffee table and an old television filled the living room, leaving just a narrow path back to the bedrooms. Beside the glider rocker was a single bookcase, floor to ceiling. All the shelves were lined with books, and there were more packed in horizontally. Amos stopped a moment and studied the titles. Fiction, almost all by women. One shelf devoted to the Brontës, Jane Austen, and Amos's own favorite novelist, Virginia Woolf. The next shelf was more contemporary, and tended toward the hopeful: Anne Tyler, Lee Smith, Amy Tan, Gail Godwin. And on the bottom shelf (what to make of this?), A. S. Byatt, Margaret Drabble, Francine Prose, and Shirley Jackson.

". . . make you a cup of tea, but I can't seem to find—" Beulah was saying from the kitchen.

"Oh, don't bother. I'm fine. Really." Amos stood, his head nearly brushing the ceiling, and walked toward the kitchen.

Beulah looked up at him and Amos realized for the first time, in the unrelenting light, that she was going blind. A certain milkiness, the way she looked just slightly past him, gave her away. In a matter of seconds he'd added it all up in his head: her Social Security checks, her arthritis, her maddeningly slow driving. They couldn't stay here.

THE SOLACE of LEAVING EARLY

"Should I take anything back to the girls, when I meet them? Anything to eat or drink?" Amos asked, hoping she'd say yes, hoping for any diversion.

Beulah shook her head. "They're not eating much. They'll eat if I tell them to, but I'm hesitant to force them."

"No. No, I'd think not."

"I'll take you back there."

Amos followed Beulah down the hallway. There was a place at the crown of her head where she'd forgotten to comb her hair. The waistband of her dress was crooked, and her ankles were swollen, but she walked without limping. He made a mental note to ask someone why the floors in her hallway might feel spongy, and what could be done about it.

Beulah knocked on the last of the three hollow, chipboard doors, then waited a moment. "Madeline? Pastor Townsend is here to see you. Can we come in?" She opened the door without waiting for an answer.

Amos ducked through the doorway. The small bedroom had been used as a storage room, perhaps for years. There were bags of material and yarn; an old sewing machine; boxes of books and old shoes. The single dresser in the room was stacked with boxes. There was hardly room to move. And there was only one bed, a twin, neatly made with a white bedspread. Both girls were sitting on the edge, holding hands. Madeline's feet touched the floor; Eloise's didn't. They looked up at Amos.

"They never much stayed here," Beulah said, as if she had become aware of the room for the first time. "I saw them almost every day, but there wasn't call for them to spend the night."

Amos nodded.

"They stayed with Gail fairly often, but not with me. Not much."

He nodded again, but he was ready for Beulah to leave. He wanted to be alone, to take them in. His heart pounded in his chest and his palms began to sweat.

"I'll leave you be, then." Beulah backed out of the doorway, but left it open.

"I'm Amos," he said. "I'm the minister at your grandmother's church." What he wanted to say was: *You* both *have her eyes*. "Beulah—

your grandma, I mean—tells me you don't want to be called Madeline and Eloise anymore, is that right?"

The numbness, the cocoon they seemed wrapped tightly in, suddenly lifted, and both girls were present. Madeline stared at him, vigorously nodding, and Eloise, after glancing at her sister, nodded too. Amos noticed the hats lying on the bed behind them.

"Yes, sir," Madeline began, then cleared her throat. "We've been given new names, and we'd like to be called by them."

"I see. Well, what are they? I'll call you anything you like."

"I'm Immaculata, like the Immaculate Conception, and this is Epiphany, like when Christ appeared to the Gentiles."

Beulah might have mentioned this little detail. Amos had assumed they'd changed their names to Ashley and Brittany.

"Goodness. What—I wonder—what do those names mean to you?"

The three studied one another. "It doesn't matter what they mean to us," Immaculata said.

An interesting answer. "Why not?"

She considered a moment. "Because those are the names we were *given*."

"Ah."

"Do you have any gum?" Epiphany asked, pointing at Amos's pocket.

"I—let me see, here—wait, yes. Yes, I do. It's Teaberry. Have you had that kind of gum before? Because it's not good for bubbles, but I like how it tastes."

They each took a piece. Amos saw their hands for the first time, the jagged edges of their fingernails, the dried blood on the sides of their thumbs where they'd picked at the skin. Immaculata's straight, nearly white hair was flat and lifeless; Epiphany still had two barrettes caught in her curls, but all the way down toward the bottom of her ears, as if they were just barely holding on. They needed baths and clean clothes.

They chewed the gum. "It's okay," Epiphany said.

"What kind of gum do you like? And I'll bring it next time."

"That kind with the moose on it."

"It's a zebra," Immaculata corrected her.

"Moose or zebra. Big mammal, with or without antlers. I'll find it."

The girls joined hands and looked back at the floor.

"I'm glad to have met you. Your grandma has my phone number, if you need anything, and also you could just walk down to my house. I'm a block and a half down Plum Street."

The girls didn't answer, so he turned toward the door.

"Mr. Townsend?" Immaculata said.

Amos turned and looked at her. She was only eight and Amos knew it, but something about her made him feel he was looking at another adult. "Yes?"

"I wonder if you could find my school books? Because I really need them. They're in a backpack shaped like a frog. We're going to have lessons in the afternoons, but I can't get started without the books."

"You're going to do school work in the afternoons, just the two of you?"

She nodded. "I've been asked to teach Epiphany some things she didn't get to in first grade. Also we have to stay caught up. For next year."

Amos promised to find them, then closed the door behind him. He told Beulah he'd be back the next day, then ran home and called AnnaLee Braverman. When she answered the phone, he just started talking: blindness, hip, storage room, school books, baths, fingernails. AnnaLee came right over, and before she was even fully in the house, said, "Amos, I have an idea."

*

Amos saw Jack only two days before he died. He wandered into Amos's office in the middle of the afternoon, without calling ahead, and Amos was so alarmed by Jack's appearance that for a moment he thought he should call someone—a doctor, Jack's mentor in Faith In Families, Father Leo—but Jack was calm and composed. He said he was hopeful that the increase in his medicine would help, and that he had begun a vigorous program of round-the-clock prayer. His hair, uncut and un-clean, hung in his eyes, and his hands trembled each time he brushed it away.

"Pray without ceasing?" Amos asked. He even smiled inwardly, thinking of Franny Glass. "It seems to be taking a toll on you. You look tired."

Jack shook his head. "I'm not, really. I feel very strong, very optimistic."

Amos sat a minute with his chin in his hands, not sure which direction the conversation should go. "And what are you optimistic about, Jack? That you'll come to terms with what's happened?"

"No, no, absolutely not. That would be total defeat. No, I'm optimistic that Alice will be guided by the Spirit of the Lord, as I have been, and that she'll bring our children and come home."

Amos sighed. "Jack—"

"—Amos, I—listen. I read the Bible every night. I've heard it all my life, and I've been in a Bible study group with Faith In Families for months now. I don't know much about the Old Testament, but I know enough. Look up the word 'marriage' or 'wife' or 'woman.' It all says the same thing. A woman is to be subservient to her husband. The man is the high priest of the home. The two shall be as one. If a woman divorces her husband and marries again, she's an adulterer. Women aren't even supposed to *speak*. It couldn't be more clear. Are you going to argue? Do you even have any grounds to disagree?"

"As a matter of fact—"

"There are laws, Amos. There are natural laws and man-made laws and marriage laws, and you know them as well as I do."

"You've made a terrible error, Jack, please listen to me—"

"Do you deny the Christian law, Amos? Just say so—"

"Jack, slow down—if you want to talk about the Scriptures, we can—look at Luke 10:25, it's perfectly clear: *love* is the final requirement of the law. Love is the fulfillment of the law. There's nothing beyond that."

"Yes, and I love Alice and I love my children, and we are meant to be together on earth as well as in heaven, and I believe God will answer my prayer and put an end to all this." Jack stood and offered Amos his hand. "I've got to be going. I believe you did the best you could."

Amos took Jack's hand and held it. "Please don't go—you've made an understandable but terrible—"

Jack pulled away and turned toward the door. "Another time, maybe. And Amos," he said from the hallway, "I love the book of Luke. My favorite verse is in there."

"Which one?"

"Chapter twelve, verse twenty: 'You *fool*. This very night your life is being demanded of you.' "

*

Amos stared out his study window at the clear night. The pups had quieted down. He remembered (tonight and often) one of the most important classes he took as an undergraduate English major, British Literature: Beowulf to Pope. He hated it at first, hated Beowulf, Chaucer, Sir Gawain, the Faerie Queene, all of it, really, even though the professor, Dr. Hempel, was gifted and passionate and funny. Then they read Marlowe's *Faustus,* and there was something from the beginning so perfectly . . . what was it? When they finished the play, the professor asked the class, "What was Faustus's real sin? Where did he really fall?" And there had been the standard answers: He was greedy. He desired power, knowledge. He was lustful and blasphemous. Dr. Hempel agreed that Faustus had been all those things, but that Marlowe had very carefully planted a clue in the first scene in the play; he had revealed the trap from the beginning.

In the text, Faustus is reading the vulgate of Saint Jerome, and comes to Romans 6:23: "The wages of sin is death," he quotes, and stops right there, despairing, without turning the page. Dr. Hempel looked out at the class. "You're all good Christians, right? What's the rest of the verse? What would Faustus have seen if he'd turned the page?" There had been no answer. " 'For the wages of sin is death, but the free gift of God is eternal life in Christ Jesus our Lord.' Don't you understand? Faustus was eternally damned *because he was a bad reader.*"

Even now Amos had to shake his head in wonder. The genius of it, to send a man to hell, and all because he failed to read a text closely. Amos rose from this desk, turned out the light in his study, and went to bed.

AT INTERMISSION

Having lost inspiration for *Tunnel,* Langston decided to take the alter-
native route, and certainly the more widely received literary wisdom:
write what you know. There were, she believed, a number of novels
available to her, given what she knew. In addition to the postmodern
subterranean novel and the academic *précis,* she also had an idea for a
book-length sonnet sequence, a dramatic psychological study of a certain type of man, written in heroic/epic form. She turned her attention
to it again, after having avoided it for a few months.

In the year she had worked on the sonnet sequence, she had only
gotten as far as the first sonnet, and then only as far as the title. She had
spent many a frustrating hour trying to produce the perfect synthesis of

form and soul. The series was entitled *The Narcissist Café*, or alternately, *At the Narcissist's Café*.

She took out the sheets on which she had been working for a year. In addition to the title she had many options for a first line, most of which had been crossed out:

We meet on your chosen firing ground.
You ask to meet on the firing ground.
The tables conceal your firing ground.
The waitresses . . .

. . . and many others, all with the requisite ten syllables, and all flubbed by the wretched meter of "firing ground." She had tried variations on the theme, by using "hanging tree," and once, "hanging judge." The margins contained her extensive notes on the themes of the poem, the matter of the beloved as judge and/or executioner; the betrayed as crucified innocent. In the progressive logic of the poem the speaker is asked to meet her beloved; he breaks her heart at her favorite table, the table he always employs for such tasks, and in the end, he asks her the same questions he has asked of all the others: How broken are you? How much have I hurt you? How long will it take you to heal? How perfect was I? This theme would be highlighted by the repetition of both "I" and "eye," employing theories of the male gaze.

Langston studied her notes carefully. She tapped her pencil on the table. She rubbed Germane's fur with her feet. The whole poem was right there in front of her. She had done the architectural work flawlessly, she felt. So where was the poem? What labor had she not performed? Perhaps she needed to do more reading . . . perhaps she needed to study with more breadth the phenomenon of narcissism. She made a note to herself to look into a diagnostic manual the next time she visited the public library in Hopwood.

She rubbed Germane's belly and thought about a certain café in Bloomington. She could see it all very clearly; the stained glass windows taken from an abandoned church. The thin, bored waitresses who studied dance. The wide plank floors, the way they held light from the Tiffany lamps; the corridor between the tables and the bar, where there remained, inset in the floor, models of human feet cast in brass. If one stepped in them and followed the pattern, one could perform a box step, or even a fox-trot. On the wall next to each table, next to the sconces that provided each table with its own circle of lamplight, were quotations about reading, her favorite of which was from Kafka: "A book must be the axe for the frozen sea within us." And another from Henry Miller: "I believe at a certain age it becomes imperative to reread the books of childhood and youth. Else we may go to the grave not knowing who we are or why we lived." And over the table in the far-left corner, the most private and desirable table, this bit of the poem "Recuerdo," by Edna St. Vincent Millay:

> *We were very tired, we were very merry—*
> *We had gone back and forth all night on the ferry.*
> *And you ate an apple and I ate a pear*
> *From a dozen of each we had bought somewhere.*

Thinking of those beautiful lines (how rich! how spare!) nearly brought a lump to Langston's throat. Her room, the world, suddenly became too saturated with meaning, and she felt she might swoon. If someone had asked her—and she almost felt as if someone were—to begin at the door and describe every inch of the café she could have, and if that person had then said, *No: more,* she could have gone on to illuminate the detail in the wallpaper and the curve of the chairs; the graffiti carved into certain tables ("Jesus is pallid impotence"); the texture of the blueberry coffee cake, which was so moist and dense it felt like butter on the tongue. She took a deep breath and reminded herself of where she really was. She memorized the smells around her, where she had come to be. All she could smell was her dog. She couldn't imagine what was wrong with her poem.

Her mother knocked on the attic door, shattering Langston's reverie, and asked her to come downstairs; they needed to talk.

*

"No no no, I can't, you can't make me do this, it's out of the question."
Her panic, her immediate sense of doom—of a struggle unnamed, unknown, long lost—caused Langston to feel as if she'd suddenly become
allergic to her own skin. She stood as stiffly as she could, rubbed her
hands up and down her arms, which had broken out in little red bumps,
then put her hands in her pockets. She pulled them out again, and just
for good measure, turned around in a circle, as if she were looking for
but couldn't find the door out of the living room.

Walt was standing behind her, miserable, and AnnaLee was in front
of her, and there was something in her mother's posture, in the way
she had made her pronouncement, that was like a cage. Perhaps one of
those terrifically primitive and suggestive cages the Vietcong employed.
Germane was pacing and making a whining sound deep in his throat,
and Langston remembered, thankfully, that she was an adult and could
make her own way in the world. She was no longer seventeen. She
pulled herself up to her full height, then forced herself to stop rubbing
her arms.

"No, Mother. I won't. I'm nearly thirty years old, and I will not take
on such a responsibility, not to mention the menial aspect of the work,
which is nearly existentially insulting."

AnnaLee looked at the ceiling and sighed. "Ah yes. The existential
insult. It's been little known in Haddington before now."

"I would not ask you, now please consider this with me, Mama, I
would not ask you to perform a task utterly unsuitable to your current
condition. I would not, for instance, request that you complete the first
draft of my postmodern subterranean novel, *Tunnel*. I would not ask
you to finish that small project I began on the indoor/outdoor nature
of revelation in Emerson. I would not—"

"I think I understand your point, Langston."

"—ask you to change your relationship to reality in order to better
suit my sensibilities. Therefore, I believe it is unjust for you to ask me
to do something I find so glaringly out of step with both my nature
and my plan for the rest of the summer. I have a *tremendous* amount of
work to do. I hope we're settled on this. I shan't, and not for love nor
money."

"That's fine, that last part, I mean, because there is neither love nor money involved. I'm asking you—no, no actually, I'm telling you—that you're going to do what's right, and it's really just as simple as that. You are not going to spend the summer in the attic working on one of your projects. You are, in fact, going to spend the summer and, depending on what happens, next school year, taking care of Madeline and Eloise. They are children, Langston, and they are in trouble, and Beulah is not—I've watched her over the past few days and she's not capable of raising them—and maybe it's okay with you to watch two little lives, two innocent babies go down in flames while you write a sonnet sequence, but it's not okay with me and I won't allow it, and this is my house."

How quickly Langston lost her composure! Within a split second she was right back to hives. "I'll leave! I swear to heaven I'll take Germane and leave, you don't have any power over me, you can't, I'll go back to—"

Walt cleared his throat. "Sweetheart, your car won't start."

She turned so quickly her vision dimmed. "*What?* I have no form of transportion?"

He nodded, sadly. "I tried to start it yesterday. It's dead as a doorknob."

"You have to *fix* it, Daddy."

"I tried. I did. It was just old." He stared at the floor.

Langston began to sob in great gasps of anguish. She was now a prisoner in her parents' home, and they had chosen to torture her. She couldn't catch her breath, even though she knew she was making an embarrassing scene. She couldn't seem to get enough oxygen, and began to feel faint.

Then her mother had ahold of her and was exerting pressure on various parts of her body, squeezing Langston's shoulders, periodically holding her head fast against AnnaLee's chest. There was a fair amount of AnnaLee, just in terms of size, and a part of Langston relaxed involuntarily, and leaned into her. Langston continued to weep with abandon; she *felt* like weeping but couldn't understand, intellectually, why she was doing so. Her synapses seemed to have skipped a crucial gateway. She was behaving as if she had received the most blood-curdling news of her life, a message that left her entirely naked, exposed to a power both random and elemental.

"Shhhh," AnnaLee whispered, rubbing the back of Langston's head. "Listen to me, your father and I love you more than anything, you are the one great treasure of our lives. And I hate to be the person to tell you this—I wish it weren't true—but you need to stay a while. I don't know why you left school and you don't have to tell me, none of that matters, and I know that the possibility of running away from, I'm not even sure what to call it, an intractable situation? has always been a great comfort to you, and I know why, I do. But really this isn't about you or me or even those children, it's about life, Langston, the way life just bears down upon us and we are forced to withstand its weight and I am *sorry*. I'm truly sorry, angel."

Langston nodded, then lifted her head, wiping away tears with the sleeve of her T-shirt. Her father was patting her back, too, and she turned and looked at him, and oh my, what a hard man he was to see. Between his handsome silence and the way he always seemed to be leaving a room, Langston often felt like a phantom fathered her. And then—those times he did come clearly into focus—he arrived like a lightning bolt: the way he was aging (what if she *lost* him?), the steep toll of the past everywhere evident on him, the bargains he'd made, his patient, plodding love.

Langston looked back at her mother, and for a moment she could hardly tell AnnaLee and Walt apart. They could say what they would, but all of her parents' best lines were in their faces.

*

She and Germane walked down to the park, Langston still periodically hiccuping with tears. Either she was exhausted from crying or else there was something soporific in surrender, because she felt almost too tired to put one foot in front of the other.

The park was almost always abandoned, and rightly so. The old basketball court was crumbling into a moon landscape, and the goal was hanging by one hinge. The merry-go-round was off balance, and set up a wail every time a wayward child tried to move it. There were no seats on the swings; the teeter-totters were splintered into dangerous propositions. Only the slide remained functional, in part because it was forged by Vulcan himself. It was a huge, hulking, rust-free piece of metal that had stood in the park since before AnnaLee was born. By July one could fry bacon on it, if one were so inclined.

Langston sat down on the merry-go-round and Germane trotted over to her with a stick in his mouth.

"Oh, Germane, let's do please try to be honest for once," she said, taking the stick out of his mouth and dropping it at his feet. He picked it up, wagging his tail. "Oh, *all right*." There seemed to be a conspiracy afoot to exasperate Langston to the edge of her tolerance. She threw the stick toward the basketball court and Germane flew after it, catching it on a bounce, then ran off after a squirrel.

At some point it becomes imperative to reread the books of childhood. They had played together here many hours, undaunted by the limitations of the equipment. Langston sat very still and tried to remember his voice; she tried to recall him cinematically, all the lovely, concrete details of the boy Taos had been, the way they both lived in their heads, was that right? Had they lived mostly in their heads? Hadn't that changed, and would she have noticed when it happened or was it something only seen much later? Taos was an indirect communication, he had been a person she couldn't know while she was in the way with him. She felt her breathing slow, she remembered, oh yes— what a wonderful thing to recall after so many years—a surprise he had given her for Christmas when she was eighteen, close to the end, two tickets to see *La Boheme* at Clowes Hall in Indianapolis. They would go together, her parents had given her a wine-colored velvet dress, it was like a date. They went in Taos's truck, and it had been a long drive in bad weather but she wasn't afraid with him, well almost never. She had slipped and nearly fallen in the parking lot, but he caught her, and she suspected, then, that things might not go well, that the whole evening had been misconceived, but as soon as the lights went down and the play began Langston loved it so much, she felt from the very beginning that she could devote her life to opera. She lost herself. And then the lights went up for the intermission, and Taos turned to her, his eyes always unnaturally bright, his hair (their mama called blackandyellow) a curly mess, and asked Langston if she was enjoying herself.

"Oh yes, I simply adore it. I'm having a fabulous time."

Taos nodded. "Let's leave then, shall we?"

And Langston simply stood up and reached for her coat. She knew exactly what Taos meant; she knew he wasn't being perverse or clever or idiosyncratic. He was handing her the sweetest possibility this life offers: to leave in the middle, while everyone else stays behind and waits for the heroine to die in the cold.

Langston kept all the letters she'd written him in shoe boxes, in a darkened corner of the attic, and she knew that AnnaLee kept them, too, hidden in her closet, and Taos had really, really meant it when he stood up and walked out. Langston thought she'd learned something valuable from him that night, something permanent, but it turned out she knew almost nothing. She knew nothing.

She stood up from the merry-go-round. Germane was on the far side of the basketball court, pawing at a half-buried toy. Langston whistled once, and he turned and ran toward her so hard and fast that his tongue flew out the side of his mouth, like a banner waving out the window of a passing train. *Exuberance is beauty,* William Blake wrote. Langston knelt down and Germane ran into her arms, nearly sending her sprawling. After she'd straightened up and brushed some dry grass from his fur, she looked up at the sky, took a deep breath, and said out loud, "All right," and headed home.

*

The girls (she'd heard AnnaLee mention to Walt that they were currently refusing to be called by their names) spent a lot of time outside, and so Langston spent the next few days either watching them from her attic window, which looked right onto Beulah's little side yard, or actually strolling around outside, trying to hear their conversation and play. In truth, she was terrified of them. She was afraid of any sort of damage: wounded animals, amputations, broken cups, torn book covers, missing buttons. And she knew from the whisperings around town that the girls were damaged, and were under the daily care of a therapist in Jonah. There had been talk of hospitalizing them—rejected by Beulah—or placing them in a foster home, also denied.

Their pattern was fairly settled: they emerged from the trailer at about nine o'clock every morning, always dressed in the gowns and hats. Langston couldn't, at first, determine whether they were wearing shoes, but eventually saw little pink ballet slippers. They walked side by side, very close together, holding hands. Conversation between them was muted; Madeline, the elder, spoke almost continuously to Eloise, who listened intently, even while doing something else. They always went directly to the small, gnarled dogwood tree at the back edge of the property, where they knelt (carefully lifting their skirts, so as not to stain them) as if in prayer. And there they stayed, on their knees, often for half an hour or more, until something moved one of them and they began to converse with the trunk of the tree. (Langston *saw* this.) The longest conversation they had with the tree was about fifteen minutes; often, it only lasted a minute or so. After they had learned from the dogwood what they needed to know, they proceeded to the sandbox, where they removed their shoes, dusted off the wooden railing around the edge, sat down side by side, and began talking again. After a few minutes, Madeline would initiate a tea party, or so it seemed, with the plastic dishes in the sand. At some point they always removed their hats, either because they were hot, or because bending over to pour sand in a pitcher they hit each other repeatedly with the pointy tops. When they removed their hats their hair spilled out like cream, white-blond. Madeline's was straight and shone like a mirror; Eloise's hung in ringlets around her wider face. Langston never saw them disagree in any way; indeed, their level of cooperation was not adult, it was unnatural.

At ten o'clock they stood up (were they wearing watches? Langston began to wonder on the third day), brushed the sand from their clothes, and set off for their daily walk around the block: south to the dogwood tree, west down the alley, north on Scarborough, east on Plum. Daily Langston sat and waited for them to round the corner of Plum and Chimney again, and every day they satisfied her: always in the same light, always conferring on a point of interest vital to their lives.

At ten-thirty, the girls climbed into Beulah's old green Buick and left for Jonah, where Langston assumed they met with their counselor. They sometimes didn't return until one, leading her to believe that Beulah treated them to lunch somewhere. Langston's heart lurched when they got home; she could hardly bear to watch Beulah try to leave her car. She had to spend at least thirty seconds just sitting with the door open, clutching the frame with one hand and the door handle with the other. Then she would swing one leg out (and from Langston's vantage point that leg seemed to weigh hundreds of pounds, such an effort did moving it require, and yet Beulah was thin and getting thinner daily), and eventually the other. Finally she would gather the strength to pull herself out, and from there she seemed okay. The girls didn't wait for her, nor did they watch her struggle. In fact, they left the car quickly, without looking back.

From one to three they remained in the trailer, where nothing stirred. (Do children eight and six still nap? she wondered. What did Beulah do with them for two hours every day—hours that were shortly to be Langston's sole province—in such a silence?) At three, Amos Townsend came strolling down Plum Street. Langston did not know how to account for his walk, his height, or his presence. She had never before seen anyone like him. His black hair, cut short but still riotous, became snagged in branches every time he approached a tree; his Adam's apple protruded; his broad shoulders only emphasized the dramatic length and thinness of his torso. And it would have been enough for him to have a long upper body, but he had to combine it with legs that seemed to belong on one of those collapsible toys, the sort Langston loved as a child. The figure (a dog, a pony, a minister) stands on a small box, all its joints connected by an elastic string. When pushed, a button retracts the string, and the figure collapses in a heap. Release the button, up pops the pony. Whatever was amusing in that concept was amusing in Mr. Townsend. Langston couldn't help but smile at the way his stride covered whole sections of sidewalk, and how he seemed to be looking straight ahead, but walked into branches anyway. He dressed casually, and in a way that appealed to Langston (although it struck her as a bit hapless and frumpy, and not at all the way she would call on parishioners): a soft, blue work shirt, khaki pants, and soft leather shoes of the sort one might garden in.

Amos knocked on the door at precisely three every day (he undoubtedly had a watch), and stayed until five. Again, there was often no movement or indication of activity in the trailer. Once, however, he walked outside with the girls. They took him to the dogwood tree, and he very carefully bent over and inspected it. Madeline talked to him a few minutes, and he nodded all the while. From Langston's vantage point the two of them appeared to be simply two adults conferring about a tree (about a fungus, for instance, or an injury), except that one was very tall and one was very short.

At five o'clock, AnnaLee crossed the street to Beulah's, carrying either dinner or groceries. She would spend the next three hours cooking, cleaning, supervising the girls' baths, and putting them to bed. Beginning the following week, she and Langston would divide the work: her mother would do all the cooking, cleaning, and organizing, and Langston would take care of the children directly. They would take turns driving them to their appointments in Jonah. This was to be Langston's summer. In the fall, someone else would determine whether they were to go back to school, or if they'd need to spend a few more months at home, with a tutor. Langston hadn't even met them yet, and she certainly hadn't begun her life of servitude, but already she was too tired to write. At night, climbing into bed with Frithjof Schuon's *The Transcendent Unity of Religions,* she often fell asleep without opening the cover. She had no idea what that book was about.

*

From the start, even from the distance of her attic window, Madeline and Eloise made Langston grievously uncomfortable. She couldn't say why. They were so quiet and civilized, nothing at all like the children one encountered elsewhere. Langston supposed she was bothered by the obvious: the girls harbored a tremendous sense of loss; their behavior was spooky; they knew something she didn't know, i.e., orphanhood—assuming Jack was gone, which he must have been—but there was something else, too.

She began walking Germane only during the hours the girls spent in the trailer, and during those walks Langston recalled the strangest things. She remembered Alice's hair, just a flash of brightness in the summer sun, as she rode her bicycle down the street, and the way they once tasted a mud pie at the same time. Alice had thrown up, Langston had not. Alice loved 7 Up and corn chips, and could read by the time they started first grade, but pretended she couldn't. She was always the third person to turn in her test paper, even if she had been the first to finish. There had been no one between them in the alphabet, Baker and Braverman, just one other *B*, Scottie Bryant, and so they often ended up beside each other in line.

And the way Madeline and Eloise held hands, for instance, or touched during tea parties, reminded Langston of swimming with Taos in a pond at the edge of town. They went there most summer days for years, or at least she thought they did, but she'd forgotten about it. How could she have forgotten? She hadn't been afraid of anything then, or at least not much. Sometimes they floated on inner tubes, sometimes they swung out over the deep middle of the pond on a rope, letting go right at the highest point. Taos loved to dive toward the bottom and scare her; he loved to float on his back; he loved to race from one side to the other. Langston never won. There was a particular silence under the water, a periodic echo she could feel more than hear, and the occasional boom—from what? And she could recall the way sunlight barely penetrated the murky water; under the branches of the tree on which the rope hung, the sunlight shafted down in stripes. There was scarcely enough light for them to see each other, even when they were just beneath the surface.

But what she recalled most of all was floating along, minding her own business, and suddenly feeling Taos grab her ankle, horrifying her. Sometimes he would touch her and then swim away underwater, and she would turn and turn, looking for some sign, some disturbance, that might indicate where he was and what he was about to do. Often he came up where she hadn't expected, far away and in the opposite direction from the one she was looking in.

And sometimes he just touched her as they swam. He held her hand, or they did somersaults around each other, and he hoisted her up on his shoulders so she could dive. Even when they were quite young he was strong enough to lift her, and she never feared for her safety when they were together. He could swim and swim forever, as long and as deep as necessary.

On Saturday Langston asked her mother if anyone ever swam in that pond anymore, and AnnaLee said sometimes, and then Langston regretted asking. For many nights she had dreams she didn't dare consider during the day: the rope, the slats of light, the echo, something waiting patiently in the blackness at the bottom of the pond. Frantically turning, watching for some sign on the surface, *get out of the water*. She tried and tried, she gave it everything she had, but she was always much too late. They were just dreams.

Chapter 13

THE GOVERNESS

On Monday morning Amos realized he hadn't checked on the Waltzes
for a week. Slim was home from the hospital, following a light stroke,
and Etta was caring for him alone, both of their children having
moved out of the state. Amos knew he should have stayed in contact,
probably should have, in fact, spent the first day or so out of the hospital with them, but he couldn't keep track of everyone. He headed
into the kitchen, trying to remember their phone number. 5232? 5523?
There were fives, and numbers that added up to five, he was
certain of—

"Yes?" The voice that answered was not Etta.

"I'm—hello—I'm sorry. I'm trying to reach Etta Waltz."

"You most assuredly have the wrong number."

"Is this 5223, or—what number have I reached?"

"In general I consider that a rude question, but I'll answer it this time. You've reached 5352."

"Oh! I called Walt and AnnaLee! Is this, then, am I talking to Langston?"

"Yes, and who's this?"

"Langston, sorry, it's Amos Townsend. I was trying to reach Etta, to ask about Slim."

"Ah, yes. Small-town names. Slim Waltz: a fat man performing a slight dance."

Amos froze a moment. "Slim isn't actually overweight, Langston. Calling a person by a nickname intended to designate the opposite characteristic is linguistically Southern, I think. He's called Slim because his younger brother couldn't pronounce his real name."

"Which is what?"

"Something with an *S*. Maybe I don't actually know." Why was Amos talking so much? "And anyway, I thought you never spoke on the telephone."

"I don't, as a rule. But just now something thoughtless and Pavlovian overcame me. I'm the only one home; I was crossing in front of the telephone; it rang; and I picked it up."

"Is there a reason you don't use a telephone?"

"Well, yes," Amos heard Langston hesitate just slightly, "there is, in fact. I have a recurring bad dream about telephones."

"Really?"

"Yes. Someone is in trouble, someone I love. For instance, I'll dream my mother is in danger, and our only hope is for me to call an ambulance, and I pick up the phone—this is what happens in every dream, with some variation—and I begin to dial the number, which is long, twenty-three or twenty-four digits, and I get the last number wrong and have to begin again, and as I'm misdialing, the person is growing more ill or the house is burning or I'm missing the last opportunity I'll ever have to reconcile with—"

"To reconcile with?"

"My only point is that I have obsessive thoughts, like anyone else, and I see no reason to encourage them if I don't have to."

"You have obsessive thoughts? Like what?"

"Like anyone else's, I'm sorry, is this news? As I'm falling asleep, or as I'm walking, or just . . . I'll see myself repeatedly turning cartwheels, for instance, in a wide, empty field. Or I hear a voice say, 'Tell the court what happened next.' I *despise* that one. Just the most standard thing."

"Hmmm." Amos rubbed his chin, trying to imagine a connection between the dreams and the cartwheels and the voice of the judge or attorney. "And would you say that—"

"Oh," Langston said, the tone of her voice completely changed. "You're quite good, aren't you? You probably know a little something about everyone in this town, you probably know things about my family—"

"Langston, I didn't intend to—"

"No, it was entirely my mistake. However, let's do hang up, shall we? I believe the Waltzes' phone number is listed."

"Wait—Langston. Wait. You're going to Beulah's for the first time today, isn't that right?"

"Yes?"

Amos could hear her try to hide her irritation at being kept on the phone, so he spoke quickly. "There are some things you ought to know about the girls. I've been with them over the past few days, and I think—"

"Thank you for your concern, but I'll be fine. I'm simply taking on the role of a governess, which I imagine I can handle competently."

A *governess?* "The situation is fairly complicated; perhaps you don't appreciate the—"

"Pastor Townsend? I'll be nannying. It isn't rocket science."

"It isn't? Do you know anything about children?"

"Only that I was one, and that I consistently see them being reared by people of subsistence intelligence. It can't be too difficult."

Amos felt something he hadn't experienced in a long time, maybe not since he and his brother were still at home in Ohio, fighting silently in their bedroom over a contraband comic book: the fluttery, sharp tingle of a lost temper. "Well. I'll just wish you the best then."

"And to you, as well. Shall I tell my mother you called?"

"No, no. I certainly didn't mean to, did I?"

*

For the next fifteen minutes Amos could barely stay in his skin. He paced the length of the kitchen five or six times, then walked out onto the screened porch, slamming the door behind him. She was insufferable. She was a thousand times worse than AnnaLee had suggested, and Amos had thought AnnaLee was exaggerating. He thought there were mother-daughter issues that clouded Anna's perception, that she was projecting some of her own fears onto Langston (because Amos knew the quality of AnnaLee's mind, he knew she was also, to some extent, a castaway), but in fact, Anna wasn't projecting, she was *protecting* Langston. She might have said, "My daughter cannot be tolerated." She could have admitted, "There is something synchronistic in the convergence of Madeline and Eloise with Langston's arrival home, but I would never expose innocent children to her." Not just innocent children, but children in trouble, *Alice's* children. And why hadn't anyone told Amos about the quality of Langston's voice, as smooth as honey and overenunciated, the sort of voice used by airlines to convince rioting passengers that the plane wasn't really going down? Extraordinary. He slammed into the kitchen, began pacing again. What was Anna thinking? What was Amos thinking, allowing AnnaLee to make such a decision without Amos first, at the very least, interviewing Langston? And Beulah! Beulah had said yes right away, even though she'd known Langston for *years*, maybe her whole life.

That's it, he thought, *I'm just going to call the whole thing off. I'll find someone else.* One of those sweet, fat women who live at the edge of town and spend their days making crafts; the opposite sort of woman from Amos's own mother, who had been thin and fastidious. Someone with a minivan and a permanent and lawn ornaments. A sweet, fat, sweatpants-and-sneakers sort of woman who will bake cookies for the girls and periodically pull them into suffocating hugs, pull them right up against her enormous breasts. Children pretend to hate that, but surely they need it, especially right now. *I'm going to* fire her, *he thought, and I'm going to hear her voice one more time,* and he picked up the telephone, dialing so fast and hard he missed the third number and had to start over.

But the phone at the Bravermans' rang and rang. Langston wouldn't answer twice.

Chapter 14

SIGHT

It was nearly time for Langston to leave for Beulah's. She and AnnaLee had decided that Langston would make contact with Madeline and Eloise sometime after they had spoken to the tree trunk, but she couldn't leave until she stopped pacing. The nerve! She was saturated with regret over what she hadn't said, sentences that included the words "impertinent" and "supercilious." And also she should have said, "Yes, please, do tell me everything you've learned about children as a lifelong bachelor." (Oh, but perhaps he'd think she was in some way referring to his sexual orientation—about which she was entirely indifferent—if she used the word "bachelor." But how else to say it?) And also: "Having this conversation with you is not making the taking on of this onerous task any more palatable." Except that was a ridiculously awkward sentence. Perhaps: "This conversation is less—" "This onerous task is even less—" She paced and wrote what amounted to a long dialogue in her head, one in which she was quick and dismissive and Mr. Townsend simply tried to keep pace, unsuccessfully. And then the phone rang again, awakening her from her reverie, and she flew down the steps and out the front door, Germane at her side.

"You think there are nuances I am unable to grasp in this situation, Mr. Townsend?" she muttered, stomping down to the sidewalk. "Perhaps, before I begin performing this unpaid and onerous task, you'd like documentation of my ability to appreciate *nuance*. Would my master's thesis suffice?" She walked so fast and hard past her backyard that Germane fell behind, keeping his distance. "It traces the tradition of the coterie poets, and then argues for such a presence in the American Romantic—" She crossed Chimney Street without either looking for traffic (there was none), or grasping Germane's collar. He loped along beside her, having decided to catch up. "Or maybe you'd like to engage in a serious conversation on the history of Western philosophy, in order to determine my ability to *babysit*—"

When she came to her senses she was standing on the sidewalk at the edge of Beulah Baker's mobile home, and the two girls were sitting frozen on the edge of the sandbox. "Oh, hello," she said, raising her hand in a friendly wave. "I'm Langston Braverman, I live across the street from you, there, AnnaLee is my mother, and I temporarily lost track of myself. I was having an interior conversation with someone I'm very, very upset with. And this is my dog, Germane. He is entirely civilized."

The older girl stared at Langston suspiciously, then slowly put down her teapot and reached for her younger sister's hand. Langston walked over and sat down on the opposite side of the sandbox, first brushing off a seat as she'd seen the children do. Germane lay down in the shade under the dogwood tree.

"You know I'm going to be spending some time with you? I'm not ordinarily so *loquacious*, it's just that I'm angry."

"Who are you mad at?" the older girl asked, still giving Langston a dark look.

"I'll tell you: Amos Townsend. What do you think of him?"

"Do you like him?" Madeline asked.

"Not today."

The girls looked at each other. "We don't, either."

"Good. Do please tell me what to call you. I understand you've rejected your names."

Madeline pointed to herself first. "I've been given the name Immaculata, and this is Epiphany."

Langston sat back, surprised. "Oh dear. How very Latin and archaic and liturgical. And also metaphorical. I too have a strange name."

"Langston, is that right?" Epiphany asked, looking down. She seemed embarrassed to have spoken.

"Yes. And don't ask me who I was named after; I've never actually asked my mother for fear she would say it was the poet of the Harlem Renaissance, Langston Hughes."

The girls were silent.

"Perhaps you're wondering why I would find that objectionable. Langston Hughes was a brilliant poet, one of the great lights in the American canon. And naming a little white baby girl after him would constitute the worst kind of co-opting of his eminence, no different than if she'd named me Duke Ellington. Tomorrow I'll bring some of Hughes's poems to read to you."

They said nothing, but Immaculata suddenly stood and said to her sister, "It's time for our walk."

Langston took out the pocket watch that had formerly served her Grandfather Wilkey. Ten o'clock sharp. How did they do that? "Shall I wait here for you?"

The older girl nodded and they set off. Immaculata leaned in toward her sister, speaking quickly and low. Langston couldn't hear what she said; they disappeared down the alley, heading west toward Scarborough Street.

*

Langston knocked on Beulah's front door and walked in at the same time. The television was on in the living room, tuned to a game show, the sound low.

"Sarah?" Beulah called, stepping out of the kitchen drying her hands on a towel. Every day she wore a dress with stockings and thick black shoes. Often she kept a sweater draped around her shoulders. Her hair, which had gone so suddenly white, was cut short, and seemed to be thinning. Langston was struck again by the dark circles under her eyes.

"No, Beulah, it's me, Langston."

"Well, where's Sarah?" Beulah stood still, perplexed, the dish towel wrapped around her hand like a tourniquet. She seemed to be short of breath.

"I'm sure I don't know. I don't even know who Sarah is," Langston said.

"She said she'd be here. She's the only one who understands this recipe."

"Oh, well, then. I can't help you. I'm entirely helpless when it comes to cooking."

They looked at each other a moment, and then Beulah's eyes, which seemed to be looking past Langston, came into focus. "*Langston*. Hello, sweetheart."

"Hello, Beulah. Let's go sit down, shall we?" What was the problem here? Everyone seemed to be coming unstrung. Langston led Beulah to the kitchen table, pulling out a chair for her. There was no evidence that Beulah had been cooking anything.

"Now," Langston said, taking one of Beulah's hands, "do tell me who Sarah is, and why you are so confused, and if, in fact, you're losing your eyesight. Because I believe your eyes are a bit cloudy. I once wrote a poem in which I said a man's eyes had 'gone milked and filmy / Like a June sky that disappoints the picnic.' "

"Oh, that's very fine. I like that so much."

"I think you'd like the whole poem. I'll bring it tomorrow. Sarah?"

Beulah sat back in her chair, then raised a hand to her forehead, rubbing it as if to raise an answer. "Sarah was. Sarah. You know that people think I was close to forty when I had Alice, yes? But in fact I was forty-five, I was just much too old, especially at that time. They told me she'd be 'mongoloid,' that was the word they used then, but I wasn't giving her up for anything. My only baby. The only time I ever got pregnant. And I don't know why Francis—Frank, Alice's father—lied to people about how old I really was. Who cares what they think?"

"Good heavens, I couldn't agree more."

"I know this about you. But he also—there were a few years, shall we say, *unaccounted for* in my youth—and he was covering those up."

"Ah," Langston said. "The Sarah years?"

"Would you like something to drink? Some iced tea or lemonade?"

"I'll get it. Go on." Langston opened the refrigerator. It was clean and bright, and there was a story in it. In a corner of the top shelf were the things Beulah had kept, just things an old woman living alone might eat: a single block of cheese, a quart container of skim milk, small bottles of condiments, and the sort of luncheon meat that came in a tube and reminded Langston of all that was godforsaken. The rest of the refrigerator had been taken over by AnnaLee: a gallon of whole milk, two pounds of butter, three different kinds of fruit juice, apples and oranges, broccoli, packages of chicken and steak, a gallon of sun tea, the whole American profusion. Langston poured two glasses of tea and carried them back to the table.

"Langston, you mustn't repeat this to anyone. Sarah and I ran away and spent three years at circus college."

Langston sputtered into her drink. "Dear me, I. Well," she said, wiping up tea with Beulah's dish towel.

"Sarah came here from Macon with Ezra Jones, he was no-account. He'd gone to Macon on some sort of gambling . . . I don't know what. And met her in a bar. They got married drunk and he brought her all the way from Macon to Haddington. She could *cook*."

"Yes, but." Macon, Ezra, no-account, gambling? "How does her cooking have anything to do with, what did you call it? Clown college?"

"Circus college. There are some excellent schools in the world that train you for the circus; the best ones now are in Russia, and France, of course. They still take it seriously there. We had a trapeze act, The Macon Sisters. Not so original, I'm afraid."

"Circus college?"

"Langston, we flew."

"My goodness." Langston sat back in her chair. "Whatever caused you to come back *here?*"

"Sarah disappeared. She took off with someone as we were shutting down in Ontario and I never saw her again, and then. My sails dropped. I got homesick, so I took a bus into Jonah and called Francis and he came and picked me up and we started over like I'd never been gone."

"For heaven's sake."

"Except we couldn't seem to have any children. He thought, well, he didn't ever say it in so many words, but he thought I'd been ruined."

"By flying."

"By lots of things, but yes."

"But then you had Alice."

"When I very least expected it. And you know, when I first saw her—she was just a normal-looking baby, but—I saw . . ." Beulah paused.

Langston took her hand again. "What did you see?"

"I saw stars. It's nothing."

Langston put her hand against her throat. "Beulah, I am *so sorry,* there's no way for me even to say—"

The look on Beulah's face made Langston afraid; it seemed Beulah might vanish completely. "You can't imagine how—"

The screen door opened and the girls walked in, Immaculata first. Langston turned toward them and started to say something, but Beulah interrupted her. "Let them go their way. They have to do everything the same, every day. Nothing can change. Right now they'll go back to their room and pray. Then they'll wash their hands for four or five minutes. They'll make sure their shoes aren't dusty, and then they'll come out and tell me they're ready to go see Lillian, the therapist in Jonah."

Langston's heart was still racing, but the girls were a distraction. "All right. I see. I have my own habits." She rubbed her hands over her arms, which had begun to itch. "Mama's just gone to pick up the car at Tim Clyde's. She was having the oil changed, that sort of thing. Then she'll be ready to drive them to Jonah."

Beulah nodded. "I'm grateful."

"You're losing your sight, aren't you?" Langston said it quietly, hoping the children wouldn't hear.

"I have cataracts. But I don't want the surgery. I don't care anymore."

*

"Well, if this doesn't just take the *prize*," Langston said, so angry she was nearly stuttering.

"Langston, please don't be angry with me, it's just that—"

Langston and her mother were standing on the sidewalk outside Beulah's trailer. "I know exactly what it is. You roped me into this, and now it turns out you lied about the requirements."

"I didn't lie, it's just that—" AnnaLee looked a bit wretched. A part of Langston felt sorry for her, and another part wanted to tell her mother to comb her hair and put on some shoes. "Your daddy dropped me off at Tim's and I was fine. And then I got in the car and I was fine. And then on the way here I started to get a little jittery, and then I thought about driving the girls all the way to Jonah and I couldn't catch my breath."

Langston looked around for someone to help her, but there was no one. Beulah's door was still shut. "Jonah is eleven miles from here, on country roads and one stretch of perfectly straight, flat highway. What? Can you not steer? Have you developed paralysis in your accelerating foot?"

AnnaLee blew hair out of her eyes, then shielded her face from the sun, which was neither bright nor overhead. "You are merciless. I'm *afraid* to drive them, Langston. If it were just the two of us I wouldn't feel that so much was at risk—"

"Thanks for that."

"Oh, stop it. You know what I mean. But what if I made a mistake and traumatized them more?"

"You are traumatizing *me* more, Mama! I was going to use the Jonah time to work on my book. I tell you, I know you don't realize this, but books can get away from one. And if my books get away, then what do

I have? And also, a vital point, this, it's *your turn*. Tomorrow is my turn."

AnnaLee shook her head. Her eyes seemed to be sloping down in the corners, dragged by some weight. "I can't."

"Well!" Langston threw her hands up in surrender. "Fine, then! I'll just go get them, and *I'll* drive them to Jonah, and then *I'll* procure some sort of lunch for them, and then *I'll* bring them back here and occupy them for two hours, and then *I'll* have to come face-to-face with Amos Townsend—"

"He called, by the way. He thinks you're not suited to the job."

Langston made a sound like a cat vomiting, then caught herself. "I beg your pardon?" Her jaws began to ache and she felt a strange itch in the palm of her hand. "He said that?"

"I told him he was wrong."

"Let me tell you something about Amos Townsend, Mama, and do please feel free to repeat it—" Langston was pointing at her mother most rudely when the trailer door opened and Beulah walked out, her sweater buttoned up in the heat. The girls were behind her, wearing their hats.

"Langston, can I speak to you a minute?" Beulah said. The girls remained on the trailer steps, as if playing Statue. "There's a slight problem. Madeline says they can't ride in your mom's station wagon because it's too long. And Eloise says they can't go without me. I convinced them to allow you to drive my car, and I'll ride along in the front seat. But Madeline has to sit behind the driver, and Eloise has to sit in the middle. And Germane can't go. And on the way we have to stop at the Milky Freeze. Alice used to take them there. And then they go into Lillian's, and you and I have to remain in the waiting room. I sit by the plant, and they'd like you to sit by the door. And—"

"For the sake of sense. Okay. Okay. We'll do it all your way, and on the trip we can speak the Arabic alphabet backward and count fence posts and only make right-hand turns. I swear."

Beulah turned toward the children. Her purse dangled from her forearm, the way old women preferred. "All right, children. It's all fixed. Come get in the car."

The children stood frozen. A panicky look crossed AnnaLee's face.

"Immaculata," Langston said. "This is no time to dawdle. Please tell your sister that we have an appointment to keep, and then come get in the car."

"You call them by those names?" Beulah whispered to Langston, worried.

"Of course I do. Those are the names they've been given." She watched them walk down the steps, carefully, holding hands. "Come, bandits. Come, beauty queens. And wear your seat belts."

After everyone was safely fastened in and Langston had gotten the old Buick started (it had no air-conditioning and no radio, but ample leg room), they pulled away from the front of the trailer. AnnaLee and Germane stood watching them in a cloud of exhaust. AnnaLee seemed abject, having told Beulah she'd take care of all odds and ends while they were gone. "Wave to Mama," Langston told the girls, who didn't move. "We don't want her to feel guilty. Epiphany, tell your sister it's polite to wave goodbye."

The little girl leaned over and whispered something in her sister's ear, and they both raised their hands in small, unenthusiastic waves. Langston noticed for the first time, looking in the rearview mirror, how very pretty they both were. There was something about Epiphany's face that was so nostalgic; the heart shape, the curls, the slight overbite. She looked like a little, blond Mary Pickford.

"Thank you for waving. Shall we sing on the way to the Milky Freeze? I know a number of fine songs from the World War II era."

Beulah leaned over and whispered, "They don't sing anymore." She sat back up. "They do count fence posts, though."

Langston looked at them in the mirror. Immaculata stared back blankly. "You'll sing, you scallywags. Just wait and see."

Chapter 15

WHAT THEN WILL

THIS CHILD BECOME?

Amos was on his knees in his garden, digging up an old flower bed, thinking about the sermon he had yet to write. The Incarnation: there was an idea. It was the hardest concept Amos had ever encountered, the true test of faith, and yet Christians talked about it as if it were the most obvious thing in the world. He knew he could ask anyone with a modicum of knowledge of church history what was decided at the council of Nicea, and they'd say, "Fully human and fully divine," as if reporting a recipe for cookies. He dug, pulling up old roots, throwing stones toward the pile next to the fence. Amos agreed with Cobb and Griffin, the Whitehead scholars, who wrote, "Whereas Christ is incarnate in everyone, Jesus *is* Christ because the incarnation is constitutive of his very selfhood." But how to preach it? There was no distance between Jesus and the lure of God toward truth, beauty, and goodness; Jesus didn't have to stand still and try to feel the tug upon his soul? That, yes, but it was immensely more complicated. *Every event pervades its future,* Cobb wrote, and Amos could see that was the case. For most people, though, the present was banal and full of error and the future it pervaded was without consequence, just more of the same. But the very self of Jesus—as the historical Christ, as opposed to the Christ incarnated everywhere else in the world—Amos forced himself not to go that direction . . . the very self of Jesus was constituted by a past response to the lure of God, which shot into the future like a mathematical vector, and inside every actual occasion until . . . Poor Mike, back in seminary, Amos thought, leaning back on his heels. How he would shudder at this line of thought.

Amos felt in his breast pocket for the pen and small notebook he kept intending to carry there. Why not make the Incarnation a cellular event, constantly occuring? He could vaguely remember, from his whirlwind tour of the world religions, a Hindu concept of Being and Non-Being: the world coming into and going out of existence, a stone moved back and forth in the hand of the god. Amos stood, brushed his knees, looked at his ravaged bed, at the deep black dirt of Indiana. None of his thoughts were very clear or coherent, but it was something like this. Niels Bohr in Copenhagen in 1927. A fundamental particle—Amos scratched his head, trying to remember the basis of quantum mechanics—could be in one of an infinite number of states or places, until observed. The world remade and made manifest in every moment, in part by our consciousness. The Incarnation of God made concrete in Jesus and in every other occasion, in every cell, every atom; and every particle of being pulled by God (God's only power, but *a really good one*) toward Beauty; in here, in this line of thought, somewhere, Amos wasn't sure exactly where to place it, there was room for miracles. They slipped in.

*

Two weeks earlier, before Langston had gotten to them, he and the girls had been sitting at the kitchen table in the sweltering afternoon light, the window air conditioner in the living room running on high, and they told him.

"She speaks to you? The Virgin Mary?" Amos sat very still, trying not to threaten or startle the girls. He addressed Immaculata; all information seemed to both come from and go through her. She didn't answer and wouldn't look at him.

"Is it Mary, the Mother of God?"

Immaculata looked Amos in the eye, nodded. Of course, Amos thought. Mary as a virgin would mean little to her, but Mary as a mother—

"She ascended into Heaven whole and without degradation where she is seated with her son on the right hand of the Father, in Heaven." Immaculata spoke in one quick, intense whisper, and Epiphany closed her eyes and began to whisper, too, as if she'd been taught to do so. "All these things were given unto Mary and she treasured them in her heart—"

"—and she treasured them in her heart," whispered Epiphany.

"And Mary said, 'My soul magnifies the Lord, and my spirit rejoices in God my Savior—' "

Amos very quietly reached into his bag on the floor and took out his notebook and pen. Resting it on his knees, he wrote, *The Magnificat, Luke 1:46–55.*

" '—Surely, from now on all generations will call me blessed; for the Mighty One has done great things for me and holy—' "

" '—holy is his name.' "

Amos tried not to breathe as they repeated the declaration to the end. The only sounds in the trailer were the air conditioner and Beulah's knitting needles ticking from the glider rocker in the living room, where she was watching *Wheel of Fortune* with the volume low. If Beulah was alarmed or surprised by the conversation in the kitchen, she didn't indicate it.

There was a moment of silence, and then Immaculata began again, her eyes closed, her hands clasped in front of her, " 'And Mary remained with her about three months and then returned to her home.' "

" '—and then returned to her home.' "

Amos wrote, *Home.* He leaned forward and whispered, "Tell me how this started, Immaculata."

"Oh, Immaculate heart of Mary, our Queen and our Mother, we seek refuge in thee. We prayed without ceasing, as You have taught us, and Aunt Gail says Not just at night but with every breath. Every breath a prayer and a heartbeat. And You told us I am coming with the clouds and Look into the place where the tree grows straight and neither the branch is bent and there I shall be also. And You said Behold the handmaid of the Lord; be it done unto me according to Thy Word, but that was not to us but to God You said that."

Amos wrote, *The Fiat.*

Immaculata opened her eyes and looked at her sister. "Mary is the model of what. You say."

Epiphany blinked and rubbed her nose with her folded hands. "Mary is the model of . . ."

"You have three seconds or else something very bad will happen."

Amos thought he should say something, but was afraid to disturb the fragile atmosphere. He sat silent. Epiphany's eyes began to shift from right to left, looking for what was coming. "Help me," she whispered.

"Mary is the model of," Immaculata began, "Faith, Epiphany, say it."

"Mary is the model of Faith she is the model of Confidence Charity Towards God Charity Towards One's Neighbor and . . ."

"Good, go on, what's the next one?"

"Is the bad thing gone?" the younger girl asked, pressing her hands against her lips.

"Yes. What's next?"

"Union of Charity of those Performing Good Works Model of Humility of Prudence of Justice of Fortitude of Tempance."

"Temperance. Don't say them so fast next time."

Beulah confessed to Amos that the first two nights were terrible. The girls shook so hard she thought they might be seizing; they refused to sleep, and when they did fall asleep, woke up screaming and tried to crawl under the bed, eventually ending up in the corner of the closet, having thrown coats and scrapbooks and old toys wildly out in the hallway. Lillian Poe had prescribed tranquilizers for them, but Gail threw the prescription away, believing that their acute pathological state was actually a profound state of grace. Beulah had been forced to call Jolene, the nurse who lived down the street. Jolene came in the middle of the night in her robe and slippers, carrying a brown paper bag filled with tranquilizers. The girls now took two and a half milligrams of Valium before bed, and half that much at lunchtime, and the nights had improved. Eloise was almost always sleepy and would have taken a long nap every afternoon, but Madeline wouldn't allow it, and Lillian Poe had suggested that they not interfere with Madeline's authority in her sister's life.

"And then You guided us to the Tree, And blessed art thou who has believed, because these things shall be accomplished that were spoken to thee by the Lord. Father Leo said that. And we knelt before the tree and prayed without ceasing and Epiphany wanted to stop because she is a baby but I said no and on the third day You appeared in Your divine grace and beauty, Mother of Jesus to whom it is given to bring forth to the life of glory all God's elect Amen."

"Amen. Do you have any gum?"

"Oh!" Amos took it out of his pocket. "Yes, look here, as a matter of fact I brought you some of the gum with the moose on the package."

"It's a zebra," Immaculata said.

"Right, here it is, then."

They each took a piece. Amos thought the gum tasted very, very good, maybe better than any other gum in his life. His piece was green, and the wrapper included a temporary tattoo. He put the rest of the pack on the table, so they could have some later.

"And then she began to speak directly to you?"

Immaculata nodded and chewed her gum. "Yes, she tells us things, and then we talk about them at the sandbox where we play Do This In Remembrance of Me and also on our walks we talk about it. And soon we'll have lessons."

Amos sat back in his chair and tapped his pen against his leg. "Would you like me to write down what she says to you every day? Are you allowed to repeat it?"

The girls looked at each other. Epiphany chewed her gum with her mouth open, then pushed her hair out of her eyes. Her hand looked to Amos as it must have when she was a toddler, except for the broken fingernails and streaks of dirt. She was just a baby. Immaculata was not; she was dexterous, in control of her movements, and capable of intense concentration. She had been in the third grade at Sacred Heart. Beulah told Amos, long before he'd ever met Alice, that Madeline had never made less than perfect grades, and had not missed a day of school in either first or second grades. Alice, Amos knew, had been confounded by her firstborn, by Madeline's love of order, her perfectionism, her faith in hierarchy. Alice had been a hapless child herself. She hadn't excelled at much and never seemed to blend in with her peers: she was outside. Eloise had been more like that, and in fact, her teachers had suggested she repeat first grade. And now here they sat, trying to decide whether to reveal the secrets entrusted to them by the mother of God.

"I won't tell anyone, I promise," Amos said, holding up two fingers in a Scout's pledge. Something had gone wrong in the tone of his voice; he sounded condescending, as if he were brokering some arrangement that would end with trinkets, or a day at a carnival; Immaculata looked at him as if he were transparent. Of course he wouldn't tell. The girls belonged to The Church, and Immaculata, for one, was aware of what that meant. Visitations, even those hundreds left unconfirmed by the Vatican, were a form of currency. Look at how zealously the pope had guarded the information revealed to the children at Fatima; the ceremony attached to the consequent publication of the predictions; the industry grown up around the cult of Mary in places like Medjugorje. What if word did get out, even in a decidedly un-Catholic place like Haddington? How long would it take for the information to spread? *Two little girls can see the Virgin Mary in the trunk of a dogwood tree. Every day Mary speaks to the children, and they answer.* First, pilgrims would begin flocking to Beulah's front yard. They would build a shrine around the tree, and keep candles lit there day and night. Father Leo would hear, and he'd activate the chain of command. Eventually, a committee would review the testimony and the physical evidence and make a preliminary report to the local bishop. . . . Amos lifted his glasses and pressed his fingers against his eyes.

He'd looked at the tree and he could see her, too—the shape of a woman—and while he was not prepared to make an objective judgment on the supernatural nature of the figure, he was willing to say the girls were not delusional, at least not about that one aspect. Millions of people see Mary on the side of a building in Clearwater, Florida? Then she's there. Mary is witnessed *daily* on a hillside in Bosnia. The scent of roses is detectable *daily* at apparation sites, and with no scientific cause. Thousands of people report having seen her image in the sky, or in the window of an abandoned house. Statues of her weep, or bleed. When Amos, looking at the outline of a robed woman in the straight, flat part of the dogwood trunk, asked Immaculata what she and her sister saw, Immaculata said: "She's in a blue robe with a white veil and her head is surrounded by stars and there are roses at her feet."

"Is she an old woman, or young?"

Immaculata answered without hesitation, "She's nineteen."

In seminary, Amos read every account he could find of both Jesus and Marian sightings—the eschatological, the apocalyptic, the optimistic—and not with an eye toward debunking them. He was not the Twin; Amos had no need to thrust his hand in Christ's wounds. He just wanted to . . . there was a pattern, wasn't there? and something great seemed to be at stake. What is at the bottom of all this, that's what he wanted to know, what is being said by the millions of faithful about motherhood, the future, our capacity to suspend our otherwise unassailable belief in the physical laws of life on earth? The conundrum he found himself in (those years in seminary) was this: If someone had written a book answering those questions, and had done so from a faith perspective, Amos would have had to dismiss it, at least partially. And if the book had been written from a nonfaith perspective, Amos would have had to dismiss it. *There is no place to stand,* he thought, struggling to keep his thoughts in order. He couldn't approach this impulsively or intuitively; he knew he had to call upon all his powers of discernment.

Amos and Immaculata began to speak at the same time.

"I—"

"I—you go first," Immaculata said.

"Don't tell me, Madeline. Because . . . you want to know why? Because I really don't know what to think of all this. And besides, Mary came to you, didn't she, to you and your sister. If she'd wanted to talk to me, well, I've got plenty of trees of my own."

Immaculata sat back in her chair, her face unreadable. "It has nothing to do with the tree."

"No. I know that."

"And that isn't my name."

The screen door opened before Amos could answer, and in the living room Beulah struggled to stand up. Her legs were swollen and causing her problems. AnnaLee walked in with the day's groceries. "Am I early?" she asked, looking at Amos and then at Immaculata. Amos knew AnnaLee was nervous around the children. She couldn't determine how to be herself; she was moved by the desire to save them, to rescue them from the flood. But she's just like the rest of us, Amos thought. The water is wide, and her boat is so small.

"No, not at all," Amos said, briefly covering Immaculata's hand with his own. He stood, touched the top of Epiphany's head. "I never take precedence over dinner." Beulah stepped in and began putting away the clean dishes in the drainer.

"Stay?" AnnaLee asked, widening her narrow eyes in appeal. "There's plenty."

"I can't. It's Wednesday already, and my sermon isn't written."

"Your sermon is never written by Wednesday."

"Nonetheless."

The girls quietly slipped from the table, ghosting past the adults in the narrow kitchen. They would wash their hands for a long time, whispering, then sit perfectly still on their bed until they were called for dinner.

"In movies, grief is so *noisy*," Amos said, taking a carton of eggs from AnnaLee and putting it in the refrigerator.

"Yes, and in movies everyone is thin and clever. You won't stay because of Langston."

"That's ridiculous. I just have to work, that's—"

"It's okay. She'd rather not see you, either."

Amos stopped moving, a box of seedless raisins dwarfed in his hand. "Pardon? How incredibly rude—"

AnnaLee spun toward him, surprising him. "Don't imagine for a moment that you're free to criticize her, Amos. She's my daughter."

"Oh," he said, putting down the raisins and holding up his hands. *No weapons.* "I'm—"

"Amos, it's okay—I didn't mean to—"

"I'm grateful she's helping you, AnnaLee, truly, and . . . What a mess."

"If you're grateful, stay for dinner. Take a meal with us."

Amos looked at AnnaLee a moment. She bargained hard and her posture never faltered. If Amos had to choose one person (he squinted at her trying to determine if he meant this), if he could see just one person approaching him in the dust of a refugee camp, or arriving at the scene of an accident in which he was informed that he'd be leaving his leg behind; if he could take only one person with him into a demilitarized zone to steal orphans . . . He squeezed her shoulder as he headed for the door. "Maybe next week."

"Mmmm-hmmm," she said, already beginning to peel carrots. "Coward."

Amos walked out into the sinking light, bright in the west, distracted. He almost didn't see Langston sitting at the picnic table, Germane at her feet, waiting for Amos to leave so she could go in and help her mother. He knew he should say something, but his shock at *her* dislike for *him* left him speechless. Sometimes, unable to sleep, he'd imagined himself confronting her, explaining to her why she needed to be nicer to her mother, why she should grow up and go back to school and stop casting a shadow over his life, and in these speeches Amos was, without failure, sanctimonious, and he couldn't stand the person talking. The inner, sleepless person. She made him . . . he'd never . . . was she reading *Frithjof Schuon?* Langston was looking right at him, he realized, over the top of her book, the look on her face one of supreme amusement.

"Pastor Townsend," she said, giving him a little Jane Austen nod.

"Mistress Braverman," he replied. He realized he'd been standing (God only knew how long) on the steps of the mobile home, gripping the iron handrail as if enduring hurricane winds. Where was his dignity? *Where exactly are my feet?* he thought, taking the last steps unsteadily. "Is that, may I ask, are you reading *The Transcendent Unity of Religions?*"

Amos saw Langston bite back her impulse to remark on the connection between the book she was holding in her hand, right in front of Amos, and the book she was, in fact, reading. "Yes. Yes, I am."

"Do you, are you enjoying it?"

"Enjoying it? Not especially. But I'm glad I'm reading it. I think his exoteric/esoteric distinction is quite illuminating, and I appreciate the idea of this brilliant light emanating from the Divine Source, transcending and unifying the world's religions. I'm just now reading the chapter 'Concerning Forms in Art.' Do you remember it?"

Amos shook his head. He had a vague sense of it, the way that the intellect was made manifest in the most perfect form available—no, he'd lost it.

"I was just reading this, um," Langston hummed through some of the text, searching for what interested her, "here:

What is particularly important to note is the fact that the 'revelation' is received, not in the mind, but in the body of the being who is commissioned to express the Principle. 'And the Word was made flesh,' says the Gospel ('flesh' and not 'mind') and this is but another way of expressing, under the form proper to the Christian Tradition, the reality that is represented by *laylat al-qadr* in the Islamic tradition.

"Langston, this is really quite extraordinary."

She looked up at him, tilting her head. "Is it? Are you unfamiliar with the precepts of universality?"

"Yes. No. Yes, I'm familiar, of course—what's extraordinary is that just this morning I was struggling over a similar question, and it didn't occur to me, this aspect, forms in art—although John Cobb addresses it brilliantly in *Christ in a Pluralistic Age*. I just. You know, I behave as if I'm writing my sermons in a vacuum, as if—"

"Everything in Haddington takes place in a vacuum."

"I don't know about that, I was just trying to say—"

"What? That you can't employ arguments by Cobb and Griffin in your sermons? Because no one in your congregation would have a clue what you were saying, apart from my mother? Are you in a crisis?"

Amos shook his head. He knew he'd never be able to reclaim the conversation.

"Because you look like you're in some sort of crisis."

"No, no I'm not. But thanks for your concern. I should be going." Amos headed down Chimney Street trying to look casual, but he wanted to kick the stop sign as he passed it, and just as he was nearly safe, nearly out of Langston's line of sight, a tree branch hit him in the head, and when he tried to back up, a twig got caught in his hair. He had to wrestle with the whole mess for more than a minute to get free. To make matters worse, maybe just in order to *mortify* himself (as the religious did in days of old), he turned back to see if she was watching, and of course she was sitting there perfectly still, her book on her lap. Watching him. She gave him a small wave, just raised her hand, really, and for a moment, Amos thought he might burst into tears.

Chapter 16

THE HADDINGTON CRIER

Taos, it has been a long time. I'm writing you today because it has been

raining for more than a week now; I have mornings to myself and ev-

erything adds up. It adds up to what I am about to say. You know I

never could abide your love of science fiction; I remember a conversa-

tion we had about the metaphorical possibilities of certain scientific

principles (the Fibonacci sequence; multiple possible universes theory;

something involving quarks). Your position was that there was little

more exciting than seeing those theories, employed as metaphor,

woven into a thrilling plot; mine was that the Fibonacci sequence *is* a

metaphor, and that what it points toward is infinitely more exciting than

genre fiction. And also, now that we're discussing it again, why not—if nonscientists are going to adopt those concepts in the name of art—why not just go directly to literature, and skip the six-headed aliens, or marsupial women or whatever atrocity so moved you about that one book? How you did go *on*. But lately I've been thinking, and I need to get this down quickly—I don't like to be distracted once the girls are awake—that grief splinters, Taos, it splits off into fragments (I think nostalgia does this, too, nostalgia being a very specific manifestation of grief), and that each of those fragments then has a life of its own. Every day is a new way to grieve, and this morning, very early, I was sitting in the attic window watching the rain and I tried to imagine even one of those splinters—could I hold on to even one? could I contain it for a day, an hour?—and it struck me as a story that could be told in science fiction. A woman loses her brother, or her brother is lost, and every moment of every day for more than ten years she rises and begins to grieve, and the grief leaves her body in something like a cloud and goes about its business. Each cloud a particularity. One, for instance, takes the shape of the woman but when she was much younger, fifteen or sixteen years old, and all that girl does, eternally, as if she's been captured in amber, is stand beneath a hawthorn tree and wait for her brother who said he'd meet her there. Her brother, who is beginning to lose his ability to keep his word. Her brother, who inch by inch is disappearing from her life and she— I don't know what I was going to say there. But do you see? A story about grief is actually a story about what is possible, multiple universes, up against the finite, or what happens when, as Tillich says, the infinitely removed makes itself felt. (The girl could stand beneath that tree forever, she is there yet today, and what can be known about the tree, the scent of the blossoms rising, their deaths, the limbs, the shade, these have become her occupation.) But really, when I put it like that, it's just a ghost story, and I never read those either. Because first I was too young to appreciate them, and then it was too late to start.

*

She tore the pages out of the yellow notebook and threw them away. Every day had been the same: she awakened as if in the grip of something—and this was a different way to work for Langston, who believed in not so much inspiration as a steady pace—and there was only one person she could talk to, she felt, and so she tried to write to her brother, as she had thousands of times over the past decade, but the tone of the letters, not to mention the content, seemed foreign to her. She barely recognized herself.

The house was quiet; Walt had already left for work and AnnaLee was gone, too, having left a note: "L. We're out of coffee—my fault—don't implode. I'll pick up more with today's groceries. Can you make it until this afternoon? You are my Sunny One, good sweet girl, xoxoxo, Mama."

"Oh, fabulous," Langston said, rummaging through the freezer, which was full of unidentified meats in butcher paper, stacked on top of those silver ice cube trays that stick to the human hand and yield not a single cube. The trays had been in the freezer so long unattended that the ice had shrunk; a sad sight. The spot in the freezer door where Langston kept her coffee was conspicuously bare, the only available place for the venison, or whatever it was, to migrate. She closed the freezer door and leaned her head against it, aggrieved. Just this one thing she continued to demand of the day, this one salvific thing, and she was to be denied it. Imagining the hours until late afternoon when her mother would breeze into Beulah's, averting her eyes from the children and generally making Langston nervous, Langston's head began to ache, just a dull whisper behind her eyes, a warning.

And where *was* her mother? she wondered, peeking through the living room curtains. The car was still parked in front, and Langston was filled with unease, imagining AnnaLee traipsing about town under her old umbrella, as she was wont to do, with her basket over her arm, barefoot. AnnaLee loved the Old Women, and nearly every day she baked something to carry to them the next morning.

"She's like a little gerbil on a wheel," Langston said to Germane, exasperated. They climbed the stairs to the second floor, and then on back up to the attic, where Langston changed from her nightgown into jeans and a T-shirt. She was able to locate her yellow raincoat in a box still packed from her apartment. She slipped the Schuon in the large front pocket, looked through her top desk drawer until she found the twenty-dollar bill her grandmother had given her, then gathered up her pocket watch and a pencil.

As soon as they stepped out on the front porch Langston realized what she was up against; the rain was falling steady and straight down, no wind, as it had been for days. The air was so warm and sodden Langston felt she was trying to breathe in bathwater. Oh, yes. This was just her mother's favorite strolling-around-barefoot sort of weather. By noon nothing, no twig, no chopstick, no tree limb would be able to hold AnnaLee's hair, and she would arrive home looking like someone escaped from a Pre-Raphaelite Home for the Deranged.

Langston patted her own hair, which was neatly gathered into her braid, then pulled up the hood of her raincoat for good measure, opened her umbrella, and started off, Germane trotting by her side through puddles that completely covered his feet. He didn't seem bothered at all.

*

At the diner Germane lay down on the front step, under the awning. Langston stepped inside and was shocked to discover the place nearly full. The air around her was humid and full of conversation, the air conditioner silent. She looked at her pocket watch and discovered it was only seven-thirty, and the place was bustling. There were all the old farmers and their sidekicks; Langston noted with alarm that nearly every man was missing at least a digit, and some, whole hands.

She added her umbrella to the four or five standing next to the door like a line of soldiers and slipped her hood off, looking for a place to sit. A number of voices said "Hey, Langston," and "Morning, Langston," and she glanced around to see who had spoken but no one looked directly at her.

"Hello. Everyone," she said, then noticed her daddy sitting at the booth in the back corner, alone.

"Is this seat taken?" Langston took off her jacket and slid it across the cracked and wavy vinyl seat of the booth, as Walt looked up from the newspaper he had spread across the table.

"Hey," he said, smiling at her. "We're out of coffee."

"Yes, we are. I wouldn't be here otherwise."

"Never seen you here before." Walt folded the paper back into its original shape, all five or six pages of it.

"That's correct. I haven't taken a seat in this diner for, let's see, probably twenty years? We used to come here for ice-cream sodas. Does Lu still make them, those ice creams with soda poured over?"

Walt nodded.

"Really, this place is," Langston began, looking around, "*exactly the same*. How is that possible? Nothing at all has changed. You didn't eat that, did you?"

"What?" Walt looked down at his plate.

"It looks to me like corned-beef hash, eggs, and biscuits and gravy. That stuff is terrible for you."

"Tasted good."

"Not my point."

"I reckon not."

Selma Sue appeared at the table with a coffee pot, a cup and saucer, and a little bowl of nondairy creamers, which she placed in front of Langston with great speed and recklessness, such that coffee was spilled on the table, in the saucer, and all over the front of the plastic menu. Langston had just enough time, before Selma swiveled and walked away, to read her button for the day: You Call Me A Bitch As If That's A Bad Thing.

"Well," Walt said, taking a last drink of coffee. "I need to get to work."

Langston felt a wave of disappointment. "Do you have to? Right now?"

He nodded, stacking his dishes and moving them toward the edge of the table. "I stay here any longer I'll be late."

"Is that, can't you just—"

"I've never been late to work. Not in thirty-five years."

"Never? Not even—"

"I've been sick, but I've never been late." He stood, stretching a little, then left three dollars for Selma on the table. He bent over and kissed the top of Langston's head. "Want me to leave you this paper?"

"Heavens no. Wait, yes, do. I'll use it to soak up this coffee."

"Good for cleaning windows, too."

Langston watched him make his way around the tables. It seemed every man he passed spoke to Walt, and Walt raised his hand in return, but none of them made eye contact.

"Ready to order?"

"Oh, oh, wait, I forgot—" Langston opened the menu, causing the coffee on the cover to stream into the booth next to her. Selma pulled a gray cloth seemingly from nowhere and swiped at the seat, raising a cloud of bleach that made Langston's eyes water. "Do you have, let's see, what sort of bread do you have?"

"White."

"Do you have waffles, by any chance?"

"Frozen. We toast them." Selma didn't look up from her order pad.

"No, that won't—"

"We've got pancakes."

"Too heavy. Pancakes make me sleepy. Is there anything you'd recommend?"

Selma glanced up. "Eggs bacon toast and juice is what I'd recommend. You look like a stick."

"Oh, well this is just my natural—and actually, I don't eat eggs or bacon, or bread if the flour was bleached. Or pasteurized juices."

"Really."

"No. Do you have cottage cheese, by any chance?"

"Not for breakfast."

"There are rules?"

"Lu says so."

"Well, then. I'll just have this coffee. You wouldn't happen to have any organic milk or cream, would you?"

"I wouldn't happen to."

Langston wrapped her hands around the cup. "Just black is fine."

Selma turned and walked away. As she passed the next table of men she poured coffee into each of their cups without breaking stride. Langston took out her copy of *The Transcendent Unity of Religions*, which was damp, and her pencil, and laid them on the table next to her coffee cup. On impulse she opened the Haddington *Crier;* it, too, remained exactly the same as when she was growing up. The first and

second pages were devoted to local news and the farm report, the third
and fourth pages were local sports and obituaries, the fifth page was
Ann Landers, Dear Abby, a horoscope, a knitting pattern, and a few
comic strips, and the back page was The Courthouse. The residents of
Hopwood County took far too great an interest in the news of the ju-
risprudence, in Langston's opinion. Who needed to know, for instance,
that all of these people had filed bankruptcy? She read through the list
but didn't recognize many of the names. Six couples had divorced; four
had applied for marriage licenses. Seven babies had been born at the
local hospital, three of whom had no father. A miracle, Langston
thought. Ollie Sproyland had been arrested for the third time in two
years and charged with drunken driving, driving with a suspended li-
cense, driving an uninsured vehicle, and a long list of other offenses,
including passing another car in an intersection. Langston had gone to
school with some Sproylands, and she tried to recall them individually,
but could not. There were many, and they did seem especially prone to
skirmishes with the law. She read: "The judge, after having granted two
continuances because of Mr. Sproyland's bad back, finally demanded
that he appear to answer charges. His lawyer answered that the only
way Ollie Sproyland would be coming to court would be on a stretcher,
and the judge replied, 'Bring him in on a stretcher then.' The following
week Mr. Sproyland appeared with seventeen family members, wheeled
in on a hospital bed which caused great consternation among the metal
detectors. The judge . . ."

"Is this seat taken?"

Langston jumped and dropped the paper. A corner fell into her coffee and began to absorb it with surprising speed. Amos Townsend tow-
ered over the table, his black raincoat dripping. There was a drop of
water on the end of his nose.

"No, no," Langston said, still alarmed. He had seen her reading the
Haddington paper. She blushed, and tried to cover her embarrassment
by pressing her hands against her cheeks, then removed them and tried
to fold and hide the newspaper before he could comment on it.

Amos took off his jacket, draping it over the back of the booth,
then mopped his face with a handkerchief. When he slid into the booth

his knees hit the underside of the table, causing more of Langston's coffee to slosh out into the saucer.

"Million-dollar rain," he said, smiling broadly.

"Excuse me?"

"It's an expression I used to hear growing up. Million-dollar rain. It means a good rain coming at a good time, not so close to planting as to wash away seeds, not too hard or too long, it'll get right down into the groundwater and keep the roots happy until harvest time."

Langston said, "And are all those variables at work here?"

Amos waved away the question. "I don't know. I'm not a farmer. But it sure *feels* like a million dollars. My garden will be happy. You were reading about Ollie Sproyland?"

"Oh," Langston looked down, busying herself with her coffee-stained napkin. "Not really. Daddy just left the paper and I was—"

"Did you get to the end? Because the best part is when the judge says, 'Mr. Sproyland, you are forthwith forbidden to pilot anything with wheels. If I catch you out on that *hospital bed* I'll put you in jail.' She always gets the best lines, Judge Latham does."

"I'm actually not much interested in the local court news."

"It fills me with pleasure, that paper," Amos said, still abundantly cheerful. Langston noticed that his hair seemed to be growing seventeen different directions at once, and that some sections, inspired by the intense humidity, were standing up like antennae. "They answer to no one, not Knight-Ridder, or Murdoch, or a conglomerate, they just print whatever they wish. The amount of lawlessness in small towns is often overlooked, in my experience."

"I don't think so. I think the whole world is aware of the criminal tendencies inherent in small-town life."

"I'm talking about a revolutionary sort of lawlessness."

Selma rattled a cup and saucer in front of Amos, dropped his menu, splashed some coffee in the general direction of his cup, then poured more toward Langston.

"Thanks, Selma," Amos said, glancing at her button. "I'll have the usual."

"That seems a tremendously naive thing to say." Langston retrieved the paper, opened it, and spread it out on the table as a place mat. "Revolution, whether it's political, economic, or artistic, has its own constructs—is governed by its own laws, if you will—as terrorism generally is. And like prophecy, a revolution can only be judged by its accuracy, not by its initial aim."

Amos tapped on his ear, as if to dislodge water. "No; yes. I see your point. I was talking about the lawlessness of the frontier or the prairie, but this isn't the frontier, is it? Not since we got cable television and the Internet. Now the world is the same all over. I guess what I enjoy are the last vestiges of . . . something."

"A dying thing."

"Vanishing, for certain. That dog of yours is wonderful. One of the best dogs in the history of the world."

Langston felt her face heat up again. "Thank you. Germane. Yes. He saved my—"

Selma slid a plate in front of Amos: eggs over easy, gelatinous in some bright yellow grease, with bacon, a biscuit, and hash browns. "Plate's hot," she said, before walking away.

"Are you not eating?" Amos asked, covering his lap with his paper napkin.

"No, no, I'm not hungry, but—"

"Oh, of course—AnnaLee has mentioned—there's nothing here you could—"

"But do go ahead yourself."

"What about oatmeal? There isn't much that can go wrong with oatmeal, is there?"

Langston hesitated. "I make it with bottled water."

Amos looked at her, his expression a question.

"I just don't trust our well water, and there's no reason to think Lu's is any different—"

"No, no, I see." But he looked away from her. "Life must be very difficult for you, here," Amos said, reaching for the salt and pepper.

"I'd rather not talk about it."

"I understand."

Langston took a drink of her coffee, which managed to be both bitter and watery at once. She thought with longing of the extra-dark

French roast her mother was able to find at a grocery store in Jonah; of her bean grinder, her coffee press, the only part of the day she still—

"May I ask you something?" Amos spread more of the yellow grease on his biscuit, from a small container barely visible in his large hand.

"I don't know," Langston said, leaning into the back of the booth, away from the table.

"The only thing I really dislike about living here is the assumption—it's the way people don't know what to make of the fact that I'm not married and don't have children. I'm marginalized, I'm treated as a vaguely pathetic . . . like a marked man."

"Is that a question?"

"Beg your pardon?"

"You said you wanted to ask me something."

"I did?"

"At any rate, you *are* marginal because you're a single man at, how old are you?"

Amos bit into his biscuit. "Nearly forty," he said, chewing.

"A forty-year-old man who has never taken a wife is a curiosity here. I'm sure everyone assumes you're gay or otherwise unfit."

"What I don't understand," Amos said, wiping his mouth, "is how people go about marriage so blithely here, and then by and large stick it out. I don't—well, it's possible, now that I think about it, that I don't understand marriage at all. Like this, for instance, like wedding rings. I look around at the people in my church, or the people I see here at the diner or in the Grocery Store or the post office, and they're all wearing wedding rings, and you can tell they don't think a thing about them. They don't consider those rings any more than they consider their noses or their shinbones. Nothing to it. But I would never *stop* considering that ring. I would puzzle over it all the time; what does this mean? I would ask myself, and How have I done it? and Am I getting it right? And that would cause me to consider my partner—the word 'wife' is another thing that stumps me, '*my* wife,'—who on earth is she and what does she have to do with me? And—"

"Wait a second, wait," Langston said, running her hands over her hair, just checking. "You glossed right over a critical element of life in

Haddington society, right at the point at which you said that people wear their wedding rings and never think a thing about them. Truly, you could stop right there and your question would be answered. The people in this town, indeed, all over the Midwest, I would venture, live lives which are entirely outward-directed; they take in and synthesize stimuli at the shallowest possible level, and simply act. They have no concept of an inner life, and so are often, in my experience, puzzled by their own behaviors when those behaviors don't fall neatly into certain preestablished categories. Look: if you said to any married couple, let's just choose those two people sitting over there, that woman with the white-blond hair and the dark roots and that farmhand-ish man sitting across from her, don't turn around—"

"That's Clint and Debbie."

"Clint and Debbie, then."

"They're not married, they're having an affair. Debbie's actually married to—"

"Let's pretend? Pretend they're married? If you asked Debbie about happiness, if she is happily married, I guarantee you'd get a look that suggested you'd carried something in on your shoe. Because Debbie isn't going to think about something as simple even as happiness, in terms of a condition of the psyche. She's thinking about getting her physical needs met, and making sure she's constantly distracted, and how to keep her hair that color without finally causing it to melt into a clump."

"I see what you're saying, but I think—"

"Happiness is a theory, and we in Indiana do not traffic in theories. We are an *applied* people. Of course no one gives a thought to a wedding ring, because it's a symbol, and a symbol represents theoretical thinking on the part of the collective—"

"Yes, but," Amos pinched the bridge of his nose, lifting his glasses, "if we asked Debbie if she is happily married, don't you suppose she'd simply say no? Because there she is, sitting with Clint for the whole world to see, while her husband drives a semi back and forth between here and San Diego. She'd simply say no."

"Ah, look what you're doing: you're confusing *what* she does and *how* she lives with how much she is willing or capable of thinking about it, and once again, you're mistaken. Just because she isn't happy and you and I can see she's unhappy doesn't mean that she would understand that or confess it. The more important thing is that she doesn't want to be asked. Trust me. She does not wish to be asked."

Langston realized with a shock, just before Selma refilled it, that her coffee cup was empty.

"How about a biscuit, Langston?" Selma asked, not looking at her.

"A biscuit? No, thank you. But it was very kind of you to—"

Selma walked away, gathering up plates from neighboring tables. Amos was nearly finished with his breakfast, although Langston had only seen him take two or three bites.

"The wedding rings aren't at the bottom of what puzzles me, anyway," Amos said, placing his knife carefully on the edge of his plate.

"No. I know they aren't."

"You do?"

"What puzzles you is how an institution can be both sacred and profane at the same time? Something like that? Or whether there is truly a transcendent element in an entirely mundane economy?"

"Yes! That is sort of what I was thinking. But also weddings, I'm very disturbed by the nature of a wedding, by the way we are forced into believing that we're witnessing a sacramental event—"

"—when we're actually witnessing an existential event."

Amos sat back, looking a bit winded. "Do you ever let anyone finish a sentence?"

"You should think faster," Langston said, picking up her book and pencil and slipping them back into her coat pocket. "And was I wrong? Or was that what you were about to say?"

"No, no it wasn't."

"Go on, then, I'm sorry."

"Never mind."

"That's what I thought." She slipped into her coat and stood up. "Thank you for your time, Pastor Townsend."

"Oh, my pleasure," he said, beginning to stand.

"Don't get up." She smiled at him and headed for the cash register.

One of the men at the register spoke to her, but she couldn't tell which one, so she directed her reply generally. Selma ambled up toward her, saying, "Your daddy left money for whatever you wanted."

Langston nodded. "Then let me pay for Pastor Townsend's breakfast. Shall I?"

She picked up her umbrella and opened the door. The rain continued to fall in heavy sheets; the sky was gunmetal gray. Germane was lying on the top step, waiting. Just before she closed the restaurant door, Langston looked at Amos, at his height, his slightly slumped shoulders, his uproar of hair. He was sitting perfectly still, staring at the opposite side of the booth, alone. She stepped out into the rain.

$\mathcal{C}hapter\ 17$

INSTRUCTIONS

Amos kicked through the rain, walking directly into puddles without noticing them. He didn't, he would grant, know very much about children, but he did know that they needed to be *listened* to, they couldn't constantly be *stepped* on. He remembered in particular a woman from his father's church, Vera Markham was her name, strange he could recall it, a compulsive talker, a woman who tortured other people with talk. She had imagined herself in a unique position to instruct, and her own children, who were Amos's age, had borne the worst of it, but no child was safe. One afternoon, just before he left for college, Amos had been in the Fellowship Room in the basement, helping a committee of people prepare for a potluck, and Vera had been one of them. She was holding in her arms a child about a year old, a little boy, while his mother ran home to get some eggs, and Amos would never forget the look on the child's face as Vera marched him around the room. "Charles, this is a *broom*. Can you say broom? We use a broom to sweep the floor. We're going to sweep up all the dust on the floor, and all the crumbs, anything we can find we're going to sweep up. I'm getting the broom out of the closet now, can you say closet? The broom stays in the closet when we're not using it. It's *good* to keep things in their proper places," and on and on she went, describing every gesture she made, asking the baby to repeat both nouns and verbs and then never giving him a moment to attempt it, had he been so inclined.

Amos began to sweat inside his black coat, thinking of Vera Markham. Thinking about Langston. If she would talk to him that way, if that was her style of conversation with him, what was she doing with the children? He stopped in the middle of the alley and tried to wipe some of the steam off his glasses with his shirt pocket, but couldn't do that and hold his umbrella. He put the glasses back on. What would she do if they tried to tell her? *Oh, of course you believe you're being visited by the Virgin Mary; it's simply a matter of reaction formation to your phobia of abandonment, and rightly so; or, Let me explain why, in terms of the literature on the subject, a Marian visitation is unlikely in this part of the world. Historically, confirmed sightings have been limited to rocky terrain which was difficult to farm, and as you've probably noticed, Indiana is . . .*

Or worse: what if they really opened up to her, what if they exposed their hearts and she interrupted or treated them condescendingly, children can't *bear* that, and these were Alice's children, they would see right through her. They would see her for what she really was and they would hear what she was saying, the depths of her tone, and they would be wounded, and he hated to cross AnnaLee, he hated to put his foot down, but Langston was impossible, he wouldn't allow it to go on. She really, really needed to go back to graduate school: it was the perfect place for her.

Amos looked up, confused and soaked to the bone. He'd walked a block past his house, as if in a dream. His pants were wet up to his knees, water flowed from his shoes with every step, and his hand kept slipping off the umbrella handle. He turned around and looked at the parsonage, gray against the gray sky, and began the walk back.

Chapter 18

THE FLEA

"Thus concludes our unit on the literature of the Harlem Renaissance," Langston said, shutting the book. "Do you have any questions?"

Epiphany was chewing on her bottom lip and rubbing her foot against Germane, periodically blinking and squinting against the bright sunshine. They had been three days without rain, and there wasn't a trace of it left.

Immaculata stared at Langston. She seemed worried. Twice she had picked at the picnic table so vigorously a piece had come off in her hand.

"Epiphany, don't chew on your lip, it's primitive. Immaculata, what's wrong with your face? Why are you squinching that way?"

"What's a moolado?" Epiphany asked. One of her fingers slipped up toward her nose.

"A *mulatto*, say it with me, mu-lat-to, is a term, no longer in use, I believe, which designates a child born of one black parent and one white parent. Younger girl, if your finger gets any closer to your nose I will have to run away screaming. Immaculata, what is bothering you?"

"Well," she said, "what about that person hanging from a tree? What does that mean?"

"Hughes is talking about a lynching, an activity formerly enjoyed by white people in small towns in the South and in the Midwest, in which innocent black men and women were hung from trees. One of the most famous photographs of a lynching, in which a whole group of handsome, well-fed townspeople are ogling the bodies of two young men, was taken in Marion, Indiana. Not far from here."

Epiphany stuck her thumb in her mouth, then pulled it out. "Were they died, those men?"

"Were they *dead*, yes, they were. Oh, but look at the time. We need to get busy on Do This In Remembrance of Me."

They stood up and headed for the sandbox. Langston took her usual seat on one side, and the girls sat down on the other. "I'd like to be the priest this time," Langston said, hoping Immaculata would say yes; she was tired of always being the parishioner.

Immaculata shook her head.

"Why not? I am perfectly capable of transubstantiating the host."

"This is for *pretend*, Langston."

"All the more reason. Plus, I know a fair amount of Latin."

"You aren't even *Catholic*."

"So."

Immaculata shook her head. "No."

Epiphany said, "No."

"Fine, then. I'll just sit quietly over here on my side of the 'church' and not bother anyone and not ask for any authority. That's what women have always done, isn't it?" They ignored her.

". . . He took a loaf of bread, and when he had given thanks, he broke it and gave it to them, saying, 'This is my body, which is given to you. Do this in remembrance of me.' " Immaculata raised the little plastic loaf of bread to the sky.

"Ding! Ding-a-ling-a-ling!" Langston rang. For some reason she was allowed to be the bell.

"And he did the same with the cup after supper, saying 'This cup that is poured out for you is the new covenant in my blood. Do this in remembrance of me.' " She raised the little pitcher with the daisy sprouting out the top.

"Ding! Ding Ding!" Langston cleared her throat. "Immaculata, I think you got some of the words—"

"Shhhhh!"

Langston and Epiphany lined up to receive the Eucharist: "Body of Christ."

"Amen."

They had barely gotten through Blood of Christ when Immaculata realized it was ten o'clock, and the girls dashed off for their walk.

*

On the drive to Jonah, Epiphany decided to randomly replace the beginning sound of certain words with the letter *b*. Her sister became Bimmaculata and Langston became Bangston, a name she found tasteless and completely unfitting.

Immaculata sat in the middle of the front seat, next to Langston, and Epiphany rode next to the door. Germane lay peacefully on the backseat, which was wide enough for him and two or three other dogs. They drove slowly along the country roads between Haddington and Jonah, the windows down, taking in the beautiful weather after the days of rain. AnnaLee had been forced to fashion outer robes for the girls out of trash bags, because they insisted on their morning tree time, even in the most inclement conditions.

"Beautiful as a June bride," Langston said, admiring the light on the cornfields.

"June is poppin' out all over," Immaculata said.

"Bune is my bavorite monf." Epiphany began to hum something sweet and tuneless.

"Okay," Langston said, returning to an earlier subject. "So you prayed without ceasing and on the third day in front of the tree, the Virgin Mary appeared and began to speak to you?"

"Right."

"Bight."

"And what did she say? Tell me what she said the first time, and then tell me what she's said since then."

Immaculata thought a moment. "Well, the first thing she said is, 'I am your Mother.' "

"Your Bother."

"And then she said, 'There is nothing but peace. Pray for peace in the world.' "

"And do you pray for peace in the world?" Langston asked.

Immaculata looked at Langston as if she were slow-witted, but still human. "Yes. That's what she *told* us to do. Mostly she says things like that, and that we must honor her son, and listen to him, and do what he says. She reminds me that no one who ever came to her for help was turned away, and that she is watching over us night and day, and won't let anything bad happen to us. One time she quoted Matthew 16:3–4, but I didn't recognize it until I came across it in my reading *that very same night*. 'You know how to read the face of the sky, but you cannot read the signs of the times. It is an evil and unfaithful generation asking for a sign, and the only sign it will be given is the sign of Jonah.' "

"*Mary* said that?"

"She was quoting the Gospel, is all. She didn't make it up. And also, I don't know what some of the things she says mean until later."

Langston shook her head. "The sign of Jonah? Don't you find that . . . ironic?"

"Swallowed up in a whale," Immaculata said, rather hopelessly.

"Ballowed up in a bale."

"I'm waiting for her to tell me to do something," Immaculata continued, "you know, like she told Bernadette to dig. But so far all she's said is Pray, Forgive, Say Your Rosary, and Eat Fruit. Stuff like that."

"Just like a mother."

They drove along quietly for a minute or two.

"Do you believe me?" Immaculata asked, looking hard at Langston's profile.

"Me?" Langston said, tapping her chest. "Do I believe you? Of course I believe you. Why wouldn't I?"

"Pastor Townsend doesn't believe us, I don't think."

Langston made a little spitting sound before she could catch herself. "No, he wouldn't. But it isn't his fault. He's jaded."

"Baded."

"What is 'jaded'?" Immaculata asked.

"It's like corruption. He's corrupt somehow, I don't know how to explain it."

"Mary ascended *un*corrupted to be seated with her Son at the right hand of God."

"So I've heard, yes." Langston turned onto the Old Dupont Road toward the Milky Freeze. "There is more in heaven and on earth, Immaculata. If I could be innocent of history, and were presented with two notions, Nazis or a visitation from Mary, I know which one would seem less likely."

"Also," Immaculata said, fiddling with the dial on the broken radio, "Lillian Poe doesn't believe us. She says that she understands why *we* might need to believe it, and that it isn't a bad thing, but that when we're better, later not right now, we'll let go of it. Of Mary."

Langston smacked the steering wheel. "She said that to you? Always always *always* it's the most dull and bereft who take money to tinker with our psyches. No one who really understood the soul would dare." She was so mad she felt a little sick. "I assume that Ms. Poe, who undoubtedly has a degree from an esteemed state university gracing the wall of her office, was never asked to read *Equus,* oh no. We can't have clinicians and behaviorists reading literature. She'll take Mary away from you, and when Mary goes she'll carry your intestines in her teeth."

Immaculata gasped. "Langston—"

"Oh, sweetheart, sorry, sorry." She patted Immaculata's knee. "I just paraphrased a line from a play. Mary would *never* do such a thing." She pulled into the drive-thru line at the Milky Freeze. "Girls, listen to me. Hand me my wallet first, and then listen to me. Thank you. Your visitations from Mary are not pathological, and they have nothing to do with illness. Lillian Poe may imagine that she can diagnose you as delusionary or exhibiting advanced defense structures or whatever she finds in those idiot textbooks, and undoubtedly she has an eye toward insurance reimbursement. But she is wrong, and every time you sit in her office and talk to her about whatever you talk about, remember that she is wrong. Mary has come to you because you are blessed and innocent and faithful, and I for one hope no one can *ever* take that away from you."

Neither girl said anything. Immaculata just stared straight ahead, clenching and unclenching her jaw muscles. Epiphany bounced her legs up and down, causing the car to rock slightly.

The sliding window of the drive-thru opened, and the same frumpy, dispirited, and vaguely rude middle-aged woman they saw every day stuck her head out.

"Yep."

Langston smiled at her, but collapsed inwardly; she lived among savages. "I'd like a chocolate dip cone, a vanilla cup with multicolored sprinkles, and an ice-cream sandwich. Thank you."

The woman closed the door without a word.

"Can we do crafts when we get home?" Epiphany asked. She wanted to do crafts every day, even though Langston found them profoundly tedious.

"Today is lessons, Epiphany," her sister said. "We're doing the Ten Commandments. We *promised* we would."

"Let's, how about this, Immaculata, let's make some crafty thing out of the Ten Commandments, a poster, or something to hang on your bedroom wall."

"Yeah yeah yeah a poster to hang on the wall, Immaculata. Do you have any gum?"

Immaculata's shoulders fell in defeat. "You have a whole drawer filled with gum, Epiphany. Pastor Townsend brings you some every day, spoiled baby."

"Boiled baby."

Surly Woman slid back the window, and handed Langston the ice cream in the order she'd requested it, and then just before she took Langston's money, gave her an extra cup with a swirl of vanilla ice cream and half a dog biscuit stuck in the top. Langston's eyes filled with tears, and she had to turn her head to hide it from the girls. *What is wrong with me?* she thought. *I've become so emotionally labile.* Before Langston could say anything to the woman, she'd taken the money and gone to get change. The girls immediately began to argue about who got to hold the cup for Germane, and when the woman came back Langston was only able to get out, "Thank you so much for that un-expected kindn—" before the window closed with a "Yep."

*

When they reached Lillian Poe's office (which occupied the front of her small, square house), Langston walked the girls into the waiting area. Lillian's door was open, and she was standing behind her desk, re-viewing notes or her calendar. Langston didn't like Lillian's officious-ness, or the severity of her haircut, which was painfully short, or the way she wore tailored suits in neutral colors, or the squatness of her fingers.

"Come on in, girls," Lillian called, without looking up. Langston didn't like that, either. She had her hands on the girls' shoulders, and she exerted just the slightest pressure, prompting them toward the door. Immaculata reached up and took Langston's hand, and Epiphany wrapped her arms around Langston's leg.

"Hey, hey." She knelt down until they were all at eye level, then wrapped her arms around their waists. "What's this?"

Immaculata had a tic under her left eye which had gotten worse over the past few days. She stared at Langston, unblinking. Epiphany bumped her head repeatedly against Langston's temple.

"Just remember what I said," Langston whispered. "Epiphany, you're giving me a concussion. Lillian can't take anything from you that you won't give her, and you don't have to see her forever. In two weeks she's going to reduce your visits to just once a week. I'm going to sit right out here and wait for you. I'll be sitting right here by the plant."

Immaculata nodded. "Sit by the door."

"Yes, bit by the boor."

Langston stood up and guided them through the doorway. "Go on then, soldiers. March on in there."

*

They skipped lunch in Jonah because Epiphany said her stomach hurt. All the way home she made little moaning sounds, some of which seemed genuine. Others had all the marks of malingering. She asked if she could get in the back with Germane.

"Sure," Langston said, at the same time Immaculata said, "No."

"Why not?"

"Because if you do," Immaculata spoke to Epiphany just loud enough for Langston to hear, "something very bad will happen."

Without thinking, Langston pulled the car off onto the shoulder of the country road. She looked at the older girl as if she were a stranger. "Immaculata! That is just patently cruel, and untrue. Apologize to your sister."

Immaculata said nothing. She stared at the windshield ferociously.

"Well, then, we'll just sit here in the blazing sun for the rest of the day. I mean it, that was unacceptable."

"No, I won't apologize! She's just faking. She's always been like this, she used to all the time tell Mo—"

They never mentioned their parents. In fact, they never mentioned their life before they moved in with their aunt, as if their mutual past had been erased.

"Okay, okay, let's just assume she means it this time."

No one moved or spoke, until Epiphany said, quietly, "Can we go now?"

Langston eased the car back onto the road. Neither girl made another sound all the way back to Haddington.

*

Langston was turning off Main Street onto Chimney when she noticed a car sitting in front of her house, a white—

193

"Oh my God! Grandma Wilkey is at our house!" Surprise visits were the worst for AnnaLee, because her mother seemed to have a sixth sense for mayhem and general disorder. Once Grandma Wilkey had shown up when the entire family was chasing a stray cat through the house, a cat inflicted with a particularly virulent gastrointestinal disorder. Another time she'd arrived at *ten o'clock at night*—Langston was certain her grandmother ordinarily went to bed around seven—and found AnnaLee in the living room with her women's support group, drunk and trying to learn to belly dance. (The belly dancing was also a very shocking sight to Langston, one that probably left permanent scars.) Oh! and the worst of all, and how she hated to remember it: Langston had come rushing home from college, certain she had cancer, having discovered a terrible, painful, unsightly lump on, let's just say, her hip. It turned out to be a boil, and her Grandma Wilkey walked in the house—walked in without knocking!—and found Langston on the sofa, with her pants down, having the boil lanced by Jolene.

"Girls," she said through clenched teeth, "I need to stop for just a minute at my house, okay? And then we'll go straight to your grandma's and fix some lunch. Is that all right?"

Immaculata looked up at Langston, worried. "What's wrong, is something wrong, what's happening?"

"No, sweetheart, no," Langston said, pulling in behind her grandmother's car. "My own grandma is at my house, and I don't think my mama, AnnaLee, was expecting her. Can we just check on her, on AnnaLee?"

Both girls nodded.

They opened the door to the living room, and it was far worse than Langston had expected. Her grandmother was sitting on the edge of the sofa in a houndstooth suit and white blouse, and AnnaLee was desperately trying to straighten up the piles of laundry covering every surface. She was now washing all of her own family's clothes, plus everything the girls wore under their robes and for sleeping, and Beulah's clothes, and as a matter of fact, there were piles of things Langston had never seen before. There were boxes everywhere.

Langston didn't know what was in them; they hadn't been there when she left in the morning.

"Hello, Grandma Wilkey," Langston said, crossing the living room to give her a kiss.

"Hello, dear," her grandmother said, turning her cheek. She smelled dry and powdery, and like mothballs. "Who is this with you?" She gave the children an automatic, feigned smile.

Langston quickly kissed her mother, who was perspiring, which of course made her hair stand out like a cloud, then stood in front of the girls. She'd made a mistake in bringing them in the house. "These are just some friends of mine. In fact, we need to be moving along."

"Darling, you should introduce them properly." Her grandmother stood, and Langston could see that she intended to see something through to the end, whatever the end was. Her flat, black purse hung from her forearm.

"Another time, Grandma. We'll just run along and go over the rules of civilized behavior on the way." Langston turned to shepherd the girls out of the house and found them frozen, wide-eyed. Immaculata's mouth was open as if she'd been trying to say something.

"What's wrong? Immaculata, what's the—"

"Langston, I think we should get the girls over to Beulah's; this isn't—"

"Girls," Grandma Wilkey said, walking toward them. She carefully skirted all impediments, including a pile of Little Mermaid panties. "I'm Marjorie Wilkey. It's a pleasure to meet you, and I just wanted to say that I was so sorry to hear about your—"

"Mama, what is in those boxes? Immaculata, look at me. Take your sister's hand and—"

Oh to have seen it from above, AnnaLee moving across the room toward the girls, Langston holding them from behind, trying to move them toward the door, and her Grandma Wilkey heading right for them, expecting them to shake her hand and be grateful for her pinch of sympathy. Langston could see so clearly what her grandmother was going to do: she was going to demand that the children accept the fact that their mother's death was just another social occasion, for which the world had developed conventions.

And then she saw it: a school backpack lying on top of two pairs of rain boots. Here was their former life, the mere suggestion of which could strike them dumb, laid open for all to see.

"Don't say another word." Langston took a step so menacing toward her grandmother that she stopped dead, her hand still extended. "Don't move another inch toward these children." She turned toward the girls, who were now looking at her, rather than at the boxes. "Immaculata, take my hand. Mama, pick up Epiphany and help me get her to Beulah's. Grandma Wilkey, don't be here when I get back. None of us has time for an unannounced visit from you. I'm terribly sorry for my rudeness, and you are welcome to take it up with me at a more opportune time."

"Langston! I will not be spoken to that way under *any*—"

"Mother," AnnaLee said, swinging Epiphany up on her hip. "You heard Langston. That's enough."

The last thing Langston saw, pushing against the screen door with her shoulder, was her grandmother standing in the middle of the living room, watching them go.

"Can I—" Immaculata began.

Langston didn't realize she was dragging Immaculata, or that she was trying to say something, until they were almost to the sidewalk. "Oh dear. I was abrupt. What are you saying, sweetheart?"

Immaculata swallowed, blinked. "Can I have my backpack?"

Langston stood up straight and let her head fall back on her shoulders. She loosened her grip on Immaculata's hand until their fingers were lightly touching. "Yes, baby. You can have anything you want."

*

"All right. What we're going to do is, excuse me? Hello? Bubble Gum Girl? What we're going to do is say the Ten Commandments. Immaculata claims that you already know them." Epiphany stared at the posterboard, breathing noisily through her mouth. She appeared to be chewing at least four pieces of gum, which she sometimes fished out of her mouth and held on the end of her thumb. "Do you know them?" Langston asked.

"What."

Immaculata was going through her backpack very carefully, taking out each item and staring at it a long time, then placing it on the table. So far she'd removed a notebook covered with sparkly stickers, a Hello Kitty pencil box, a red hair ribbon, and a Tweety Bird Pez dispenser. She looked at the things spread out in front of her the way Langston had seen, in news clips, family members examine items retrieved from suitcases after a plane crash. Not certain whether Immaculata wanted to be alone, Langston had asked if she'd like to take the bag to her room, but she'd shaken her head no.

"The Ten Commandments. Do you know them? Because we're going to say them, and if you forget some, I have them written down right here. And then we're going to write them on this posterboard, this is the 'crafts' portion of lessons, Immaculata's going to do that part, and you're . . . you, Epiphany, are going to use this stamper and stamp on pictures. Then you can fill them in with your markers. I swear I'm talking to a . . . Bepiphany?" Langston knocked her on the head. "Are you in there?"

Epiphany laughed through her nose, and her gum fell out of her mouth.

"Shall we, then?" They began to speak in unison, although sometimes Langston didn't have a clue what Epiphany was saying.

"You have only one God.

"Don't use God's name the wrong way.

"Make time for God.

"Be good to your mother and father.

"Don't kill people.

"Love your own husbands and wives.

"Don't steal.

"Don't lie.

"Love your own wife and family" (clearly a mistake, this repetition, Langston thought).

"Don't take things that belong to other people" (ditto).

When they finished, Immaculata slowly and carefully put her belongings back in her backpack and placed it in the corner of the kitchen. There was a brief but intense scuffle over whose elbows went on what corner of the cardboard, but soon enough that was solved and the girls were working quietly. They had only an hour before Amos Townsend appeared. Beulah was napping in her bedroom; she had been short of breath for the past two days, and her ankles were swollen.

"I heard something," Immaculata said, a bit under her breath.

"What?" Langston said, looking around. "What did you hear?" Germane was asleep by the front door.

"I heard my grandma tell someone on the phone that you were in Haddington because you quit school."

Epiphany looked up. "Oooooooo! Laaaaaangston!"

"Oh, for heaven's sake." Langston sat back and crossed her arms over her chest. "Yes? So? Yes, I did quit school. I was studying for a Ph.D. at a university far away from here and I left. End of story."

"Hmmm." Immaculata gave her a look, then went back to her lettering.

"I had to leave, if you must know."

The girls remained silent. The periodic screeching of a Magic Marker over cardboard was causing Langston's spine to tingle in a singularly unpleasant fashion. "Well, I didn't *have* to leave, no one *asked* me to leave, I was a star. As you can probably imagine."

She crossed her legs and bit the inside of her cheek.

"I was compromised, since you've asked." Langston let her head drop into her hands. "Oh, the politics! They are so terrible in an English department, so very much worse than Machiavellian. Life in an English department *never* rises to the level of Machiavelli—that would be such a welcomed evolution—no, no, it's more like an inner-city riot; fires burning in the street, looting, horribly misconceived slogans."

"Go on," Immaculata said, without looking at Langston.

"Look. I tried to stay above the fray, I did. I could see the smoke in the distance and tried to avoid the conflagration. All I wanted was to live the life of the mind, and I know it's a terribly shopworn thing to say, but there you have it. I didn't stand in any camp, I wasn't a formalist or a feminist, I didn't want to call myself a reader-response person or a deconstructionist or a poststructuralist. I wasn't a Marxist or a proponent of queer theory, or a Freudian, a post colonialist, or God help us! there was a black man in our department, a graduate student like me, who wanted us to start a movement to rename Multiculturalism 'Slave Studies.' He believed there was some sort of cleansing, revolutionary power in the 'ironic distancing,' that's what he called it." Langston took a deep breath, then sighed, remembering it all. "And no one could say anything to him, because we had no authority—that's the key to the recent developments in the critical tradition: if you're inside—and believe me, academia is nothing but a cult of expertise, it is the only religion alive and well—only if you're inside do you have any authority, and if that's the case, no one can speak to you. Your *curriculum vitae* becomes your fortress. Epiphany, try and resist stamping on your arms or your . . . Look, there's the poster and that's your, sweetheart, stamp the poster. Thank you."

Langston poured each of them a glass of lemonade and carried them to the table. Epiphany still preferred a sippy-cup. Everyone preferred that Epiphany use a sippy-cup. "Let's say I had decided to go the way of theory, and had chosen a camp; naturally, I would have had enemies in every other school of thought. But guess what happened instead? I tried to stay neutral, and had no friends."

*

Langston was the locus, and she didn't believe this was an exaggeration, of the collective anxiety of the entire department. Some people hated her because she was arrogant, or believed to be so; some hated her because she didn't speak enough in class, thus revealing her faux humility. She wasn't clever or ambitious enough for theory, or she was too ambitious for theory, and had a nefarious plan up her sleeve to overthrow the power structure. Because she didn't wear T-shirts bearing the likeness of Emma Goldman or Eudora Welty, and because she didn't have any posters hanging on her office door proclaiming, "If you can walk, you can dance. If you can speak, you can sing," or whatever that saying was, she was considered an enemy of women, and because she was not sexually available, she was the enemy of men. Even in that environment, she survived. She believed she'd make it to the end.

And then she took the John Donne seminar. She'd waited until her last semester of course work, because she knew it would be one of the highlights of her graduate school career, taught, as it was, by Jacques Perrin. Jacques Perrin. Second-generation French American, past president and solar flare in the International John Donne Society. An expert not on Donne's love poems (that would be too obvious) but on the Holy Sonnets. Author of *Resurrection, Imperfect: Divinity in Donne,* and *Little World: The Abridgement of the Universe,* along with countless articles and conference presentations. Perrin was one of the many scholars, scattered across England and America, who had been working on the Donne Variorum for years.

Jacques was not so tall, not quite six feet, and compact. Spare and athletic. He rode a bicycle to school all through the reasonable months. He had short, dark hair, and a black beard streaked with silver, which he kept cut close. On the first day of class that year he'd worn black dress slacks and a black turtleneck under a black cashmere sport coat. Cashmere.

They'd moved their chairs into a circle, with Dr. Perrin right in the midst of them (no podium for him), and he took attendance, making certain they all knew each other (they did, unfortunately). He said he wanted to perform a little test, and leaning back in his chair, resplendent and at ease, he'd recited Donne's most famous sonnet, "The Flea." They were all perfectly, respectfully silent. Some were, perhaps, even moved by his rendering.

" 'Three in one,' Donne says, your blood and mine combined with the flea's. The Trinity. What could be more intimate than that? This is a poem of seduction, of course, in which the woman's honor is stolen as soon as her blood mingles with that of the speaker. And since she has nothing left to protect, why not? Why not give herself entirely to him?"

The students continued to watch him, rapt, even though what he was saying was certainly not news to any of them.

"What I want to know is this: does it work, not as a poem, but as a seductive argument? Raise your hand if you would say yes to a man or woman who'd spoken these words to you."

And, oh Lord, what was Langston thinking? She wasn't thinking at all; her defenses had been lowered by a number of factors, including a head cold, and before she knew it her hand shot in the air, and at the same moment, at the exact same moment she raised her hand, she realized that everyone else's hands remained decidedly on their desks. Her fellow students grimaced, and all for different reasons, but Dr. Perrin threw his head back and laughed, even applauded a bit.

"Good for you," he said, and with such happiness Langston had blushed scarlet. She didn't look up from her book for the rest of the hour, and as they were preparing to leave, she heard Dr. Perrin say, "Miss Braverman, could you stay after class a moment?" Her fellow students traded knowing glances, and it was as simple as that. She was Next Year's Girl.

*

"Next Year's Girl?" Immaculata asked, having long ago given up the pretense of coloring. Epiphany had, at some point, crawled into Langston's lap and was now leaning against Langston's chest, sucking her thumb.

"It's a figure of speech."

*

There were things Langston didn't want to say, details she preferred to omit: the dinners, the firelight, the smell of woodsmoke on his skin in the morning. He lived in the woods outside town in an angular, modern house; he drank martinis and collected African art and recordings of famous poets reading their work. He owned an album of Richard Burton reading Dylan Thomas. There was a grown daughter in another state whom he never saw, the unfortunate product of his seduction of a *nun*. (Jacques had insisted they name the baby Dardenelle, but when he refused to marry the mother, refused, in fact, to live with her or love her or make any sort of commitment to the child, the fallen woman had taken the baby to her parents' home in the Pacific Northwest and quietly renamed her Nancy.) He berated himself, he excoriated himself for his treatment of the woman and the child, but it was too late to fix it. He'd been young and foolish.

Langston didn't want to tell Immaculata how Jacques had taken a sabbatical and she'd requested a leave of absence from the department and they'd spent an entire year traveling. A week in San Francisco, a week in Manhattan for an academic conference, three days in the mountains of eastern Pennsylvania. They were always back home by the end of the week, so that Jacques could work on his latest project, something about Donne and Paracelsus (alchemy, probably; everyone was doing alchemy that year). Walt and AnnaLee had no idea Langston had been gone.

She didn't want to tell the child about what she called the Heraclitean Mobile that hung above Jacques' bed: stars and fishes. The upward and downward way. Or how they had, most mornings, spent three or four hours at the breakfast table, drinking coffee and reading the *Times,* talking. Langston had told him everything.

*

"He was your boyfriend?" Immaculata asked.

"Yes, that's one way to say it."

*

In May, after they'd been together sixteen months, Jacques took her to the café, took her to her favorite table, and broke up with her. He'd come home from a conference in Chicago irritable and distant, so unlike himself, and there was nothing Langston could say or do, there was no way to get through to him, and within twenty-four hours she was standing in the room she'd kept in the graduate student dormitory, a room she hadn't even visited in months, with everything she'd had at Jacques' house, every shoe, every framed print of famous Italian operas, every book and bottle of shampoo. And she certainly couldn't mention to Immaculata how she'd spent three days under sedation at the Student Health Center, carefully watched by a young psychiatric resident named Elise, or how Langston had followed Jacques all through the summer, calling his house every hour all night, how seriously she considered suicide when he began to be seen around town with a beautiful young colleague, newly arrived from Japan, named Song. Jacques never called the police or took any legal action, although he could have. He did something far worse, something more damaging and permanent: he told everyone in the department. He told them everything about her.

*

"He didn't want to be your boyfriend anymore?"

"That's right," Langston said. Epiphany's hands were covered with Magic Marker. Langston rubbed the side of her face.

"So what did you do? What happened next?"

Langston sighed. "I took an apartment at a place called the Greene Arms, and went to the pound and got Germane," who lifted his head at the mention of his name. "And then I went back to school, and I tried, I did, I thought—well, I knew that there were far worse things than losing a lover, and so I just avoided him assiduously, I studied for my prelims and assembled a dissertation committee and completed my proposal, and then I showed up for my orals and he was sitting there with Song. They had recently married, and she was pregnant. In a black silk dress. He was giving me this paternal look—paternal, Immaculata? fatherly? like a priest?—and I could see that he was trying to say something to me, something about how he'd found me and saved me, he had, in some measure, made me what I was, and he had come because he was proud of me."

"And?"

"And I only had two choices, and neither one was tenable. I could let him watch me fail, or even worse, he could see me succeed. I just walked out. I left." Langston took a deep breath, swallowed, shifted Epiphany's weight. "But enough about me. I want to ask *you* something. Why do the two of you wear these robes and hats every day?"

Immaculata looked up at Langston, and it all happened so fast. Her eyes got wide and she tried to take a deep breath, but no air seemed to

203

pass her throat, and the same thing happened to Epiphany, whom Langston had thought was asleep. Whatever was happening to them was worse than the worst asthma attack Langston had ever witnessed (which had been on the subway in New York, a little Hispanic boy). The girls couldn't breathe.

"Beulah!" Langston screamed, lifting Epiphany with one arm and wrapping the other around her sister. She somehow managed to carry them both to the couch, and by the time she'd gotten across the living room, Beulah was there with pills and inhalers, grim but calm. The rest was a blur; all Langston remembered later was Beulah working on Immaculata while Langston held the inhaler to her sister's mouth; how Langston's hands shook; how Epiphany tried to say the same thing over and over, a sentence that began, "We forgot to close the—" and how, every time she said it, Immaculata's eyes rolled back in her head as if she were suffering a seizure.

"*Please,*" Langston said, begging them to breathe. And then everything just stopped, the way a tornado is simply gone, and Beulah and Langston found themselves in a tangle of little girls, their faces streaked with tears, their bodies hot and trembling. "I don't know what I did," Langston said to Beulah, blinking back her own tears. "We were just talking, and I asked Immaculata why—"

Beulah put her hand on Langston's arm. "It's all right. None of this is your fault."

The trailer door opened, and Amos Townsend walked in. It was three o'clock.

*

"I hold you entirely responsible for this," he said, in a low voice which, nonetheless, conveyed the depth of his anger. They were standing face-to-face on the sidewalk outside Beulah's trailer. The girls were asleep and Beulah had gone back to bed.

Langston was still shaking, and somehow her panic rose up through her body as rage. "Oh! Oh, is that right? And on what grounds, given that you don't even know what happened? Or does your position as a pastor in Haddington, Indiana, grant you omniscience?"

For a moment he seemed tongue-tied, then was able to say, "What I *know* is that there are two little girls lying in bed nearly comatose, children who had been left in your care."

"They're going to be fine; Beulah said this has happened half a dozen times before, and while we're on the subject of children left in incompetent care, why don't you explain to me why you don't believe they're talking to the Virgin Mary?"

"Why I don't, what are you—"

"Are you going to justify your skepticism with the Protestant Revolution, or have you consulted the patriarchy and gotten a thumbs-down?"

"Who in the *hell*—"

"Or are you threatened? Is your authority threatened? Are you afraid the housewives of Haddington might stop baking you cookies if they think the Queen of Heaven is speaking from a tree in Beulah's yard?"

By this time they were standing only about six inches apart. Langston had inadvertently begun poking Amos in the chest with her index finger.

"You aren't fit to take care of those children, and I'm going to talk to Beulah this afternoon about keeping you away from them," he said, his voice shaking.

All the blood in Langston's body seemed to hit her head in a rush. "If you," she said through clenched teeth, "try to take those children away from me, listen to me, Amos. If you make a single gesture to keep me away from the girls, I will take them and run. I will *take them* and *drive away*, and you'll never see them again."

Amos shook his head, his hands on his hips, then turned to walk away. He'd gone only about three steps when he made some decision, she could see it travel up his spine, and he turned and strode back so fast Langston stepped backward, afraid.

"Everyone protects you, Langston," he said, right in her face, "your mother, Beulah, Walt. They protect you the way they would a wounded animal. But I think they're wrong, I think your shell of denial and self-protection, your amnesia, are all guarding what is essentially psychosis. Your mother told me you still don't even know how Alice died, you still insist it was cancer or some disease, wait, don't even think about walking away. Madeline and Eloise lying tranquilized in a storage room, those children you think will be fine? Their father, Jack, shot their mother, Alice, twice, no wait, wait, get this part: Alice was standing right in front of the children—her blood hit them in the face. And somewhere between Jack's first and second shot, or maybe they fired at exactly the same moment, Robbie Ballenger isn't sure and it doesn't much matter now, anyway, Alice blew off the back of Jack's head with her own gun, children still present, mind you, and after both bodies had fallen the girls had to run past their dead parents to reach the front yard, and hold on, what about this? Their shoes were soaked with blood, they had blood in their *hair,* when the police and the ambulance arrived they were standing in the front yard screaming, clinging to each other, they'd left bloody handprints all over each other's clothes, and at DSS all they had to change into were those costumes they won't take off because Alice made them. *Those,*" he spit at Langston, "those are the children you're threatening to steal, the children who are going to be fine."

Langston saw her own hands fly into the air, and then the sky, and then nothing. She fainted.

Chapter 19

THE TASTE OF NEW WINE

There was no question. He would resign, and he would do so tonight, after he finished this bottle of wine and felt capable of facing his own shame. And what would he say, in his letter to the district? He would say, "I am like an officer at Gettysburg; I have destroyed my own troops in the name of a lost cause." During the past few weeks, minutes, some- times whole hours, passed when he forgot he was responsible for Alice's death (and for Jack's—he mustn't forget), so taken up was he with the lives he was trying to save. But every crime was returned to him tenfold in the moment he saw Langston begin to lose her balance, the way she blindly reached for him, but missed: reached for him! the man who had tried consciously to destroy her. And then, when he somehow managed to catch her before she hit the ground, and he felt in his hand the curve of her ribs, her narrow waist, he realized there was almost nothing to her. She had been, all this time, making her way through the world with just this slight . . .

He shook his head. It had felt like holding a bird. Amos's thumb had gotten caught in a narrow strip of elastic in her bra, and then he had begun to pray, probably out loud, *Forgive me forgive me forgive me.* He recalled the famous photograph of a firefighter carrying a dead toddler out of the bombed Murrah Building in Oklahoma City, and how Amos's eye had been drawn not to the child's burned skin or missing hair, but to the single article of clothing still recognizable on her body: a little white sock. Only an artist (this nearly made him laugh out loud, so gruesomely perfect an example it was of the problem of evil) could have imagined such a scene: the square-shouldered fireman, his face heroically impassive; the dead child; the viewer's eye drawn, the mind pulled straight down into grief, not by the scene *in situ,* but by one little flash of white.

His whole life, Amos decided, had been a single, long war of attrition. His father and mother were gone, his brother was gone, the whole of the Mt. Moriah Christian Church: vanished. Alice and Jack were dead, the children could not, perhaps, be rescued, and Langston, although she was conscious, hadn't moved since Amos carried her into her house, followed by a frantic Germane. It had been eight hours since he lay her on her bed in the attic, nearly undone by heartsickness, and she hadn't moved. He called AnnaLee every hour until ten, when she said she'd call him if there was any change. She hadn't called. Amos had asked: Does she have a doctor? No. Does she take any kind of medication? No, never, not under any circumstance. Is there a friend, a lover, someone from school, someone she grew up with? No, and no. No one.

And Beulah. Beulah was going; Amos had seen the signs. She had given Amos power of attorney, and named him the legal co-guardian of the children (with Langston, who didn't know it) in the event of Beulah's death. And she'd stopped checking on the girls' aunt Gail, who was in a private, Catholic institution almost a hundred miles away. Gail was not her problem, Beulah said, shaking her head. The last time they spoke privately, Amos asked her what she thought had happened in those days the girls were alone with Gail, after Alice died, and Beulah had sighed, disgusted and weary.

"I don't know," she said, finally. "I think whatever Gail did to them started years ago, when they were going to church all the time and spending nights with her. But the girls could take it then, you know, because they were strong and normal and had a happy life. And then—" She stopped. Amos knew what she meant to say. It didn't matter so much, what happened in those last days. Beulah and Amos were seeing the full flowering of seeds planted long ago.

"Do you know that each year during the Lenten season, Alice let Gail take them to Mass every day? They hadn't even taken their first Communion! What was the point? They attended the first service of the morning, at six forty-five, and then Gail would take them on to school. And every year I'd say, 'Alice, I think this is a mistake.' And she'd give me that look of hers. She was an innocent, Alice was. Never thought for a moment that anyone might have motives less pure than her own."

That was another way Amos knew he was losing Beulah, because she could talk about Alice so calmly, with such philosophical detachment. *She was here, and now she's gone.* When he asked Beulah how she'd managed it, the first time Beulah brought up Alice's name without tears, she'd said, "Well, I just realized I couldn't have taken her with me where I'm going, anyway."

And then, and Amos simply had to allow himself to enjoy the irony of this, Beulah had started asking, nearly every day, for someone named Sarah. No one seemed to know who Sarah was or what she meant to Beulah, but the name certainly meant something to Amos. Sarah had been the name of his first lover, all the way back when he was an undergraduate at Ohio State; they'd met their sophomore year in a history class. They were both virgins, and had figured it all out together, the whole mess, with a noisy, giddy, acrobatic joy.

Amos never thought of Sarah. He hadn't remembered her for years, and he had come to believe, with a paranoid certainty, that Beulah resurrected Sarah on purpose, to remind him of something, to point out that the past isn't dead (it isn't even past, as Faulkner said). In the last two weeks Amos was able to remember Sarah in such vivid detail that he felt punished, all over again, for what happened, forgetting, naturally, his own dictum in pastoral counseling, anytime a congregant bemoaned mistakes or expressed deep regret: "It was just your life. You were just living your life."

Sarah was short and curvy (she was overweight, really, but Amos didn't mind a bit), big-breasted, with bouncy red hair (curly—wild—she could do nothing with it) and freckles. She was freckled everywhere. There was a gap between her two front teeth, and she was loud. She had a big laugh and she talked so fast sometimes Amos would begin to laugh regardless of what she was saying, and then she'd punch him in whatever part of his anatomy was closest to her, hard. She'd grown up in a big, sprawling, noisy Irish family in East Chicago, and had come to Ohio State because her father had graduated from there, and it was the only school he'd pay for. She was studying social work, but wasn't ambitious; in fact, she never finished anything she started (but loved starting). Amos knew Sarah would never graduate, knew she was just biding her time until . . . what? He asked her repeatedly, but she'd learned early in life to change any subject, and so he'd let it go.

Maybe he had been confused about what they were doing, or maybe there had been a miscommunication, or maybe these were just the lies he perfected all those years ago, after they'd spent a thousand nights together in either his dorm room or hers (he thought of it that way: a thousand nights), after they'd fought and wrestled like puppies and learned how to be a man and a woman in the process. Sarah had taken the child out of Amos, he knew it even as it was happening, and raised him right up. She did it naturally and painlessly; she was gifted from all those years with siblings. It was love (what she felt for Amos, what she did for him), and he had allowed her to love him with the whole of her bounty, even though he didn't love her in return and knew he never would. How could he have taken her into the future as his helpmate, a pudgy little woman with an industrial accent and no sense of decorum?

By the time Amos graduated and Sarah didn't, he'd known he was going on to seminary, and when Sarah asked Amos what he thought she should do, he said, "I think you ought to go home for a while." What had she thought he meant by that? he wondered now, twirling his wine glass in his fingers and looking out at his dark garden. He had meant: go home, think about it, then get on with your life. They'd helped each other pack, and he'd loaded her things into her father's station wagon, and Sarah had sobbed, she'd wept with such abandon, Amos had never seen anything like it. He pitied her, but in a distant way (he was already a professional, really), and mostly he wanted her gone, so that he could go about his own business undistracted.

There were letters (he no longer remembered this part very clearly), and desperate, pleading phone calls—threats? did she threaten him, maybe?—over the summer, and Amos somehow held her off, kept her at bay. By the time he was installed in seminary, Sarah had nearly given up and Amos had nearly forgotten her. When her name did occur to him, then and over the years, he always felt the slightest shudder. They would have been entirely wrong for one another, as adults. They were both lucky it had ended when it did.

Amos poured himself another glass of wine and added Sarah, as Beulah had done, to the list of charges against him. He knew he hadn't loved her, he knew he would leave her, and had slept with her, anyway, for three years. He knew every inch of her freckled body, and had taken all she could possibly give, and now didn't know if she was alive or dead. Hadn't thought about her for years.

*

Smooth, blond, cool Alice. In his letter of resignation—not just from the Haddington Church of the Brethren, but from the ministry in general—Amos would write: "I chose to counsel Alice and her husband, Jack, now both deceased, because I thought Alice was my soulmate. I believe now that all the honorable intentions I fabricated at the time were merely that: fabrications. And at a critical juncture in the story, I urged Alice to leave Jack, which precipitated her death. *Moreover,*" . . .

He'd gone out to her new house, at Alice's invitation, for a cup of coffee, after the girls were asleep. The house was quiet and warm, and there was a sense of sweetness in everything: the homemade Mother's Day cards on the dining room table, and the smell of the girls' bubble baths still radiating from the bathroom. Amos felt happier—no, no, that wasn't exactly it—he'd felt closer to domestic happiness than ever before in his life. He felt as if it were just within his grasp. They had talked, he and Alice, for probably an hour about everything except her pending divorce (Jack's name was never mentioned, and neither seemed to find that suspicious). Alice had confessed her love for all things Frank Lloyd Wright, even the fountain pens, and Amos had admitted that for years, all through his undergraduate studies, he hadn't understood Emerson.

"And then when I was in seminary, I don't know why, but I took his essay on nature into the bathtub with me. I was maybe a little ridiculous at the time. And I read it out loud, every word of it. When the water got cold, I'd let it out and run more, I just wanted to . . . I just wanted to stay until I got it."

"And did you get it?" Alice asked.

"I . . . do you know what Emily Dickinson said about poetry, her definition of poetry?"

Alice shook her head.

"I can't quote it exactly, but it was something like: 'When I feel like the top of my head will blow off, *that* is poetry.' "

"And that's how you felt that night?"

Amos nodded. "There were sentences, whole paragraphs, maybe, I couldn't read out loud because I was so moved and stunned. Emerson is an indictment. Who said that, do you remember, that beauty is an indictment?"

Alice looked confused. "I don't know, I've never heard that before."

"Pound? Pound said it, I think, or else someone said it about Pound."

Their conversation had gone on this way for an hour, and then a storm blew up out of nowhere. Rain began to slant against the windows, and Alice remembered she'd left her car windows down. Amos stood to go roll them up, but Alice ran out the door before he could stop her. She hadn't been wearing any shoes, and the rain was cold, and Amos saw more of her in that gesture than in anything she'd said during the evening: her ease in the world, her lack of fussiness and self-protection. Impulsiveness. And that's what did it, the realization that she was impulsive, that made Amos consider, for the first time, what kind of lover she might be. By the time Alice came back in, soaked to the skin, her teeth chattering, Amos was in a state of desire so acute it felt like despair. He'd gone into the bathroom for a towel, and when he saw her standing in the doorway, dripping, he'd crossed the living room in two steps and wrapped her up so tightly she couldn't move. Alice tipped her head back to look at him, and he pressed his body against her, and then she was leaning forward, her lips about to touch his, had they touched his? and one of the girls called out, and Amos took a step back so far his head hit the doorframe.

"Whew. It's become a dark and stormy night," Alice said, unwrapping herself, looking away.

"Yes, yes, I should go." Amos took his car keys out of his pocket, his hands unsteady, and then looked once more at the kitchen, at their two cups on the counter, the cupcakes in a plastic container, the copper teakettle, so many things that belonged to her, that were a part of her life with her babies, he wanted to inventory them all.

She didn't say *Don't go;* she didn't stop him with a touch or a look or a word. She smiled at him and thanked him for the visit, said she'd be in touch, and he had tried, fumbling to shoulder as much of his professional mantle as possible, but he knew right then. There was a world inside her, and Amos had been seconds away from becoming a fool in order to find it. Within days she was dead.

"There was a world inside her," Amos would write, "and I destroyed it."

*

Music, Amos thought, standing. He'd become a bit blurry, maybe, but not drunk. Not exactly. Walking through the back door he weaved, bumped his shoulder on the doorframe. "Whoa," he said out loud, and remembered his best friend in college, Daniel, saying, "Brother Amos, you're listing starboard." He laughed out loud; it was a *great* thing to say when they drank, a bunch of Ohio farm boys who'd never been near a boat. Daniel was great. For a moment, a wave of adolescent male glee welled up in him: *I'm free. I'm listing starboard, and I'm free.*

What music to resign to? he wondered, walking toward his small,

portable stereo. What was Daniel doing these days? Whatever became
of him? Berlioz, something dark? Or sacred: Bach? Something pre-
dictably resigned: Mahler? Delicate and passionate, like Segovia, or dis-
turbing, Schoenberg or Cage? Something to make him regret his wasted
life, and also enjoy the regretting? Coltrane?

When Amos saw it, he knew. His favorite, the most reliable sorrow-
ful composition on his personal soundtrack. He put in the CD and hit
the repeat function so that it would play through the night, if necessary.
Stood too quickly and nearly lost his balance, then had to make his way
back to the screened porch with the aid of doorframes and chairbacks,
but no matter.

He sat down heavily; his bones seemed to have added some density
in the past few months. Two or three mornings a week he liked to go
for a run just as the sun was coming up, out past the edge of town. A
farmer out that way kept donkeys, and Amos loved to study the foals.
He'd seen only a few, but surely they were one of the hallmarks of
God's benevolence: their eyes, their absurdly long ears, the swing of
their tails. But running had hurt the past few times Amos tried. He
couldn't find his stride and his chest began to ache almost immediately.

This wine is *good*, Amos thought, raising his glass, what the hell, it
was a drunken, dramatic gesture, the sort of thing one might see in a
movie or onstage. No one was watching him. "Blood of Christ," he
said aloud, the way one might say To your health. His church had a
Love Feast (a meal, a foot washing, and Communion), but no consub-
stantiation, no transubstantiation, no mystery of the Host. Suddenly the
gesture didn't strike him as either funny or acceptable. *You don't believe
them*, Langston had said, and that was the real reason he attacked her,
wasn't it? It wasn't because she threatened to steal the children; they already belonged to her. She saw right through him. Amos could say anything he wanted about Incarnation, God in the world, the feminine
aspect of the Holy Spirit, Sophia. He learned it all, and could recite it:
God as Mother, God as Lover, God as . . . he couldn't remember the
rest . . . Postman? Undersecretary? And he'd read *The Chalice and the
Blade*, his intentions were good, he recognized the difference between
the cult of the goddess and the cult of death. And yes, yes, Yahweh was

a warrior and Job's suffering was unaccountable, and there was something in the story of Jesus of Nazareth that rang of cosmic child abuse. It was a cult of death: in the end there was no symbol in human history more disconcerting to Amos than Jesus on the cross. Amos was drunk, okay, he would admit it, but he loved Jesus, he loved the doomed baby and the serious little boy in the temple addressing his elders, and he adored the man Jesus became, the crafty magician sneaking into villages and healing the least of his brethren and whispering *Tell no one I was here.* Amos could think about Jesus for hours, how he inverted the status quo and begged us to lay down our weapons, how (and this is a stunner, as far as Amos was concerned) one of the tests scholars apply to the Gospels, in trying to determine what might be legitimately ascribed to Jesus, is this: what speech, what gesture, is the most *unlikely* in first-century Palestine? Find those, and *ecce homo,* you've found the Man.

Amos loved the character of Jesus, but there was no question in Amos's mind that Jesus was dead and had been dead for two thousand years. He died just like any other man, and he never rose again, and there wasn't a shred of historical evidence to suggest that he did, regardless of what fundamentalists liked to pretend. (They row as fast as they can, just like the rest of us.) And any time one of the faithful had suggested to Amos that Jesus had appeared, or spoken, or guided, or touched, Amos feigned happiness, but in his mind he asked, "What is at work in this person? What need, what sort of imagination? How can I help them?" The dead return, oh yes they do. They come in dreams, and in fits of memory so potent they can double a grown man, but that wasn't the same thing as an apparition.

And Mary? Amos knew nothing about Mary, even after all his reading and contemplation. She seemed less real to him than a thousand other women, much less real than Ariadne, abandoned at Naxos, or Medea, boiling up her children. At one point in seminary he became convinced that the trick of Mary is precisely that: to be nothing, to be an empty canvas on which the hopeless faithful can paint the portrait they need. She is the woman dreamed in every orphan heart, and Amos didn't need her, he didn't know her, he didn't believe.

That crafty Langston, Amos thought, stretching out on the wicker loveseat, dangling his legs over the end. All that masterful denial of her own past, her own damage, and she looked right into Amos's life and called him by name. *No doubt about it,* Amos closed his eyes and began to drift, his favorite music mourning in the background: *she nailed me. I am finished.*

Chapter 20

THE LONG LOST AND
THE NEWLY GONE

Taos, when you and I were little. Once upon a time, when you and I were little, we were in Daddy's truck, we were seven and five, or eight and six. We were on our way to Jonah to . . . pick something up from the hardware store? to buy groceries? I wish I could remember. I wish memory were a more steady, more physical artifact. It's just a breeze, or a scent barely detected and fading. I know it was summer, but not whether it was late or early, I don't know if we'd just finished the school year or were about to start. Where was Mama? What was occupying her? You and I, Taos, were an army of two. You were my playmate, my constant companion, strange, wavy hair that Mama called blackandyellow, and green eyes, like a cat. And a face like a cat. A narrow chin and broad cheekbones. A scar in the middle of your forehead shaped like Italy, from when you fell on the corner of the coffee table, and a strawberry birthmark on the back of your neck that brightened when you were mad. I could be scared of you, you weren't above scaring me with your temper, I could be scared of your slightest displeasure. When you were mad at me I had no one, and I would never have anyone, because we were all alone, but I was the most alone. Mama had Daddy, and you had Mama (so she had two), and to some extent you had Daddy, you were men together. And you had Nan Braverman who told you you hung the moon, and Grandma Wilkey, who adored you. I don't believe she ever loved another. But I didn't have Daddy, and I didn't have Mama, certainly not. The whole of her heart belonged to you. You argued at dinner, you sat on the swing and talked and talked, all hours, she would read a book in a day and give it to you and you would read it in a day and you would talk and talk. Charles Hartshorne and Teilhard de Chardin, Augustine, Proust, Hegel, linguistics, Restoration drama, until I thought I would weep or drown or run away, but I didn't, there was no end to your conversation, I can almost hear it now, although I thought I had forgotten. Most of those books are gone now—she donated them to the library in Hopwood. And once we were in the grocery store, Mama and I, and ran into her high school physics teacher, an old man, and he stared and stared at her, he was looking for a clue and I wanted to say, *Forget it, you'll never find it.* "Your mother," he said to me, "understood physics the way other girls understood knitting." I nodded. I nod. I know she did, and so did you, once when you were sitting at the table surrounded by dirty dishes and open books, arguing about something, Mama tipped her head back and howled—was it happiness, or grief, or laughter?—and said, "You are a mind without end, Taos." She didn't want to go to college, that's all, she said, she didn't want to, and you understood, you didn't want to either. You didn't want to go to elementary or middle or high school, but you made your way through, you eased through. *What did you want, what do you want?* I used to ask Mama, exasperated, and it was always the same answer: I just wanted to think, and to talk, with no one telling me what to do. You could be mean, Taos, and you were growing tall, getting muscles from running running running everywhere you went, and pounding a hammer, and climbing ropes and ladders and trees, and although mostly no one ever talked to me, sometimes at school I heard things about you, about how you were reckless and would take any dare, how you were itching to get going or get somewhere, and I'd see you walking down the street ahead of me in your striped T-shirt and old blue jeans, your body hard and unforgiving, that crazy loping walk you had. And I worried, but I didn't know what worried me. They named you Taos because that's where they went on their honeymoon, and there was something in it, something beyond the sentimental or nostalgic, they were trying to say: once we went so far. And you were how far they went. There is no more distant star, I now believe. You were sweet, too, and tireless if you loved someone, you bought thoughtful gifts, oh you were a surprise. You were the greatest surprise of my life. My lying down and rising up, my all in all. I've forgotten, or thought I had, nearly everything, and which is worse? To forget it, or to remember, as I fear I might? Because, well, like this. I didn't know I knew, I didn't know I could remember that truck ride with Daddy when we were sitting side by side, two years apart, some year, in the summer, and there was a stretch of straight country road, broad fields on either side, just a slight rise where the road approached a railroad track. A hawthorn tree before the tracks, and a falling-down fence, a stand of trees in the distance, and just as we approached the tracks, a bird fluttered down out of a tree, we both saw it at the same time, a bluebird, a bluebird was dipping toward the road, and then we were on the tracks and you and I turned and looked behind us, and there was the bird in the road. Daddy drove right on like nothing had happened, or more likely as if he didn't know that something had happened, but I felt faint, my stomach simply flipped upside down, and the first thing I did was look at you, I looked at you to tell me what it meant, but you just stared straight ahead, your jaw clenched. Nothing had ever scared me more, not the swirl of blue feathers in the road, not the fact of the bird, but that look on your face, Taos, as though you were collecting evidence against the world and here was an exhibit. It's what we do, Epiphany does it too, the younger, the lesser, the least qualified, looking to the elder, the bitter straight and smarter one, to tell us, just in case—just in case we're the only ones left someday—precisely what the *fuck* we're supposed to think.

*

Now she wrote to him only in her head, which saved time and paper. She was still lying on top of her quilt in her clothes, as Amos had left her, except that her mother had taken off her shoes and socks, and Langston knew he'd meant it, she knew Amos was going to take the children away from her and just as well, but there was something she wanted to do before she left in the morning with Germane.

She got out of bed quietly and turned on the light on her desk. There was a book somewhere in the west eave she wanted to look at; she needed to confirm something that had been gnawing at her, a nameless thing. She dug around in the dark, trying to locate the book by its spine: a tall, thin, coffee-table edition with a gold cover, *Images of Mary in the Old Masters*. She took it to her desk and sat down, turning the pages slowly. There she was, by Raphael, Mantegna, Botticelli, and Rubens, just an introduction, these pictures, the standard stuff, her face flat, her eyes downcast in utter humility and patience. Amazing. And the baby Jesus with the face of an old man. Langston couldn't imagine that the artists had gotten him right; some of the infants looked like exhausted, angry little bankers.

Carpaccio's *Birth of the Virgin:* Mary, conceived without original sin (that's the actual Immaculate Conception, not the conception of Jesus); Mary as a young girl, rosy-cheeked, in the temple, by Titian. Her wedding to Joseph, a middle-aged widower who had to be convinced, in Raphael's *The Marriage of the Virgin.*

The Annunciation: Gabriel announcing to Mary the hard fact of her fate. She was, what have scholars decided, twelve? Certainly no more than fourteen. In the Fra Angelico, Mary and Gabriel could be twins; in the beautiful Rossetti, Mary is shrinking into a corner, perhaps because Gabriel's feet are on fire. And a lovely rendering of the time Mary spent with Elizabeth, *The Visitation,* by Jacopo Pontormo, in which the women are mirror images of one another, old and young, and stand grasping one another in the classical pose of the Graces.

The Nativity, lots of paintings of this event, of course, by La Tour and Dürer and Botticelli. The flight into Egypt; beautiful, some of those. *The Presentation of Christ in the Temple,* by Jouvenet, in which mother and son are surrounded by sacrificial animals. Mary searching for Jesus, and finding him in the temple, preaching; the wedding at Cana, where she said, like a good mother, "Hello, Jesus? They're out of wine. Could you do something about that, Mr. Smarty Pants?"

And oh. It always happens, even when you forget its inevitability: the Crucifixion. (Once on a flight to Seattle with Jacques, Langston read a new biography of Sylvia Plath. They got caught in a holding pattern above the airport, and she was able to finish the whole book, and she remembered so clearly how she felt when she realized Sylvia was going to do it, she was actually going to kill herself and no one was going to catch her in time. Langston had been deeply shocked that the story turns out the same every time.) Mary at the foot of the cross, old now—although she would have been only forty-five, younger than AnnaLee, aged decades in the hours it took her son to die. In Perugino's *The Deposition from the Cross,* Mary's face is shades of green and gray, in stark contrast to the bright red robes and pink ribbons around her. The Apostles fled, but the women remained at Golgotha until the end, Mary the Mother and Mary the Other, and who knows how many more. In every picture the women are there, in Pontormo and Bouts. Ghastly. Jesus's broken chest and upturned eyes, his bloody hands and feet, she hadn't looked at any of these paintings in years. And then Caravaggio's *Deposition;* no one in history ever had his vision, or his touch, Langston thought. Caravaggio gives the scene a black background, and in this painting Jesus is no metaphor, he's A Man, with a carpenter's broad chest and muscular arms and great, thick hands. He isn't saintly or fey, he's huge, three days on the cross couldn't bend him. Jesus is being lifted off a table or a stone slab, his head turned, his eyes open, his veiny right arm reaching for the ground. And yes, Caravaggio got him right, in this painting he does look like a man who could turn history upside down, but it's the mourners Langston found most interesting: the complete devastation revealed in the faces of the men, who looked just like men you'd see anywhere, like Herschel Lewis in the diner, or Walt Braverman, or AnnaLee's high school physics teacher. A beautiful girl with a strawberry-blond braid wrapped around the top of her head is there, and Mary. Langston wondered how Caravaggio could have finished this painting, in the way she didn't understand how Tolstoy could have written the end of *Anna Karenina*. Doesn't it, at some point, just become too hard, witnessing the agony of your characters? Who would have blamed Caravaggio if he'd left Mary's face a blank white egg on the canvas, if he'd simply said: *I can't. You have a mother, fill in the blank.* After many minutes, Langston turned the page. In Bellini's *Pieta*, Mary's eyes are bruised with grief, and there's something in the way she supports her dead son's body that caused Langston to look away, as if she'd walked in on a scene of shocking intimacy.

Here is Mary at the tomb, the first to realize Jesus's body is gone, and then many images of the Assumption; Mary being carried into the sky by the angels; Mary crowned the Queen of Heaven; Mary among the cherubim. And isn't it interesting that in all the Assumption images, in Titian and Velázquez, in Botticelli's *Madonna of the Magnificat*, she is no longer old enough to be the mother of a grown man? Her youth has been restored to her.

Langston turned back to the work that interested her the most. The editor had chosen to devote an entire spread, both pages in the center of the book, to a single painting: da Vinci's *Annunciation*. Langston studied it a long time, then sat back in her chair and looked out at the night sky. She wasn't sure she'd found what she was looking for, but it was a start. Gabriel is on the left, with the high forehead and pouting lips of a Renaissance man or woman, either one. Protruding from his shoulder blades are small but very dense and muscular gray wings. He's kneeling on the ground, and has one hand before him as if he might be offering a proposal, as if he's saying, "No wait, just hear me out." Mary is sitting at an outdoor table in a stone courtyard, dressed like royalty; she's blond and regal, and looks to be nineteen or twenty. The expression on her face is priceless. She's neither alarmed nor surprised. The news of her imminent liaison with God seems to mean nothing to her. She's just listening politely to what the angel has to tell her, as any well-bred young woman would have done; she's maybe even humoring Gabriel. That's the look on her face. She's waiting for him to finish his spiel and move on. Her left hand is raised as if to make a point of her own, but her right hand is poised above the book she was reading before she was interrupted, one long, thin finger saving her place.

Langston rubbed Germane with her bare foot, and thought of how much she'd like to show this painting to Taos, and to Amos, and to the little girls, to AnnaLee and Beulah and Alice. To Taos she would say, *There was also* this. She would tell Immaculata and Epiphany that by one very grim yardstick, they were lucky. Because we're bound to lose our parents—we may even lose our children—but we should get to keep our siblings to the end, and they got to keep each other. Langston would put Amos and Beulah and Alice together, a little trilogy, and she wouldn't say anything, because they would understand. Alice would understand. But Langston would give this painting to her mother, if she had the original she'd hand it right over to her, and she'd say, *I'm so sorry that if one of us had to go, it was your beautiful, perfect son. It should have been me. I wish it had been me, instead.*

*

She must have drifted off to sleep, because when the children first began to scream, she was sitting at her desk with the book open and the light still on. She jumped up so fast she slammed her kneecap against the underside of the desk, but couldn't feel any pain. Germane was already down the steps, and Langston went running after him. By the time she got the attic door open and hit the hallway in the second floor, the light was on in her parents' room, and before she could knock, they both came running out the door, pulling on clothes. There wasn't time to say anything. They nearly tripped down the staircase, all three of them without shoes. Langston could hear the children through the opens windows of her house, screaming something unintelligible, and then she and her parents were through the living room and out the front door. Langston had never seen anyone run as fast as her father did, and right past the girls—who were in the middle of Chimney Street, clinging to each other and turning around in circles, wailing like sirens—

straight to Beulah's trailer. He jumped, landed on the top step, and opened the door, all in a single, fluid motion.

Langston and her mother reached the girls. She tried to lift Epiphany, but couldn't separate her from her sister, and AnnaLee finally said, "Let's just lift them up together and carry them into the house," and that's what they did. Lights were coming on in other houses. As soon as they reached the couch, Langston left the girls to her mother and ran across the street, and she, too, leapt to the top step. Inside, Walt was on the floor with Beulah, performing CPR, and Langston had to jump right over them to get to the bathroom where the inhalers were kept. Her hands were trembling, and she kept seeing little dancing pinpoints of light, but she knew she wouldn't faint. She felt remarkably clear-headed. She grabbed the inhalers and jumped over her father a second time, then leapt straight to the sidewalk from the door of the trailer, skipping all the steps.

In the house AnnaLee was trying to hold both girls, who were limp and gasping for air. Langston handed her the inhalers and AnnaLee said, "Go get Amos, Langston. He isn't answering his phone. Run."

Langston ran out the door and headed down Chimney Street, Germane at her side. They reached the corner of Chimney and Plum and Langston saw the wide, dark street ahead of her, lit by streetlights and patches of moon, and she felt like she could fly. She felt like Beulah or Sarah, one of the Macon Sisters. She hadn't run so hard or so fast since she was a little girl, racing Taos down the very same sidewalk. She always lost. Her feet were bare but she couldn't feel anything, no stones or broken pavement, and just when she began to wish it could go on forever, that she could run straight out of town, Amos's house came into view, and she stopped in her tracks. AnnaLee hadn't been able to get him to answer the phone, but all his lights were on. His windows were open, and Langston could hear music, and this was the strangest thing: a moment of awareness can only contain so much—it is finite, after all—and Langston was overloaded. She wasn't really certain who she was anymore, and she had only the vaguest sense of what she was supposed to do. She had forgotten everything but *Run*. But as soon as she heard the music, she thought very clearly, as if a voice had spoken it to her: that's Schubert. The trio in E-flat, Opus 100, one of her favorite compositions in the world. She stood still a moment and listened to the texture of it, the way the cello creates an illusion of sadness that is really just an implausible . . . She even closed her eyes and took a deep breath before she remembered where she was.

"Amos!" she screamed, running toward the house. "Amos, wake up, it's the girls, it's Beulah!" She pounded on the front door, but he didn't answer, so she ran down the sidewalk and around to the screened porch, and just as she started up the steps, the screen door opened and there he was, fully dressed, his shoes and glasses on, looking like two in the afternoon.

"Get in the car," he said, without a hint of worry or vexation.

"Amos, we can run and get there faster! Drive if you want to, but I'll just—"

"Get in the car, Langston. Your foot is bleeding profusely."

She looked down, and he was right. Blood had pooled where she was standing, and just like that, as soon as she saw it, she could feel something embedded deeply in her heel. It *hurt*. She got in the car.

The Rabbit was reluctant to start, and Germane was panting; Langston's window wouldn't roll down and a piece of the roof seemed to be stuck to Amos's glasses, but he remained quite collected. The engine finally caught, and they drove off with a shudder.

"You've called an ambulance."

"Jesus. Yes. And Daddy's doing CPR."

"The girls are with your mother?"

"Amos, are you *retarded*? Yes, the girls are with Mama, and she has the inhalers, and there. Listen." An ambulance was on the way, blaring down the highway between Hopwood and Haddington.

Just before they pulled up in front of the house, he turned to her. "Langston, I need to say something to you, please. It's about what happened between us, the things I said, and about Beulah's—"

She held up a hand to stop him. "Save it, if you would. The Amos Townsend Show was yesterday. I'm much more interested in what's happening to the children."

Langston jumped out of the car and limped through the front door. AnnaLee was sitting on the couch with the girls, who were crying, but breathing. When they saw Langston, they both sprang from AnnaLee's lap and grabbed her, and she still had enough of the strength she felt when running to lift them off the ground, resting one on each hip.

"Langston, we found Grandma on the floor!" Immaculata wailed, her face shiny with sweat and tears.

"Langston, she is died!" Epiphany pressed her face into Langston's neck.

"Shhhhh," Langston said, kissing first one and then the other. "Don't worry. I'm right here, and Amos is here, and nothing, *nothing* is going to hurt you." She glanced at Amos, who was watching her with an expression so pained and tender that she felt something travel up her spine, a jolt of recognition, news; no one had ever looked at her that way. Not once in her life. He took Immaculata out of her arms, and they headed for the car, AnnaLee following with a towel for Langston's foot. The lights from the ambulance made the whole of Chimney Street look like some gorgeous emergency: the red trailer, the red dogwood tree, Langston's empty, red backyard, the red sky.

Chapter 21

WORD I HAD NO ONE LEFT
BUT GOD

Amos paced like an expectant father for a solid thirty minutes, right up until AnnaLee said she would call security if he didn't stop. They were the only two people in the Intensive Care waiting room in the small hospital in Hopwood. Walt had gone home to get some sleep, and Langston was with the girls in a room on the pediatric ward. A television, suspended from the ceiling, was on and couldn't be turned off, at least by mortals. The sound was mercifully low.

"What do you make of this profusion of televisions in the hospital? They're everywhere," Amos asked.

AnnaLee put her book down, a collection of E. M. Cioran. "I think

it's sinister, frankly. I feel like we're in a Ray Bradbury short story."
She went back to reading.

Amos tapped his fingers on his bony knees. "Why do you have a
book and I don't?"

"Because I'm a woman, Amos."

"Yes, but why do you have a book and I never do in a situation like
this?"

AnnaLee put the book down. "I carry a bag. I also have safety pins
and emergency money, and a package of those little wet towelettes. We
live in Indiana. I could get stopped by a train, I could get bored. I always carry a book." She went back to reading.

Shuffling through the pile of magazines on the table at the end of
the sofa they were sharing, Amos was disappointed to find nothing
changed in the past ten minutes: *Parents, Money,* and *Sports Illustrated,*
and a *Children's Book of Bible Verses.* He sat back. "Have I ruined your
daughter?"

AnnaLee gave him a look of great forbearance. "No, Amos.
Langston is fine, this was nothing. She had a single bad afternoon and
night." She checked her bag for another book, but didn't find one. "I've
always thought that the thing she does, this minor catatonia, is just a
way for her to gather up some time. She needs time to process things.
You should have seen what happened to her two years ago, when her
affair with the Donne scholar ended."

Amos felt his breath catch. "She had an affair with a Donne
scholar?"

AnnaLee nodded. "Jacques Perrin."

"Jacques Perrin? I own his two books, that's just—" He stopped,
unclear about what he wanted to say. "Was it serious?"

"Oh, yes. At least from Langston's point of view it was. They lived
together, in essence, for quite a while, although she never told us that.
We never met him—I think he didn't want the entanglement of a family, of her family. And she took a year out of graduate school to travel
with him. She adored him. Amos," she said, touching his arm, "don't
mention to Langston I told you about this."

He shook his head, "No, of course not. He broke up with her?"

"Brutally, I think. She was one in a long line."

"And she didn't take it well?"

"No. No, she didn't take it well."

"What happened?" Amos turned to face AnnaLee, which required the folding of a leg. "I mean, did she—"

"Amos? Are you preparing her dossier?"

He shook his head, looked at the floor.

"You know what I think?" AnnaLee asked, slipping her book into her bag. "I think what you're really asking is not whether you broke my daughter, but how she got broken. You want to know what's wrong with her. Is that it?"

"No! Okay, yes, I have wondered, in passing." Amos paused. "Am I pushing you?"

"No, I'm past all that, really."

He believed her. Amos had become accustomed to the undisguisable fragility of the bereaved; he'd welcomed women back to church after miscarriages and stillbirths and SIDS; shaken the hands of men who had just buried beloved wives or parents or children. And always there was the slight nod in the grief-stricken, he wasn't sure how to describe it, a primitive fear or wariness. Amos spoke to them and they tried to look directly at him, but their eyes constantly shifted, as if they were looking for a door—a psychic door—a way into or out of their own condition. Beulah had it in the beginning, but didn't have it anymore, and Langston had an embedded form of it, but AnnaLee didn't have it at all.

"Taos, my son, was . . . I didn't love Taos wisely, I'd have to say. There were no role models for me, I was just winging it. If he'd been normal I think my instincts would have been okay, but. He was a child who *strained,* I've thought about this for years. When he was born, all he wanted was to roll over, and when he could roll over he wanted to sit up. You can see where this is going. He wanted not to walk, but to run, he yearned. And then," AnnaLee pinched the end of her earlobe repeatedly, a nervous gesture Amos hadn't noticed in her before, "you know. He was bright. I've probably mentioned that. He reminded me of my father, David. David Wilkey. There's a point in that, in the way they were alike. My mother adored my father but she destroyed him, she went at him with her great guns every day, every day of his life, and she did so because my dad was smart and kind, a reader and thinker, even though he was just a farmer. And there was something in the way he stood in relation to the world that made my mother *insane* with, I don't know what it was, maybe he made her own life look trivial by comparison. Though my dad never would have said such a thing. And I had an older brother, or I would have had an older brother, he choked to death at the dinner table when he was a baby and neither of my parents could save him, and that was really the end for them. For my mom and dad. I did nothing. My coming along did nothing to help them." AnnaLee reached up and let her hair down—there was some strip-of-leather-and-chopstick combination involved, the likes of which Amos had never seen before—and then in one fluid motion, twisted the hair back up and replaced the stick and everything was perfect.

"And then Taos was born, and he was so pretty and robust, he was a fabulous, strong little boy, and Mother preferred men to women in any case. And he turned out to have that mind, that same searching, curious mind my dad had, and what do you know?" AnnaLee laughed, still amazed. "Mother adored him. What she loved but had to destroy in my dad she loved unconditionally in her grandson. Do you know, listen to this, that Mother threw away all of my dad's books when he died? Didn't even offer them to me, wouldn't sell them, wouldn't give them away."

Amos had long wondered whether Tolstoy was right about the difference between happy and unhappy families, and had come to believe he'd never be able to test the theory, having never, *ever* encountered a happy one.

"So my mom loved Taos too much in her brittle way, and Nan Braverman loved him too much, but like the other sort of grandma, the grandma everybody dreams of. And Walt and I were young, we didn't know anything, and we were liberal, progressive, especially for Haddington. We thought we could . . . we thought if he wanted to run, we should say run. And we did, we said run, we said climb, jump, swing, sing, you name it, *eat*." She laughed. "I called him 'Zorba' when he was little, he was the life force, Amos. You should have seen him."

Amos watched her, struck again by how exquisite the stories were the people around him carried, and mostly silently, the lives they'd lived and endured, the sweetness and loss.

"He was two when Langston was born, and Amos. How to say this?" She paused. "Taos was the love of my life, I honestly believe, I truly believe that people who never have children, or who never love a child, are doomed to a sort of foolishness, because it can't be described or explained, that love. I didn't know anything before I had him, and I haven't learned anything of importance since I lost him. Everything that isn't loving a child is just for show. This is a terrible confession, it's the worst confession I could possibly make, but Langston was born, and," AnnaLee swallowed, "I loved her *better*."

"What?" He was stunned. "But I thought—"

"She, Amos, the moment I laid eyes on her in the hospital she was just my favorite, there was no way around it." Her eyes filled with tears. "When Taos was born my instinct was to nurture him and help him grow up into what he wanted to be, the man he could be, but Langston. Her head was so small, and so perfectly round, and when she slept her eyelashes touched her cheeks, and the first time, the very first time she looked at me I could see *her* in there, not just a baby but a great, extravagant soul inside the body of a sparrow, it was like a fairy tale, she weighed so little."

Amos nodded, remembering.

"I named her after a doll my dad won for me at the county fair, my most precious toy, how's that for a metaphor? And when we got home from the hospital, you know, I thought I'd gone crazy. Because I wanted to hurt people who got near her, I didn't trust anyone to hold her. I wanted to stare at her for hours and hours and breathe her air. I had a dream once that I was holding her and an animal suddenly appeared from the shadows, like a combination of a dog and a lion, and it took a single step toward us, crouched to spring, and do you know what I did, in the dream?"

Amos shook his head.

"I ate it. So you can see. There was trouble everywhere. Taos never stopped moving, and I could sense this thing around him, not a shield really, but more like a repellent field, and no one could penetrate it, and it seemed to get stronger every day, after Langston. He knew, he sensed in some way, that my heart had turned. I was afraid of what I was going to do to them, what I might do to them with my *love*, Amos, imagine that."

"You don't have to tell me how much damage love can do, AnnaLee."

She patted his arm. "No, I don't." She paused, thinking about what to say next. "I just, you know. Taos started talking, and then I knew. I knew what to do with him. When he wanted to run, I had said run, and so, when he was three I said, 'You want to be a genius? We'll be geniuses.' And I made a place that was just for the two of us, and I closed Langston out of it. I thought she could have everything else, and I would save Taos this way, but it didn't work. Because he was insatiable, and I had to struggle to keep up, and oh, please, I'd be a liar if I didn't admit that once I realized what we were doing I simply dove in. I gave him my worst self, Amos, as a gift. And I saved nothing for the child I loved best, that delicate little girl standing at the edge of my life."

Amos closed his eyes as the story became clear. In the insufferable woman, a nearly weightless child. They were just ghosts, he knew, just spirits, the young mother and father, the hard little boy, but it seemed to Amos the past was right there with them, shimmering on the surface of everything AnnaLee said.

"So guess what she did? Guess how Langston tried to save herself? She turned to her brother, wouldn't you just know it, and he wasn't . . . he wasn't the sort of person you'd want raising your baby. But he took her in, I'll hand it to him. He never turned her away, he never said no, protected her from other kids. And she was sweet, Langston was, and she gave all that sweetness to him, and it became something else, I don't know."

AnnaLee leaned up and pulled her sweater on. It was so late, and they'd both had too much coffee, and Amos thought AnnaLee must have been feeling terrible, physically. He did.

"They became parallel lines, those two, like railroad tracks. Taos was on one rail being destroyed by me—I'm telling you, Amos, I protected him from nothing. If he said, 'But what about evil?' my response would be, 'We'll spend a couple of weeks on Nietzsche, and then a month on the Holocaust, beginning with the historical causes and the roots of German anti-Semitism, Hitler as an Enlightenment figure, and ending with the liberation of the camps and a discussion of whether Roosevelt should have bombed Auschwitz-Birkenau.' He was twelve when we had that lesson. I was like some dark wizard, or a bad fairy godmother, I gave him everything he asked for."

"And what, what did you think you were doing? I mean, not what did you do, but what was your intention?" Because it did seem very odd to Amos, it seemed like a mistake, but he didn't want to say so.

She shrugged, hopelessly, as if he'd asked her the most impossible question, and then shook her head. "I don't know. I don't know what I was doing. I do, actually, I know what I thought at the time. Don't . . . I started to say don't laugh, but that seems unlikely. Amos, I thought I could give Taos *all*, the face of God, whatever. I thought he wanted it all, and I honestly . . . I believed then, I believe now, that in the end the information balances, and that he'd see that for himself. I was trying to lead him to Beauty, if you can swallow it, and I was willing to get there by any means necessary, including terror."

"The sublime."

"Kant, yes. That's the sort of terror I mean." She paused. "And so Taos is on his rail, and he's moving fast, he's hell-bent, and on the other side is Langston. And here's an interesting thing, an example of the crazy sort of upside-down life we were living: Langston was an A student, and no one noticed. Walt noticed, of course, and he tried to let her know he knew, but I don't think Langston ever really saw Walt. She was *his* favorite, too, but he couldn't tell her."

"He's a mystery, that Walt."

AnnaLee nodded. "Still waters run deep, as Nan Braverman used to say. Walt's my favorite secret. He . . . here's, I think, the strangest thing about him: He's steady as a rock, I know this, I've been married to him for thirty-three years. The man cannot be rolled. And yet he lives life without any guard, he feels and sees everything. Nothing gets past him. I can't reconcile the two things in my mind, because at the moment I'm most open to experience, I'm also the most paralyzed. He hates working at the plant; he's farsighted, you know, and he has a mind for math—categories, strata—and so he could, if he wanted to, but he doesn't, lay out for you or me the various concerns associated with pesticides in a rural community. He could delineate the economic impact either way, use or nonuse, the short-term benefits versus long-term effects, etc. And then he'd toss in the possibility of birth defects or miscarriage as the result of pesticide contamination of the aquifer, and the great likelihood that chemical contaminants can't be removed from fruits and vegetables with any amount of washing, meaning they lodge inside babies and children, eventually flicking little DNA switches that will change the course of human evolution. Not to mention the evolution of parasites."

"Walt? Walt could say all that?"

"Absolutely."

"Has he?"

"No, never."

"Then how do you know?"

She looked at Amos with a bit of disappointment. "Because I know. Because he's my husband. So imagine that, what Walt knows. And yet he gets up every day and goes without a word of complaint. He does it for me, for our family. He'd defoliate this county with his bare hands for Langston. He'd walk on broken glass for her."

It's Langston who walks on broken glass, Amos thought, remembering the piece removed earlier in the emergency room.

"There's Langston, earning straight A's and doing everything right, and after she and Alice stopped playing together—"

"Alice and Langston were . . . they played together?"

"Oh, sure. They were best friends, well, as much as those two could have a best friend." AnnaLee shook her head. "Misfits. Literally, they, Alice and Langston, did not fit with other children, and so for a while they had each other and they didn't really fit there, either." She rubbed her thumb up and down the length of her palm, distracted. "Anyway, Langston was earning straight A's and doing everything right, and she's running along beside her brother as fast as she can go, and what is her family doing? We're all saying, my mother included, 'Good for you, Taos, that you flunked the eighth grade. You're obviously just too smart for public school.' And everyone has to have something to rebel against, it's an existential requirement, so when Taos turned sixteen he rebelled."

"How?" Amos nearly laughed, imagining a world so wide open and welcoming there was nothing to push against.

"County boys, at first, drinking. All those farm boys prowling around out there, not the sort you see in church, Amos, but the other kind. The ones who brag about having sex with pigs, the shotgun-toting, beer-swilling end of the world. And they loved him. They ate him up. He had a peculiar metabolism, Taos, and he couldn't self-medi-cate like a normal boy, couldn't sleep at night, and he could drink and drink and not feel drunk. And then he'd just collapse in a heap. He was great fun for them, for those boys." AnnaLee looked down at her hands in her lap. "Langston worried about him so much she started to get physically sick, a whole collection of symptoms; stomachaches, numbness in her legs, double vision, our doctor could never find the source of her illnesses. And then Taos found this dog, a big, white mutt he named Strife. He became Taos's soldier, he was mean and un-predictable, a cat killer, and we were all afraid of him. And you know, I saw through that in about three seconds, I took one look at that dog and said, 'You picked him out on purpose, Taos, and you want him to be dangerous, because you're afraid of something.' But by that time no one could get through to him. He was out of school, working with Doc Fielding at the veterinary clinic and as a hand on Nathan Leander's farm part-time. He was still living at home with us but al-most never there, and when he was home he was out in the barn—there used to be a barn in the backyard?—with the doors bolted shut from the inside. And when he was with us he was this person none of us knew, a sort of mad, handsome rogue; he could imitate anyone, and the four of us would be sitting at the dinner table—but he hardly ever ate anything—or on the front porch and Taos would tell us stories about his exploits, imitating all his brain-dead cronies, and the three of us, Walt and Langston and I, would laugh uncontrollably. We laughed like we were in a panic. He had a robber's smile, those last few years."

Amos watched her. There was no sign she was talking about the love of her life. "Life is robbery," he said, quoting one of his favorite ideas of Whitehead. He meant it to comfort her, but he wasn't sure how.

She made an exasperated sound. "Quote the rest of it, Amos, '. . . *and all robbery requires justification.*' That's the part that really mattered to Whitehead."

Amos was speechless. How many times (he was humiliated, thinking back) had he done this exact thing, and not just to AnnaLee, but to everyone in his life? Using bits and pieces of better men and women to shore up his authority, his wisdom, to people who were too kind to correct him?

"Taos wasn't justified. That should be said right up front." Anna-Lee stretched, rubbing a fist against the small of her back. Amos's back began to hurt. "He had been good in chemistry in school, and somebody, probably one of the uncles of the farm boys—they all seemed to have these uncles who were unemployed, veterans, some of them, living in shacks in the woods, staying afloat by running traplines—one of the uncles gave Taos methamphetamine, and that was it. I don't know when or how it happened, but he set up a lab in the barn and he was making it out there, and at first we really didn't have any idea. Can you imagine us, ten years ago? A homemade laboratory in our barn? I don't know what we thought he was doing in there, but he didn't get it right at first, not until he got ahold of a recipe called the Nazi method— please, Amos, I know," she shook her head, then squeezed her earlobe, " which uses anhydrous ammonia. He was able to get it from the tanks at Nathan Leander's, just a gallon at a time, but we could smell it. Everyone could smell it, the whole town. For almost a year we walked around afraid of him, afraid of what was happening. He was either working or driving back and forth to Muncie and Indianapolis buying supplies, good Lord you should have seen what was in that barn. Hoses, coffee filters, tubing, hundreds of boxes of cold medicine, muriatic acid, starter fluid. He never slept, none of us could sleep, and then word started to get out. I guess he had been selling it to people at work, and they started showing up here, and one of them, a boy named Derrin, was coming out of the barn and saw Langston in the yard, watching. She hovered, she was always trying to figure out how to get to Taos. And Derrin grabbed her—when we saw him later, on the street, his skin was gray, ash—"

"He *grabbed* Langston, what do you mean—" Amos felt a flutter in his stomach, wings, or stage fright.

"He shook her, yelled in her face. I wasn't home, but Walt was, and a lot of things happened very quickly. Langston shouted and Walt, I think he must have looked out the window and seen them in the back-yard, grabbed a shotgun, and of course Derrin let go of her as soon as he saw the gun. Walt walked past him toward the barn and Langston followed, and Strife flew out the open doors at them, Langston told me later that all of his teeth were bared and he was barking so hard she could feel it in here," AnnaLee tapped her chest, "like a bass drum. Like percussion. And Walt didn't hesitate. He just raised the gun and shot Strife in the chest."

Amos opened his mouth, closed it, opened it again. "Oh boy."

"Yes, it wasn't good. Not a good moment for Langston. Then Walt stepped into the barn, saw what was there—but he didn't know what he was seeing, not really—and stopped Taos from what he was preparing to do, which was to blow it up. He was going to blow the barn up, he had gallons of anhydrous, along with the muriatic acid and the starter fluid—can you imagine? Jolene's house would have been gone, ours too. The windows would have blown out of the church."

"But, wait. Would he have killed himself, killed Langston and his own father, is that—"

AnnaLee shook her head, "I don't know, I don't know what he was—his thinking was very disorganized by that time, and he'd become paranoid—it didn't matter, anyway. Walt dragged him out of the barn at gunpoint and held him until the police came."

"Oh boy."

"My mother posted his bail. She who keeps a ledger of every pair of gloves she's given me at Christmas, every ten dollar bill tucked inside a birthday card, just withdrew twenty-five thousand dollars from her sav-ings account and got Taos out of jail. We brought him home, he went to his room, and within a day, maybe a day and a half, he was gone. He was facing a long prison sentence."

Amos sat back in his chair. On television a man who seemed to be wearing a Frisbee on his head was healing a woman on crutches. Amos blinked; it was just Frisbee-shaped hair. "Ten years ago? And you've—"

"Not a word. He just vanished. And no, we're not looking for him anymore, either. My mother paid a private detective from Indianapolis for two years, but he never turned up anything, not a trace."

"I wonder," Amos squeezed the bridge of his nose, where a headache was taking shape, "if it's harder for you, not knowing? Would it have been better if he'd been sent to jail, or if—"

"I know, I think I know the answer to that. I think it's best that he's gone, best for everyone, really. Because after a couple years we were free to . . . reinvent him? do you see what I mean by that? But if he'd gone to jail and then come home . . ." She shook her head. "I can't imagine. And he freed Langston, although I don't think she knows she's free. I think of him every day—"

"Of course you do."

"—and do you know what I always think? 'He's twenty-seven now,' or 'He'd be almost thirty.' If he's alive, he's thirty-two years old now, Amos, he's a man. And that makes me shudder, trying to picture the sort of man he might be."

Amos was silent.

"I'd like . . . I'd like to face Jacques Perrin just one time. I have a very strong sense of him from his two books, and from things I've heard from kids around here who went to Bloomington. He fancies himself such a dangerous little scholar; he left that trail, you know, and Langston was one of them. But if I could say just one thing to him, it would be: 'You are an amateur. You can't imagine what kind of love she's capable of.'"

AnnaLee, it seemed to Amos, was sending him a message, but he didn't understand the content. "What are—"

But she had turned away, and was settling herself against the arm of the couch to go to sleep. "Listen to me. You asked me about Langston and I answered you with Taos. If that doesn't just tell the whole story."

"I heard her, though," Amos said, "in there. She's in there."

AnnaLee closed her eyes. "We tore the barn down. That's probably the end of the sordid tale."

"I can see why you would."

"It smelled to high heaven. I couldn't stand it."

*

In Introduction to Pastoral Care, Amos had been taught to say, "Thank you for trusting me enough to share your story," as opposed to "That story reminds me of all the reasons I'm planning to die young." But he didn't say anything to AnnaLee when she finished the tale of her children, and she didn't say anything more, either, just closed her eyes and fell asleep. For a few minutes he watched the Frisbee-headed man declaim, exhort, and smack innocent people on the head. Amos had missed so much without a television set. Finally, he let his head fall back against the couch, and the next thing he knew, AnnaLee was shaking his arm.

"Amos?" she said quietly, trying not to startle him. "The doctor's here."

He tried to gather up his dignity and meet the man head-on, he was a minister, after all, and the clergy never sleeps. But he had a few problems remembering how to stand up, and then when he did get to his feet, nearly involuntarily, he rose and rose like a helium balloon. His head felt very small, and his ears were ringing, and he was so tall he could barely see the small people staring at him in the waiting room.

"Mr. Townsend?" The doctor, an older man with a kind, exhausted face, held out his dry hand. "Mrs. Braverman, I'm Dr. Harrison."

Amos shook his hand, and Dr. Harrison delivered the news, and the three of them talked for a few minutes, and on the whole Amos comported himself as if he were in his right mind. When the doctor left, Amos turned to AnnaLee and said, "I'll go tell Langston," and ran out the door before she could stop him.

*

Pediatrics was on the second floor, and Amos took the stairs down instead of the elevator, grateful for the chance to use his legs. He opened the door to the long hallway, and heard again over the intercom something he'd heard twice already tonight, but had barely registered.

At the information desk a lone nurse was entering information into a computer. She was overweight and had one of the dreadful haircuts Amos secretly referred to as "local," plus she was wearing a smock covered with teddy bear doctors and nurses, and for just a moment he was tempted to feel sorry for her, but the moment she looked at him he was chagrined (for what had to be the twentieth time in a single day): she was pretty, and her smile was joyous, and if he had sick children, he'd want her to take care of them.

"Can I help you?"

"Yes, I'm looking for my . . . I'm looking for Madeline and Eloise Maloney."

The nurse looked at a chart, then said, "They're in 211-B, just around the corner on the left. Are you with Langston Braverman?"

"Yes, I am, and thank you," Amos said, heading for the room. He stopped after a few feet and turned around. "Can I ask you one more thing? Three times tonight I've heard, out of the blue, a little piece of Brahms' lullaby over the intercom. What does that mean? Is it a code of some kind?"

She smiled, the looked back at the computer. "Sort of. We play it every time a baby is born. New moon. Busy night."

Amos nodded but didn't say anything. He felt shaky, walking toward the girls' closed door. Two children were born in the time he sat with AnnaLee, right in the same building, and another as he bounded down the stairs. Brand-new lives.

*

He opened the door quietly. Langston had left the curtains open, and a security light across the parking lot was shining in the room, enough that he could see all three of them clearly. Epiphany was on one bed, asleep on her back with her mouth wide open. One arm was above her head, and the other was resting on her stomach. Immaculata was in the other bed, curled up on her side, breathing deeply. Langston had pulled the lone, uncomfortable chair up to Immaculata's bedside, and fallen asleep with her head on her outstretched right arm.

Amos walked over quietly and knelt beside Langston's chair. There is nothing in the world, he thought, quite as strange as watching another person sleep; the way they are both present and not. Langston couldn't know her own face at that moment, couldn't know how young she looked, or how innocent, but Amos knew. Her braid was hanging down the side of the bed like a rope a suitor might climb to meet her in a tower, and he was just beginning to think, he'd just had the slightest glimmer of a thought, but before he fully grasped it, Langston's eyes opened, and she was looking right at him. An amazing thing, the way she went from being sound asleep to wide awake.

"Good morning," he whispered.

"Amos, I was having a dream," Langston said quietly, without raising her head.

"What was it?"

"I was in the yard at Beulah's, sitting at the picnic table; the girls were on the sidewalk, pretending to be a marching band. And I saw this butterfly, a very big, beautiful butterfly, sailing around the roof of the trailer and up near the power lines. I called out to the girls, 'Look! It's a monarch! You might never see another of these,' but I couldn't get their attention. And then it flew toward me, and it was really quite big, like the size of a small cat, and landed on my arm. It was very light. I called the girls again, but they still wouldn't look. So I picked it up by the body part, you know, not the wings, and raised it up to look it in the face, and it was a woman, it was Mary, I recognized her right away. She just looked at me, she didn't say anything, but I realized I'd been wrong about her, I could see it in her face. That whole humility and patience thing? that's completely bogus, that's not her at all. She's quite competent and smart; she has a lot on her mind, and she wants us all to get busy."

"She didn't speak to you?"

"Didn't open her mouth."

"And then what happened?"

"And then you woke me up by staring at me." Langston sat up and tried to straighten her spine.

"Beulah is alive."

Langston stopped moving. "She is?"

"No—I mean—*yes*. We all thought. She had a heart attack, but the damage wasn't—I can't remember the words he used. She's very tired, feels terrible, the doctor said, but she'll probably be home in a week or so. On medication. Diet and exercise and do something about her cholesterol, he said."

She sat back in the chair, watching him.

"Langston, we need to talk, and my knees are starting to worry about how long I might stay on the floor."

"Here," she said, scooting her chair back. "Sit on the edge of the bed. You won't bother Immaculata."

Amos sat down and rested his elbows on his knees. He found it difficult to face Langston in this half-light; he didn't know if he could trust himself to speak. "The girls can't live with their grandmother anymore," he began, and Langston nodded. "She has named us, you and me, I mean, their legal co-guardians."

Langston blinked repeatedly, and Amos hadn't expected this, this frightened look. He thought she'd come out swinging, especially when she realized they had equal power, that Amos couldn't make decisions about the children without her.

"And so, it's going to be your decision, too, where they live, and maybe you think they should move in with you and Walt and AnnaLee, but I've been hoping—"

"I don't want them to live there," she said.

"Well, now see, I don't want them to, either. Because it wouldn't be, I don't think it would be fair to your parents, and also the parsonage is so big, I have three bedrooms and that great big study, I just rattle around—"

"No, no, that's good. That would be perfect for them."

"Wait, it's not just—" Amos actually reached out and rested his hand on her knee, not caring if he crossed boundaries or behaved inappropriately. He was so afraid she'd misunderstand, then flee before he could mend the damage. "—it isn't just the girls I'm thinking of here, Langston. I think the three of you should stay together, anything else would hurt them immeasurably, and what I want is—"

She didn't say anything, just continued to stare at him (her eyes were the oddest color, some crazy mixture of green and gold and dark brown), and so finally he just said it. "I want you with me, I want us all together, the four of us, and you can—oh, and Germane! of course, I want Germane there, too—and you can share my study. You can work right at my desk, and I'll add more bookcases, I'm gone most days, but! but I can be in and out and do anything you want, I'm very self-sufficient, I would be responsible for all the housework and the cooking, I would never see you as a—"

And before he knew what had happened, before he saw it coming at all, Langston had her face buried in his shirt, she was crying so hard the whole bed began to shake. So he stood and pulled her to him, as close as he'd ever held another person, and she cried and cried, there seemed to be no end to it. He thought she might very well cry until morning, and he wouldn't have minded. There were worse ways to spend the last hours of a long night.

"This is a small town," he whispered into her hair, "and we can't just live together. Do you understand what I'm asking you?" She nodded.

He could cover her back with his hands, he could enclose the long, thin nape of her neck with just his fingers, the back of her head could rest in his palms. They stood that way a long time, Langston crying as if she would never recover, and Amos standing still and taking his measure of her.

EPILOGUE

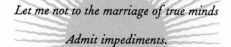

Let me not to the marriage of true minds

Admit impediments.

WILLIAM SHAKESPEARE

LANGSTON

"To be perfectly honest, I never thought I'd see the day," Grandma Wilkey said, taking the lid off the box Walt had carried down from her attic.

"No, neither did I," Langston said, sitting on the edge of the chair in her grandmother's bedroom, a beautiful rocker trimmed in mahogany and covered in dusky pink velvet.

"You never seemed much the marrying kind."

"No, I'm really not."

"Here it is," her grandmother said, taking out a yellowed newspaper clipping sealed in plastic. She handed it to Langston.

Rev. W. T. Thompson, pastor, read the vows. The setting for the cere-

mony included palms and two baskets of Fall flowers. Illumination was provided by tapers in candelabra.

"The veil isn't usable, of course, even though I had it cleaned
and placed in storage right after the ceremony, and it's been packed in
mothballs ever since. But look here, it's completely, what's wrong with
this, good heavens."

*The bridal colors in the flowers and gowns were shades of brown gradu-
ating from deep brown to copper to beige.*

"But the dress is . . . here, let me unfold this . . . Langston, dear?"

*She wore a gown of ivory satin with a small train and portrait neckline.
The veil of white net embroidered with flowers fell from a braided white
satin coronet of seed pearls.*

"Just like new. You're a bit thin for it, of course."

*She carried white roses on a white Bible with rosebuds knotted in white
satin streamers.*

"Do you want to try it on?"

"This was all so long ago," Langston said, still looking at the newspaper announcement. *For the ceremony, the bride's mother chose a cocoa colored gown accented with gold beading at the neckline. Her corsage was white
gardenias.* "It all seems so . . ." She lay down the newspaper and pressed
her fingertips against her eyes. When she opened them, for a moment all
she could see were ghosts: the glowing outline of the oval, full-length
mirror; her grandmother in the bright afternoon light, holding the dress
aloft; spots in the air, floating like flowers. "Oh," she said, blinking,
"that's beautiful, Grandma, what a beautiful dress." Langston stood and
walked toward it, the slippery satin spilling from the hanger like milk.

"We'll have to take it in at the waist," her grandmother said, gathering up an inch on each side. "Women were more substantial in my day."

Langston held the dress up in front of her as her grandmother continued to sort through the contents of the box. The dress would be perfect, after the alterations.

"Your mother tells me you've asked her just to plan everything?
You're not taking any role in your own wedding?"

Langston shook her head. "I wouldn't have the first idea how to
conform to the mores of small-town weddings, Grandma. I know

there's supposed to be that white cake and the icing made from Crisco, but that's all. Oh, and the nuts and things. But I wouldn't know whom to invite, or if one simply issues an invitation to the whole town, or how far afield I should . . . yes. Yes, I've asked Mama just to take care of it all."

Her grandmother sat down on the edge of the bed, smoothing out her skirt. *For traveling, the bride changed to a three piece navy and white checked suit. Her hat was navy blue velvet and her other accessories were navy.* "Sit down here with me, Langston."

Langston sat down, reluctantly.

"You may know that when your grandfather proposed to me he already had two hundred acres of land, and a fair amount of livestock, nearly three hundred head of Hereford cattle, and I came with a hundred acres as a dowry."

"I didn't know that, no."

"Your grandfather and I worked on this farm from the day we married; three hundred acres isn't much, and we had to be smart. But we started out knowing what sort of plan we had to follow and how to go about it. We were thrifty and worked as a team."

"I'm not exactly profligate myself."

"I never said you were. I just wonder if you've really thought about this, about what it means to be someone's right hand. Amos Townsend is a decent man, I'm sure, but his prospects—"

"You find it hard to imagine me a preacher's wife?"

"That's the long and short of it, yes. I wonder if you know what it entails? I wonder if you know about the church picnics and the phone calls in the middle of the night—"

"Grandma," Langston began, holding up her hand.

"Do you realize that he'll never earn a decent wage, that you don't own your own home, that you'll never have anything but secondhand cars? And now you'll be raising someone else's children?"

Langston felt as if she'd been slapped; or worse, as if Amos and the girls had been slapped in front of her. "When you got married, Grandma, did you know you'd lose a son? And that your grandson would become a manufacturer of drugs and flee the family? Did you know you'd outlive your husband by so many years? Didn't you fail to reckon on far greater griefs than church picnics and banal sermons?"

Her grandmother looked away from Langston, her back stiff. "I never said anything about banal sermons."

"I'm sorry. I'm sorry I said all that."

"Langston, just tell me this one thing," her grandmother said, looking her in the eye. "Are you doing this for those children, or for yourself?"

Langston stood, then bent and kissed her grandmother's cheek. She thought of the things she might say: *I'm doing it for all of us,* or *I'll know who I am because I did it.* But all she said was, "I don't know, Grandma, honestly. Whoever knows what they're doing at a wedding?"

*

At the Holiday Dry Cleaners in Hopwood, Langston asked the teenage girl at the counter if she could speak to the person who did alterations, and was led back to a small room. A Korean woman in her late sixties stood up from her sewing machine, a tape measure draped around her neck, and offered Langston a slight bow.

Langston bowed in return. "Hello," she said.

"Hello, I am Mrs. Li." She bowed.

"I'm Langston Braverman," she said, bowing.

"You have a dress?"

"No. I do, but I don't think I want you to change it."

"Yes?"

"I'd like a new dress. I'd like for you to make it for me."

"Make a new dress? You have a pattern?"

"No, there's no pattern, but I have it in my mind and I can tell you all about it. I'm sure you can do it. All you need is a good eye and a steady hand."

"Okay." Mrs. Li bowed.

Langston bowed and drew her a picture.

*

When Langston got home the girls were on the front porch playing with the new dolls Amos had given them, Astronaut Barbie and Doctor Barbie. Germane lay beside them, in the shade. Langston sorely disapproved of the whole concept of Barbie, and was able to quote at length the many feminist theses on the early identification with distorted body image (including the well-worn statistics of what Barbie's measurements would be if she were a real woman) and had explained as much to Amos, who listened with care and then asked the children if they wanted to play with the Barbies and they said yes and so he gave the dolls to them. There were bugs to be ironed out yet in their arrangement.

"Hello, chiclets," she said as she passed them.

"Hello, Langley," Immaculata said, as Langston opened the screen door.

"Hello, Spangston."

She stepped back out onto the porch. "Did you say 'Spangston'?"

Epiphany nodded.

"I rather like that one."

Inside, her mother was sitting at the dining room table going over the guest list. In the past few weeks AnnaLee had taken to wearing reading glasses of the half-moon variety, which Langston thought suited her splendidly.

"Mother, I'm not wearing Grandma Wilkey's wedding dress."

AnnaLee looked at her over the top of the glasses.

"And I don't want that Crisco cake or any nuts or lard mints. And I'd like to decide what will be said at the ceremony—along with Amos, of course—and I don't want any traditional wedding music, none at all, I want only the Schubert in E-flat, and also the aria from *The Marriage of Figaro*. And I'd like to have the reception outside, in the meadow next to the church, under a tent."

"Is that all?"

"I would like Giant Fizzies available for the children. And we can have cake, but not that kind."

"I understand. Has something happened you'd like to tell me about?"

Langston shook her head. "No, nothing has happened."

251

AnnaLee looked back down at the notebook on the table. "Would you like to go over the guest list with me, then?"

Langston waved the list away, heading back outside to the children. "Mama, I *told* you—I don't care who you invite. This is essentially your social affair." She stepped outside, and then back in. "But make sure you invite Dr. Harrison, because he's been so good to Beulah. Oh, and send an invitation to Aunt Gail, just as a gesture."

"Aunt Gail is crazy, Langston."

Langston stopped, half in and half out of the door. "Half of the people you've invited are crazy, Mama. We must not let that stop us from having a good time."

AMOS

In the weeks that followed his wedding, Amos lay awake at night trying to remember every detail. He went over it in his mind step by step: the hot August breeze, the walk to the church, the murmuring in the room off the vestibule where Langston dressed. He had waited in the wings just like a groom, adjusting his tie and pacing, while the minister who would marry them, John Wagner, his mentor and old friend, talked easily with Walt. Amos had heard the Schubert begin to play on a borrowed stereo, and then felt certain he couldn't go through with it, that his life was proceeding as if in a dream. He couldn't go through with it. There was a water fountain just outside the Fellowship Room and he walked to it feeling dizzy. He was a man who lived alone, a disciplined man, and the last time he heard the same song he had been drinking red wine and composing his resignation; he was a man who lived alone. He took a drink of water and thought of all the things he wasn't. The water was cold, and he remembered listening to the song as he fell asleep that night, and awakening to Langston's cries, the brightness of the moon, she called for him and he rose right up as if he'd never been asleep; he could see her again as she looked that night, breathing hard and leaving a trail of blood, the light in her gaze. He took another drink of water, unable to go through with it. What would he say to Walt, to AnnaLee, to John Wagner, to the girls? How would he ever face her again?

And then he heard Walt walking down the hallway toward him and Amos turned to face him. There were a few things about Walt, things Amos was unable to articulate. He kept imagining Walt with the shotgun, raising it first at ashen Derrin, and then firing it, unblinking, into the chest of the dog Strife. Because it was Langston. Because Langston was in danger. And it had been Walt who called the police and turned in his son; Walt who had awakened in the night and given Taos enough money to leave; Walt who watched Taos drive away; Walt who took down the barn. Now he placed his hand firmly on Amos's shoulder.

"Are you ready?"

Amos nodded.

*

He remembered walking to the front of the church, behind John Wagner and before Walt, as the aria from *Figaro* began, how it soared into his body and reminded him again that he couldn't go through with it, and how he was running out of time to say so. Because he could listen to this particular piece of music alone, he could listen to it as he failed to write his sermon, or as he failed to save someone else's marriage, but he couldn't listen to it with another. It simply wasn't possible. And especially not with her. Because when he looked into her eyes he saw *her* in there, an extravagant soul, and there was no chance she wasn't listening, and all that was most moving to him was in that song and she would hear it, too. It was one thing to be moved, lying alone on a back porch on a summer night, drinking wine and composing an unsent letter. But it was another to be seen.

And then the girls started down the aisle, Epiphany first, wearing her pink robe and her pink hat with the trailing ribbons, carrying a little basket of red rose petals which she dropped, six or seven here, none there, a dozen in another spot, as she made her way to the front. She smiled at Amos all the while, and not just because he gave her gum, but because she'd lost her first tooth, right in the front, and she loved the way the breeze blew into her mouth.

Immaculata was next, in her lavender robe and her hat with the trailing ribbons, carrying a basket of white rose petals which she dropped with a mathematical precision, her face so serious, her blonde hair pulled back into a braid just like Langston's. Amos watched her and decided that if he ever needed anyone to run his company, Immaculata was the one. Or if he needed a Chancellor for his university, or a Secretary of State, he'd call Immaculata first.

Now, he had thought. *Now I will simply say that I made a mistake; we should all go home and forgive ourselves later, or not at all.* AnnaLee was sitting in the front row with Marjorie Wilkey and Beulah, all of them crying and patting each other on the knee, and she must have practiced, Langston must have practiced when she would walk through the swinging doors into the sanctuary, because just as the aria began its ascent she stepped inside and Amos saw what she had done. She was wearing an ivory robe just like the girls, made of the same inexpensive, durable fabric, and an ivory hat with streaming ribbons, and she carried a single white orchid. That was the moment he remembered with the greatest clarity, the moment he realized that she was the last woman he would ever love; that every storm between them would be a confection, that their bed would be his grave.

I will, he had said, and he meant it. He meant it.

*

Langston stood at the bottom of the stairs, looking at her watch. "Ragamuffins! Problem children! The Jesus Train is leaving the station in five minutes!" Upstairs the girls were singing some ridiculous song about learning to tell time. Immaculata was insistent that her sister be able to read a clock before she finished first grade, to which Amos replied, Fat chance. Epiphany didn't even realize time was passing; he'd seen her sit on the back step with Germane an entire hour without moving, the two of them just staring out at the garden.

Amos washed his hands at the sink, after cutting some flowers for the kitchen table. Langston gathered the breakfast dishes and began to stack them in the dishwasher.

"After I drop the girls off at school I'm going to do some home visits, then I'll be in my office all afternoon with counseling appointments, then I'll go back and pick them up again. Is there anything you need today, anything I can do for you?"

Langston thought a minute. "Oh! yes. Take this audio book to Beulah. She's exhausted all of her others from the library and refuses to let me read Proust aloud to her. She'd die before we finished *Swann's Way*, she claims."

"Probably true."

"Undoubtedly. And she's also craving deviled eggs. I explained that preparing such an item does not fall within my purview, and so Mama made some. Just ask Beulah if she got them, and if they were to her liking. Mama can be heavy-handed with the nutmeg, or whatever that brown powder is."

"Got it."

"And lunch? Shall we?"

"Absolutely. I"ll meet you here at noon. What are you up to today?"

She drank the last swallow of her coffee. "Editing." She was reluctant to talk about the book: *Apostrophe,* or *Letters to a Missing Person,* but Amos had seen the manuscript grow in height daily on the edge of the desk.

The girls thundered down the stairs, skipping the last two steps, then lined up, so Langston could inspect them. Their school uniforms seemed to be in order; the white button-down shirts with "Sacred Heart Academy" stitched in green above the pockets; their khaki shorts; white socks, and tennis shoes.

"Do you have all your books?"

"Yes," Immaculata said.

"Yes," Epiphany said.

"Do you have your lunch money?"

"Yes."

"Yes."

Langston knelt down in front of Epiphany. "Sweetheart, where is your lunch money?"

Epiphany stared at Langston, breathing noisily through her mouth, but didn't answer.

"Look, no look at me, it's right here in this little zippered pocket—Epiphany, look at me, sweetheart, not at Germane. Germane! for heaven's sake, how rude. Emily Dickinson's dog would never—Epiphany? Where's your lunch money?"

"In the little zipper."

"In the little zippered *pocket*." Langston sighed. "You're going to starve. You'll develop scurvy and trade your kingdom for a lime. In the meantime," she leaned over and kissed the top of Epiphany's head, that wavy miraculous hair, as soft as a baby's, "in the meantime I love you, I'll miss you, have a good day. And you, Miss Immaculata. I'll go over the study guide you left me and hang your new poster. Let me just say now, in front of these witnesses, that there is nothing so perfect, and I'm talking about in all God's creation, than a fourth-grade girl. You should be the president. You should be Queen of the World."

"You said that yesterday," Immaculata reminded her.

"All the same."

"Go on, then," Amos said, pushing them both toward the door. "Get in the car, and I'll be right out." They ran out the door, fighting about who got to sit in the front. Immaculata won. Amos turned and looked at Langston, who was standing at the foot of the stairs, one hand on the newel post, one resting on top of Germane's head. Her posture reminded Amos of AnnaLee, moving like a ship through calm water. "Do you know?" he asked. "Do you know what moves me most about you today?"

Langston shook her head, then narrowed her eyes at him.

In his mind, Amos ran through the list of all he might say to her: How her hair at night, undone, trailed across her pillow like a sheet of black silk. The way she read so fast. The quality of her attention, the birthmark on her back, her long, long stride. The way she met him like this, unblinking. "Today, what moves me most, is just the *slope* of you."

And then she blinked, that slow, languid look she had that no one saw but him, and took a step toward him, pulling open his shirt between buttons, kissing his chest.

He walked out the front door and headed for the car; it was just another Wednesday, nothing to it. And then she ran out the door after him, he'd forgotten Beulah's tapes, and as he got in the car, adjusted the girls, checked seat belts, and drove off down Plum Street, she was still standing on the porch with her dog, her arms crossed over her chest, watching them, and he thought, as he thought many times a day, *Thank you, Thank you.* He couldn't imagine how he earned this little piece of luck. She was just another possibility in the mind of God, one of many potential universes, and somehow, in a trick, a tug, she arrived. Love, Amos thought, didn't always harvest the world's riches. It didn't happen often, but sometimes two people woke up, and they were home. And sometimes they just walked away free.

ACKNOWLEDGMENTS

I would first like to thank John Miller, who was one of my professors at the Earlham School of Religion, for reading this book in draft for theological content. He clarified and corrected my thinking with ease and graciousness. I will always appreciate this and other gestures he has made toward my betterment, including those he didn't know he was making. All remaining errors are my own.

My godmother, Dorothy Kennedy, after listening to me bemoan the sad fact that I'd never write a doctoral dissertation on Alfred North Whitehead and the nature of grief, said, "You could always write it as a novel." (Forgive her: she knew not what she said.) Thank you, Dorothy.

Thank you to the students, faculty, and administration of Immaculata Catholic School, for allowing me to spend a day observing.

The International John Donne Society welcomed me at their annual conference, although I was completely unknown and not even remotely a John Donne scholar. (Langston originally was, however, and the Society lent their expertise to her development.) John Donne scholars *rock.* Thanks especially to Judith Herz, Ernest Sullivan, Graham Roebuck, and Achsah Guibbory, as well as the incomparable Thomas Hester. In addition to being the king of all things Donne-related, it was from Dr. Hester I heard the idea about Faust's ultimate flaw. And deepest thanks to Nate Smith, gentleman and scholar, who knows a Holy Sonnet when he sees one.

In the writing of this book—as in all other aspects of my life—I received the unqualified support of my mother, Delonda Hartmann, and my sister, Melinda Frame. As Donne said of his wife: they are the Most Beloved and Well Read. My babies, Katie Koontz and Obadiah Kimmel, sweetest and most lovely, never complain about the work I have to do, plus they are both really funny. I thank them from the bottom of my heart. Ben Kimmel has done so much for me I stumble in my gratitude, and the same goes for Don and Meg Kimmel, who keep all of us afloat and aloft, while also offering lessons in Living Really Well. My excellent neighbors, Ann Gleason and Gary Patilo, offered me every kind of support while I was writing this book, including soup. Thank you.

Thanks as ever to Tom Koontz, who shared with me his greatest treasures; Beth Dalton, an inspiration as a writer, a mother, and a friend. Thank you to the Adorables, Maia Dery and Senga Carroll, who came into my life like oxygen; my kind and *very* good editor, Amy Scheibe; Chris Litman, for all his help; my agent and friend, Stella Connell; Lee Smith, Keebe Fitch, Fred Neumann, Jesse Kimmel, Murray Wagner, Jay Alevizon, the good people at Grapevine Print and Design. Lawrence Naumoff, I hope someday to be half the writer you are. My dearest gratitude to James Baumann (it's a novel of ideas, actually). Thank you to Eddy and Shirley Cline, and in memory of their daughter, Donita. Tom Milam lent me books on post-traumatic stress syndrome in children (thank you, Tom), and Noelle Milam was just the best at all things. Thanks to Jody Leonard and Lisa Kelley, proprietors of the Mast Gap Inn, who gave me a much needed weekend away. Thanks to Mary Herczog, Kindred Spirit, whose correspondence rivals Christabel's own in grace and wit.

And thanks most especially, as always, to John Svara (rarest of creatures): *My ragges of heart can like, wish, and adore, / But after one such love, can love no more.*

8/11-30